CW01263762

THE FOOTAGE

STUART JAMES

This book is dedicated to the wonderful Teresa Barun.
You are so very sadly missed by all of us.
Also to my incredible wife, Tara, and my beautiful children, Oli and Ava.
I love you all so very much.
And of course, my parents, Jimmy and Kathleen, who I absolutely adore.

Copyright © 2024 by Stuart James

All rights reserved.

No part of this book may be reproduced in any form or by any electronic or mechanical means, including information storage and retrieval systems, without written permission from the author, except for the use of brief quotations in a book review.

PROLOGUE

FIVE YEARS AGO. A MONTH AFTER THE FRIENDS DISAPPEAR

'Everyone says it's cursed. Are you sure you want to go in there?' Eugene stopped at the brow of the hill, waiting for his friends and seeing their concerned faces. 'Come on. The last one pays for breakfast on Saturday.'

The pedals of his mountain bike spun as his feet rested on the red frame, and the handlebars shook in his hands. Wisps of his curly black hair fell over his face as he charged along the road towards Sheers Woods.

Mia and Simon struggled to keep up with him. Their mountain bikes were older and had fewer gears.

As he gripped the brakes, the bike skidded sideways, and he came to a halt at the entrance. Watching his friends pull up beside him, the heavy panting sounds pushing from their mouths and beetroot-red faces, Eugene asked, 'Are you sure about this? Have you seen the clip on social media? The four friends who disappeared from the lodge.' The fields were bathed in the soft light of the full moon as he pointed to a narrow road winding around the woods. 'It's along there.'

'Do you think it's real?' asked Mia, her voice rife with concern and the cold air catching in her throat.

'Course it's real,' Simon added, standing on his bike pedals and trying to balance. 'And the crazy thing is it only happened a few weeks ago.' Getting off the bike, he walked to the entrance, adjusting his cap and turning the peak behind his head. 'I think the lodge is closed now. I can't imagine anyone would want to stay there after—'

'Come on, let's go in,' Eugene ordered. 'Unless you're both chicken.'

'Do you want to, Mia? You don't have to if you're scared. I'll look after you,' Simon offered.

'I'm not scared. It's just so... dark.'

'All the better then. We can keep hidden.' Eugene adjusted the gears and cycled along the road leading up to the lodge.

His friends followed close behind.

'They haven't been found, have they?' asked Mia, adjusting the light on her bike and gazing into the bleak fields. She didn't want to be here. Eugene and Simon were her best friends; she'd known them for a couple of years since starting secondary school, year seven. But the boys competed too much. The dares were often ludicrous. Who could ride their bike longest with no hands? Who would kick a football across the road between vehicles? But this was a step too far for her. She'd heard rumours about it being haunted. Loads of the kids at school had said it, and most wouldn't dare venture into Sheers Woods after dark.

Pulling away, Eugene rounded a bend and dumped his bike on the grass. As his friends approached, he jumped out from behind the bushes and screamed.

Mia's handlebars shook, and she fell off the bike.

'You're such an idiot at times. What's wrong with you?'

Simon got off his bike and held out his arm. 'Are you alright?'

'Thanks,' Mia said, brushing mud from her jeans. 'I'm okay.' Aggravated, she grabbed Simon's hand and pulled herself up. Looking at Eugene, she spat, 'Why do you have to act so stupid?'

'It's just a joke. Lighten up. Jeez.' Eugene turned, glimpsing along the narrow road. 'There's a weird glow up ahead. Look.'

'No, there isn't. You're trying to spook us. Come on. Let's go. This place creeps me out.' Simon got on his bike and steered it towards the entrance.

'I'm serious. Look.'

Turning, Simon gazed to where his friend was pointing. 'It looks like a lantern. Is it a person? I can't tell. There's more of them. Quick, the lights are coming this way.' He suddenly felt faint, and his mouth became dry. 'Let's get out of here.'

As the three rode along the path towards the entrance, a shadow seemed to cross in front of them and race into the fields.

'What was that?' Mia shouted, gripping the brakes.

Her friends stopped beside her.

'Did you see that?' asked Simon. 'Shit. There's someone there.'

Muted by fear, Eugene sat on his bike, his torch facing the bushes. Suddenly, they rattled as if someone or something was hiding.

Then, a voice, sharp and intense. 'You have to help me. I don't know what they've done to me.'

As Eugene pulled away, a low growl emitted from the edge of the field, and he was thrown off his bike.

'Quick. We have to leave. Get up.' Simon lifted his friend,

and the three of them cycled along the road to the entrance of Sheers Woods.

1

PRESENT DAY. WEDNESDAY EVENING

'Night, Jess. Can you turn the lights off when you leave?'

The sound of squeaky wheels rolling over the carpet resonated through the small local newsroom as swivel chairs edged away from desks. Work colleagues were deep in conversation, bidding goodnight as they shuffled out.

'Yeah, no problem, Doug.' Watching from her desk as her boss walked towards the door, the smell of his odour pushed through her nostrils and slowly worked into her lungs. Doug's dull grey trousers slid further down his backside, revealing his grubby white underwear. His swept-back, greasy black hair glistened in the light as if it were recently dyed. At the door, he sneezed, spraying phlegm over his jacket.

As he wiped it off, Jess called out, 'Oh, Doug, did you think any more about the documentary?'

He turned, irritated, his mouth opening as if giving it a second of his time. The deep sigh and the stained sticky hand working through his hair made her regret asking. 'I'll give you an answer tomorrow. Your contact, Philip Lawson. The new owner. I've emailed him.'

'What did you say to him?'

'I said we're a local paper and explained how we'd like to feature the place. I mentioned nothing about what happened there. If he finds out our intentions, there's no hope of a story. The lodge exchanged hands a few weeks ago. I think he's in Spain, so he shouldn't bother you. If my answer is yes, he can't know what you're doing in terms of filming a documentary. I'll have to deal with the repercussions afterwards.' Doug wiped his thick brown moustache, and crumbs dropped to the floor. 'I must admit I have concerns. Let me sleep on it, okay?'

'Okay,' she answered, trying to stem the excitement. 'What concerns exactly?'

Opening the office door, he looked back. 'It's dangerous. You know that, right? Investigative journalism often is. It comes with the job. Oh, I'm not saying the footage is genuine. Far from it. Most people believe it's a hoax, including me. But I have to say the buzz it's created, the views on social media, it's blown up and could be a winner. No one has stayed at the lodge since the incident. You don't know what kind of weirdos could be hanging around or making your stay more uneasy. It's risky.' He watched Jess nod, then continued. 'Anyway, let's speak tomorrow.' Looking towards the back of the office, he said, 'Night, Ruth.' With his eyes back on Jess, he grinned. 'Have a good evening.'

With a finger hovering over the laptop, she cleared her throat, biting her bottom lip. Jess could smell her colleague's fruity perfume; notes of citrus and berries were apparent, and she felt the warm breath on the back of her neck as she sat behind her. Ruth was in her mid-thirties, always dressed impeccably, and resembled a young Naomi Campbell. Jess thought so anyway. They had so much in common: boxsets, films, the theatre, shopping, food, and she and Jess hit it off instantly. From the first day Ruth started, Jess was her backbone, showing her the ropes and helping however she could, explaining the pressure of deadlines, the barriers she'd face, and convincing sources to come forward with information.

'I don't know about this, Jess.' With the flat of her hand, Ruth rubbed her navy-blue skirt, trying to rid the creases. 'I hate this stuff.' She smiled nervously and continued. 'I'm freaking out, and you haven't even pressed play.' Placing her hands on the side of the swivel chair, Ruth pushed her heels against the floor and wheeled herself closer.

The office was empty; everyone had gone home for the evening. Outside, through the window, Jess saw Upper Street, the busy main road in Islington, North London, already jam-packed. Rain was spraying from vehicle tyres, and umbrellas were bouncing as people made their way home in the dark.

Glancing towards Ruth, she saw the hesitation in her eyes. She had to say something and put her at ease so she didn't feel pressured. 'Look, it's fine, honestly. If it's too much for you, I understand.' Her shoulders dropped, and she turned back to the laptop and closed it.

'No,' Ruth said. 'Play it. I won't be able to rest until I've seen the footage. Go on, I'm ready.' Ruth giggled to ease her tension. Her frame relaxed as she pushed back into the chair. The warm leather padding created a sense of security, enveloping her body.

She and Jess worked as investigative journalists for The Islington Gazette, a local paper. Ruth had worked there for a few weeks, Jess almost six months. The money was good, and the job was exciting, but the demands made it stressful.

Jess hadn't produced a gripping story in weeks; the page views on her authored stories had dropped by 30%, and her boss, Doug Hargreaves, was breathing down her neck, telling her to produce something, anything, to save her job and possibly her career.

This was the story Jess assured him would turn things around.

The documentary had gone viral on social media. It was first posted on a YouTube channel called The Chilling Floor. Shortly after, more people posted it on their channels and social media accounts. It became an overnight sensation. Everyone was talking about it.

After gruelling research, Jess discovered that Philip Lawson, born in Islington, had purchased the lodge, hence the angle to persuade Doug to go with the story.

Taking a deep breath, Ruth fought the trepidation. 'Go on, Jess, press play.'

'Are you sure? It's a tough watch. I don't want you having nightmares,' she said with a hint of jest.

'Um, I... yes, go on. I'm ready.'

Smiling, Jess opened the laptop, connected to YouTube, and clicked play.

2

WEDNESDAY EVENING

White noise pushed through the laptop's speaker, harsh on their ears. The picture flickered, vertical lines moving upwards as a grainy image appeared. It resembled an old B movie filmed on a low budget that had been watched dozens of times on a video recorder—that worn, jumpy effect. Smoke clung to the air, and it was difficult to see anything at first.

Pushing her body forward, watching the screen, Ruth could suddenly make out the inside of a camper van. There were four people in total. Two men and two women. As a window opened, the smoke cleared, and she saw tanned thighs and sliders.

One of the women drove.

The second woman sat in the back, and as she declared her excitement for their stay at the lodge in Sheers Woods, Ruth's skin felt icy cold, and goosebumps developed on her arms. The voice sounded dubbed, artificial, almost robotic, as if someone was using a disguise at the end of a phone. Her face was distorted, with swirling shadows shrouding her appearance. Only her long blonde hair and clothes suggested she was female.

'Oh, come on,' Ruth laughed. 'You can clearly see this is bullshit.'

'Keep watching,' Jess replied. 'I've seen it loads but still can't make up my mind. So many people believe it's leaked.'

'Yeah, whatever. It's done the trick, though. How many views has it had on social media?'

'A few million at least,' Jess responded. 'Predominantly YouTube, Facebook, and Instagram, but more recently on TikTok. It's been shared by thousands of accounts.'

'The creator must be loaded.'

'That's the thing. No one knows who posted it.'

The recording stopped for a few moments.

White noise.

More lines floated to the top of the screen as the picture focused.

The camera was stationary and looked as though it rested on the kitchen worktop.

The two men were on the sofa, their faces grainy and distorted. One had their legs over the edge, swinging back and forth. The other man was lying down, talking to the women. Although his voice was mechanical, you could make out his words.

'Shall we have a barbecue this evening?'

The woman who'd been driving wore a dressing gown, drying her short black hair with a towel. 'Sounds like a plan.' Again, her voice was disguised.

The second woman wore a tight T-shirt and shorts and appeared excited, waving her hands, and eagerly bouncing on her toes. 'Good idea. I'm up for that.'

Ruth's lips pursed as she squinted her eyes, finding it

impossible to make out any of their features. 'You really are falling for this, aren't you? Come on. It's so fake.'

Leaning back on the chair, Jess stretched her arms to the side, pushing her chest out and hearing a bone crack. 'All I'm saying is watch it. Then make up your own mind.'

The women disappeared from the clip as the men sat on the sofa drinking.

'Are their voices dubbed throughout?'

'Uh-huh. That's the weird thing, crazy, right?'

'Why can't we see their faces?' Ruth asked.

'Some believe the clip was released by the person or persons responsible for their disappearance. Others say the group loaded it before vanishing. It's like they're reaching out, begging to be found, and needing their story heard. There are so many comments on social media. Many believe something menacing awaits anyone who enters Sheers Woods.'

'Like, paranormal or a cult?'

'It's a possibility.'

'And where's this lodge?' asked Ruth.

'Bucks. Amersham. It's around an hour from London.'

They both jumped as, once again, white noise sounded through the laptop speaker.

The group were outside, throwing an inflatable ball to each other. The grass was short, the hedges trimmed and shaped. The sun was low in the sky and about to set, glistening on the camera lens, and a corner of the lodge was visible behind them.

They were laughing and appeared happy, enjoying each other's company.

Again, the camera was perched beside them, filming everything.

As the inflatable ball was tossed between the four of

them, one of the men was smoking and pretended to poke the lit cigarette into it.

The woman with long, blonde hair said, 'Don't, you arsehole. What's wrong with you?'

The man responded, 'I'm joking. Come on, I'm hungry. Are we going to eat?'

'Watch this,' Jess said.

'Watch what?'

'Here. Watch here.' Jess touched the laptop screen with her finger.

As the group finished throwing the ball to each other and walked back inside, a plaque with the words "Sheers Lodge" was visible. Beyond the lodge, a lone figure stood in a field, watching them.

The screen went blank.

'Holy shit. Now that's creepy,' responded Ruth. 'Who is it? One of their friends, possibly?'

'No one knows. Spooky, huh? I've zoomed in countless times, but it's hard to say.'

'Okay, I'm invested now. It's clever; I'll give you that.'

'You haven't seen anything yet.'

As the following clip rolled, the group were outside.

One of the men played a guitar, and the others were drinking, singing with him, and taking turns checking the food on the barbecue. Again, their voices were distorted. A campfire roared, and beyond them, the beautiful orange-coloured sun was dipping behind the hills.

The man placed the guitar on the ground and stood, poking at the barbecue. Smoke spilled into the air as he sat back against the tree, tuning his instrument.

The blonde-haired woman coughed, prompting the man sitting beside her to lean across and put his arm around her. They appeared to kiss, faces always ebbed out, and then both of them stood up, taking charge until the food was cooked.

'Right, who wants a burger?' the man standing at the barbecue asked.

They all nodded, and the couple proceeded to toast the buns, cut them open, and place the burgers inside them.

The four sat, chatting and laughing. The distorted voices added a menacing perspective to anyone watching the documentary.

The clip continued with more laughter, music, and chatting as the campfire roared, the flames dancing with the slight breeze. The darkness gave the clip a more eerie feeling.

Suddenly, a piercing scream rang from the surrounding fields.

Ruth felt a chill wash over her. Although Jess had seen it many times, she felt her skin get hot and clammy.

The group jumped up and stood by the fire.

Guitar man picked up a torch, shining it into the fields. What the fuck was that?'

The blond woman was visibly shaken, her body quivered as she moved from one foot to the other. 'I don't know. Someone's in trouble. It sounded like a woman in distress.' Pulling a mobile phone from her pocket, she held the screen in front of her. 'Still no reception. Christ! What is it with this place?'

'I don't have any either,' the other woman responded.

'I say we jump in the van and get help?' guitar man suggested. 'The nearest town is only a couple of miles away.'

'Someone help me; I'm begging you.'

The four of them stood momentarily, too frightened to move. Then, the second man spoke.

'We have... have to help her. She's in trouble.' Turning towards the voice, he shouted, 'Where are you?'

The place was silent. Only their shallow breaths as they appeared to consider their next move.

Guitar man shone the torch, watching the light dance along the ground, through the bushes, and back into the barren fields. 'Can you tell us where you are? Hello? We're going to help. Just tell us——'

Another scream ripped through the air, causing them to step away.

'I want to go home,' the blond woman shouted.

The second woman faced her, placing her hands on her shoulders. 'Look, we're going to get help. We'll drive the camper van into town and call the police.'

Charging out of view, guitar man returned seconds later with the keys and tossed them to the woman who'd been driving. Then he grabbed the camera, continuing to film everything.

After turning the key, the engine churned over several times, and smoke billowed into the air. 'Yes,' the black-haired woman shouted, thumping the steering wheel. 'This thing is temperamental at the best of times. Right, every-one pile in and lock the doors. We'll drive to town and get help.'

The others joined her, and she rolled the camper van along the grass at the front of the lodge.

The picture was erratic, jumping between blurred faces as the camera holder sat in the back.

Ruth squealed as she heard the tyres blow, and the camper van abruptly stopped. 'This can't be happening. They've gone to a lot of expense to try and convince us it's real.'

'Keep watching,' Jess said. 'You need to see all of it before making up your mind.'

More white noise, and as the next clip rolled, Ruth found herself clutching the edge of the chair, her nails buried deep in the leather material.

The camera appeared to rest on the kitchen worktop.

The four of them remained muted, most certainly from shock.

The front door pounded. Five raucous thumps in succession.

Guitar Man turned to the others. 'Maybe it's help?'

'Don't answer it?' the girl who'd been driving insisted.

Again, five bangs on the front door.

The tension was evident, the atmosphere sombre as guitar man eased to the front door, opened it, and stood outside. 'Who's there? Leave us alone, do you hear me?'

'Come back inside. Lock the door, please,' the driver pleaded.

The next couple of clips were short, chaotic, and genuinely terrifying.

Firstly, someone came rushing through the front door. The clip had been edited in such a way it was difficult to see the figure.

Frantic voices followed.

Then silence.

And finally, the clip ended with screams coming from one of the rooms at the back of the lodge, the camera jolting as if someone was running, deep, frightened gasps, desperate to escape.

Then, the recording finished.

3

WEDNESDAY EVENING

Ruth sat beside Jess, her mouth ajar and clutching her chest, listening to the rain pelting against the office window. The footage was raw, and although tampered with, there was something so realistic about it. The video clip had gone viral and accumulated a few million views on social media, and Ruth could see why.

'So, what do you think?' Jess asked, concern evident on her friend's face.

Ruth's eyes squinted, her brow furrowed, and lines appeared on her forehead. 'Honestly, I don't know. I have so many questions.' Standing up, she pushed the swivel chair back and walked over to her desk, grabbing her coat. 'And they've been missing for five years? No one knows anything about them—their story or why they were making a documentary?'

'So, here's the thing. I did lots of research. As you know, I'm hooked on this story. Initially, I contacted Thames Valley police, and they clarified that no one had come forward to confirm they knew the missing friends. We'll assume they're friends by how they acted in the clip. This led me to believe that because their identities were concealed, no one recognises them. Another angle is that they were backpackers from another country. It's possible family members have passed away or maybe haven't seen the clip to either confirm or deny the mystery. So yes, in answer to your question, no one seems to know anything about them. That's what makes it so intriguing.'

Walking back across the office, Ruth was hit by the sudden smell of detergent as the cleaner entered, spraying the air with freshener. Although a smoking ban was in place, their boss, Doug, often had a sneaky cigarette at his desk. Seeing the elderly lady grimace, Ruth flicked her eyes upwards as if to side with her.

'That bloody arsehole,' Maureen sniped. 'I've told him so many times. What's the point in me spraying the place? He'll only fill it with his toxic fumes in the morning.'

'He doesn't listen; you're wasting your time and energy on him,' Ruth stated. She turned back to Jess, watching her slip into her coat and grab her handbag from her desk. Ben's picture, her boyfriend of almost a year, had been placed in a new wooden frame. Jess's parents, Bob and Carol, were in another frame beside him. 'Don't you think it's suspect?' Ruth asked. 'I mean, okay, it's done well. I can see how it's had so many hits, but why the dubbing and distortion? And why did someone tamper with it? If you're going to upload a clip onto YouTube, post the real one.'

'That's why there's such a debate. An ebb of mystery. No one knows why.' Jess walked past the empty desks, the swivel chairs tucked neatly underneath, pictures of family and friends perched on desks, and mugs with motivational quotes filled with pens, paperclips, and elastic bands. She nodded at Maureen, who pushed a trolly filled with jay cloths and polish, its wheels spinning like a dog chasing its tail. 'Hey. How are you?' she asked. 'We're talking about that documentary. You know, the one filmed in Amersham. The group of friends who went missing.'

'Oh, I saw that on Facebook the other week. Freaked me right out. I showed Al, and he said it was bullshit. It's done well, though. Makes you think, don't it? I only remember it because it was so close to home. I hate those things. Don't like anything scary, me. Gives me nightmares. I saw people coming at me with pixilated faces for nights after while I slept, although I know it's not real.'

'It's what I was telling you,' Ruth emphasised. 'So, you think the town has some kind of sinister secret?'

'I think something's going on in Amersham,' Jess stated, 'that's for sure.'

Spraying polish over the desk closest to the door, Maureen began wiping its surface with a J-cloth. She turned to Jess and Ruth, wisps of her long grey hair hung over her face, her bright red lipstick smudged her teeth, and her dull green eyes almost screwed shut. 'I saw comments on Facebook. People were saying that it's cursed.'

'Oh, come on,' Jess said with a nervous laugh. 'Cursed?'

Spraying more polish, Maureen filled the air with the aroma of beeswax and turpentine. 'I know I wouldn't go near the place if you paid me.'

Outside, the rain lashed so ferociously it appeared to bounce off the ground. Opening her umbrella, Ruth shielded them as they ran to Jess's Peugeot.

Grabbing the keys from her handbag, Jess unlocked the car and opened the driver's door. 'Thanks. I really appreciate it. Where are you parked?'

'Just there.' She pointed to the corner of the car park at her four-seater Mini Cooper.

The women hugged as a bus passed on the road, the water spray almost catching them.

'I'll see you tomorrow,' Jess shouted over the rain, realising how loud she sounded. 'I hope the footage didn't freak you out too much.'

Ruth fought with the umbrella, the wind turning it inside out as she struggled to hold the stem. 'It would have if it were real. Anyway, enjoy your evening.'

The usual forty-minute drive home from the office in Islington to Cricklewood in North West London was nearly double due to the bad weather. As Jess sat in traffic, watching vehicle lights blink as cars stopped and started and aggravated drivers continuously wiping condensation from the windows, she thought about the footage. Although she'd seen it many times before, it still freaked her out, seeing the friends so vulnerable. She pictured the short scenes. The group chatting, throwing the inflatable ball to each other, the barbecue, the woman crying for help, the screams coming from one of the back rooms, and finishing with someone running through the lodge, desperate to escape.

Jess swerved and slammed the brakes as a cyclist emerged from a side road. *Shit. Get it together. Concentrate on the road.* Watching as he turned, the camera on his helmet pointing straight at her before giving her the V sign, she felt agitated, pushing her body back against the seat. 'Oh, nice. So mature. Yeah, go on arsehole, put it on YouTube and blame me.' Tapping the brakes again, Jess stopped, aggravated by the strain on her right leg. As she sat alone, a sense of failure worked through her body. Her boss had been giving her a hard time lately. He was unimpressed with her work ethic; that much was clear. The cruel jibes, the sarcastic remarks. *One day, you'll be early and shock us all. What, going home already? You've barely been here today. If you spent as much time writing as you did talking, you'd go far. Right folks, your wages are in, don't spend it all at once. Jess, don't you feel guilty getting paid? Money for old rope, hey.*

She'd just turned twenty-two and had worked for The Islington Press for almost six months after spending two years in sixth form and a further three years at university studying journalism and getting her bachelor's degree. But Doug was making it difficult to stay motivated and keep turning up. She felt harassed and often violated. She'd suffered severe bullying at school, which led to her being prone to bouts of depression, anxiety, and panic attacks. Her parents had pulled her through and been her rock, getting her the professional help needed to cope. That, and listening to her, always reassuring Jess how strong she was and her ability to cope with anything thrown at her. But the pressure of work and Doug's cruel snipes triggered her childhood struggle.

This documentary had to work. Jess had to pull it back and win his respect. Jobs were difficult to come by, and Doug was the type of prick who'd call her new boss and spend half the day slagging her off.

She was going to make it work.

In her addled mind state, Jess almost missed the turning and hit the brakes, hearing a driver behind honk the horn. Lifting her hand, she waved an apology and turned into a side road, pleased to find a parking space close to her flat.

The rain had finally eased as she opened the driver's

door. Grabbing her handbag from the passenger seat, she stepped onto the road and closed the door, hearing the short, sharp beeping sound as she locked the car.

Jess rented a ground-floor flat in an adequately sized semi-detached house, thanks to her parents helping with the costs. She rarely saw the neighbours due to the long working hours, and her evenings were spent either researching stories or catching up on projects and writing reports. It was a huge commitment, often without pay for the extra time consumed, but Jess loved the challenges her work presented, such as research, conducting interviews, and the social aspect.

Ever since her childhood, she'd wanted to be a journalist. This was her first job, and she was determined to win Doug's respect.

For this assignment, she aimed to conduct and film interviews, write a gripping article, and uncover the truth about what happened in Sheers Woods.

As she opened the front door, the automatic sensor activated the lights.

Letters and flyers slid under her heels, and Jess bent down, seeing a couple of envelopes with her name on the front. Once she'd grabbed them, she unlocked the inside door to her flat.

The lights were on in the hallway for security purposes, as she disliked the dark. The walls were painted a bright grey, displaying family pictures and an award for passing her journalism course.

Jess removed her high heels, punched in the alarm code, and walked barefoot into the kitchen, passing the bathroom on her left; the diffuser filled the flat with a pleasing scent of lavender.

In the kitchen, the recessed LED lights cast a warm glow

as she filled the kettle with water and turned it on. Grabbing a mug from the cupboard overhead, she placed it on the polished granite worktop, peering at the letters and throwing them onto the breakfast bar behind her. There were no alarming signs like "urgent" or "do not ignore" marked on the front of the envelopes, and her mind was too preoccupied to open them this evening.

Her night was already planned.

Jess was going to research the documentary and see if anything new had been posted regarding its authenticity.

Standing by the worktop, the kettle hissing, she peered at the breakfast bar surrounded by tall red stools and popular kitchen quotes hanging in frames on the white walls.

Mama's Kitchen.

Happiness is a small house with a big kitchen.

My kitchen, my rules.

Don't like the heat, get outta the kitchen.

The solid wood fitted cupboards housed a washing machine that rumbled loudly on its final spin, possibly the drum, and Jess was pleased she lived on the ground floor, not wanting to irritate neighbours underneath her. Next to it was a dishwasher. To her left was a modern electric hob, and underneath were large drawers for her utensils, fitted with a push-sprung sliding mechanism.

As the kettle boiled, Jess grabbed a spoon from the top drawer, dipped it into the coffee jar, and tipped it into a mug, pouring hot water on top and stirring the contents. Adding a dash of cold water, she sat at the breakfast bar, opened her laptop, and went onto YouTube.

After tapping the words "Amersham, found footage" into the search bar, Jess clicked on the most viewed video, seeing the clip reposted many times by loads of different accounts. She scrolled, seeing all the recent comments.

Although she'd viewed it many times, the sense of danger seemed more real. It felt more personal suddenly, knowing it could be her next assignment.

Everything depended on Doug's decision tomorrow morning. She'd tracked down the new owner, and he'd emailed, awaiting their response.

It was Jess's time to shine. To step up.

She began reading the latest comments on the found footage.

Stevothecelt

Nice try, people. But it's fake. Why aren't they celebrities already?

Clownprince501

Moron, have you seen their faces blotted out? No one knows who they are.

Doggyfresh

It's my sister and her friends. They're fine. No harm done.

This comment made Jess smile. She continued to scroll.

Maydayo1
I wonder what happened to them. If it's real, it's fucked up and proper scary. A bit like a horror movie if you ask me.

Manbat1957
Yeah. Love this. I've seen it so many times.

Druidic
Fake.

Stationchick
Totally made up, and you're all falling for it.

Jakerake99
Bullshit alert.

Scrolling back to the top of the page, Jess sipped her coffee and clicked the video, wanting to see something, anything that could give her a clue to its authenticity.

The familiar white noise crackled through the laptop's speaker, the lines moving up the screen as the inside of the camper van came into focus.

Jess found herself pausing every few seconds, zooming in, looking for something she'd missed to indicate whether it was real or fake. A smirk due to a glitch in the recording while they were under pressure, a clue in their mannerisms, how they acted. It was impossible to tell.

I guess that's why there's such a buzz about the record-

ing, Jess thought. *No one really knows, it's what makes it so intriguing. Very clever.*

Clicking a little further along, still looking for tell-tale signs, Jess jumped to the part of the clip with the group outside, throwing the inflatable ball. The edge of the lodge was visible in the corner of the screen. Tapping the mousepad and slowing the footage down as they walked back inside, she paused at the part with the shadow behind them, resembling a person or persons watching them. Pinching the mousepad, Jess zoomed in closer. The larger the picture became, the more pixilated it looked. It was impossible to tell what it was behind them. *A large shadow figure, perhaps? Possibly a creature or ghostly apparition? No, come on. Someone or something is watching them,* Jess thought. *Why? Why are they being watched? Did they piss someone off on the way there? Get into a fight while driving through the town? Cut someone up on the road?* Grabbing a notepad from the drawer where she sat, Jess began writing.

Ask the locals. Someone may know something. A raised voice in a shop, a road rage incident. Anything to detect something happened while they drove to the lodge.

Looking at when the footage was originally uploaded, Jess opened a new tab. Into Google, she typed "road rage, Amersham, Bucks," and entered the date. The local paper reported numerous road rage incidents but nothing in or around the time in question. She typed "fight," knowing if she'd searched for the words "argument, pub, shop, Amersham," the chances were slim of finding something significant to make the papers. Again, a few incidents of street muggings and an organised prize fight back in the sixties—nothing to indicate anything relating to the group in question.

Next, Jess moved her finger along the mousepad, and the

video cut to the barbecue, one of the men playing the guitar while the others sang. Again, robotic voices. They sounded like the munchkins in *The Wizard Of Oz* telling Dorothy to follow the yellow brick road.

Suddenly, a distant scream pierced through the speaker, causing Jess to jolt. No matter how many times she viewed it, the footage still affected her. Scrolling back slightly, she listened again. The person, most certainly a woman, was desperately calling for help as if their life depended on it. This part didn't sound artificial. It seemed genuine. Again, Jess scrolled back, turning the volume up—the scream.

So chilling.

So incredibly eerie.

She almost leapt off the seat as her mobile phone rang from the worktop.

Leaning against the back of the stool, feeling its soft cushion, Jess took a deep breath, laughing to herself, and grabbed the phone, pleased to see Ben's name. 'Hi, babe. Wow! You frightened the life out of me.'

Ben's voice was comforting, deep, smooth, and a welcome relief from the tense footage she'd been watching.

'I frightened you. How?'

'Oh, I'm watching that footage again. You know, the one where the group goes missing from the lodge.' Hearing him sigh, she knew he didn't like her watching it and scaring herself.

'Jess, you're getting a little fixated with this. I'm worried about you. Please don't ask Doug again. I don't want you going anywhere near the place.'

Stretching, knowing she needed rest, she stemmed the yawn, not wanting to sound rude. She'd been working long hours, and her body needed sleep. 'I... I asked him again.'

'Who?' Ben queried.

'Doug. He's gonna let me know tomorrow. It looks like he's up for it.'

'You're joking, right? Tell me you're joking.' When Ben heard the embarrassed silence, he continued. 'I thought this... I thought you were fooling around. I didn't think Doug would be up for it. I'm sorry, Jess, but I don't want you to go. I can't get out of work as we're on a deadline to finish the set. Macbeth starts in a couple of weeks, and I'm running the team. Please don't do this.'

With a raised voice, she answered, 'My career is on the line. I'm not performing as I should, and I know Doug is getting fed up with me. I'm already hanging on by a thread.'

'So, get another job?'

'You know it's not that easy. And I think Doug will make it difficult. He's sneaky. I hear him slagging me off to anyone who'll listen in the office. This could be my big break. I know I can do this. I know the story inside out. I've seen the footage dozens of times. People are obsessed with it.'

'No, you're obsessed with it. It's all you've spoken about recently.'

That hurt her. After a short pause, she continued. 'Doug has emailed the new owner of the lodge. They're possibly going to let me stay there for a couple of nights. It's the first time it's opened since—'

'It gets worse. I thought you were going up there for a couple of hours, ask some questions, and bolt.'

'I want to stay there. I need to find out the truth.'

'Jess, I'm begging you. At least wait until I'm done with the set. And if you're still determined, I can come with you.'

'I can't. Doug is about to sack me. I have to prove my worth.'

'You're worth ten of that idiot.'

'Thank you, Ben. I appreciate it.'

'Can I come over?' he asked. 'I'll be done here around half ten.'

'I'm going to do a little bit more research; then I'm going to bed. I'm knackered, but I'd love to see you tomorrow.'

'Okay, fine. I have another long shift, but I'll come over after work.' Ben's deep sigh indicated his irritation. 'I'll be over around eight. Is that good for you?'

'Yes. I can't wait to see you. It's been days.'

'Love you, Jess.'

'Love you too.'

After making another coffee, she grabbed the laptop and walked along the hallway and into the living room, eyeing the flat-screen TV to her left on a metal stand by the window. More pictures of her and her parents hung on the wall opposite. A day at Brighton Beach, Jess was digging the sand with a plastic shovel, her mum and dad stood behind her, and a stranger captured the beautiful moment. Another at their favourite Italian restaurant, her prom night showing Jess and her school friends entering a flashy white limousine, her parents on either side, proud smiles on their faces, and another of her graduation day, as she'd finally passed her exams, with her proud parents behind her, placing their hands on her shoulders. As Jess stood, looking at the photos, she fought the lump in her throat, suddenly feeling neglectful. She hadn't spoken to them for a couple of days. They always had her back and were a part of everything she achieved. Guilt suddenly festered, causing a knot in her stomach. Work, the footage, pleasing Doug, and the worry about keeping her job consumed every moment of her life.

As she stood over the sofa, the conversation with Ben ran through her mind. Yes, she knew he was worried; that much was obvious. But Jess had to do this.

Staring at the photo of her at Brighton Beach, she swallowed the lump, struggling to control her emotions, and sat, the images so vivid of her as a little girl, maybe six or seven, imagining the warmth as the sun shone high in the sky, the smell of candy floss and toffee apples, the waves lapping the shore where she crouched, seagulls crowing above, her father in long shorts, socks, and sandals, her mother in a summer dress and a large straw hat on her head to avoid getting sunstroke. Jess imagined that little girl clutching the sand, seeing it evaporate through the gaps in her fingers.

Now, her job felt the same. Slowly disintegrating in front of her. *What would I tell that little girl if I had my time back?* Jess asked herself. *To be brave. Don't listen to anyone who puts you down. You can do this, Jess Turner. You can achieve anything you want. Oh, and by the way, your crush, Stephen Ebson, forget it. He's a minger now. I saw him in town recently. Yuk.*

Opening the laptop, Jess clicked back into the YouTube video, desperate to find something. She ran it from the start, frustration working through her body as she became giddy, tapping her feet on the wooden floor and biting her nails.

With her forefinger tapping on the mouse pad, she stopped the recording every few seconds, dissecting the main parts frame by frame.

The camper van.

Throwing the inflatable ball to each other.

Spreading her fingers across the mouse, she zoomed in, watching as the ball floated majestically in the air. She dragged the mouse to where the figure was standing behind them. Someone or something was watching, but it was so hard to tell what it was—a mere shadow. Jess had lots of questions. Many of the previous comments on YouTube had claimed it was an entity. Something demonic. Could that be what happened? Had the young friends been stalked by something sinister?

Stop. Enough. Your imagination is running wild. It's not possible. But the more she gazed at the figure, the more convincing it became. Maybe there was something paranormal haunting Sheers Woods.

A shiver powered through her back, her shoulders jolted, and her skin went cold.

Come on, Jess, get it together.

Scrolling down the page, she found previous comments regarding the shadow in the fields.

Geezerfridgefreezer

There's definitely something there. But it's concealed. The uploader is fucking with us and doesn't want us to see who or what it is.

Robthesnob08

Fuck, man. That's some freaky shit right there. Someone watching them, and they don't even know. I can't watch past this part. Forget it.

Cassthelass39

That poor group. God help them if it's real. May they rest in peace.

.   .   .

Rudedude

    Mate, are you serious? It's completely fake.

Mackthefork

I think the town has some kind of urban legend, and this is a warning to keep away. I wouldn't venture up there for all the money in the world.

The last message resonated, and she'd thought this herself.

What if the town has some kind of urban legend and the video clip is a warning?

4

THURSDAY MORNING

'Jess, have you got a moment for a chat?' Doug Hargreaves stood at the office door, wearing the same trousers as yesterday with the soup stain down his left thigh. His blue shirt was damp under the pits as he gripped the top of the door frame. Although it was cold, his forehead glistened with sweat, and one corner of his moustache was stained with ketchup from his breakfast.

Slowly, Jess rose from her seat and made eye contact with Ruth, seeing the apprehension on her face. 'Of course,' she answered.

'Good luck,' Ruth mouthed.

'Thanks,' she replied. As she walked towards the office, trying to read Doug's face, she felt as though her career depended on the next conversation. Through the glass, she watched Doug stroll across his office floor, sinking into his swivel chair.

After tapping on the door, she entered the office, the stress almost unbearable, as if she were about to audition for the X Factor or waiting for the jury to give their verdict.

The smell of smoke and stale coffee hit her hard as she looked towards him; the usual smirk adorned his face. She wanted so badly to grab him by the shirt, pin him against the wall, and scream, *Don't fuck me around. I don't need it. You know I'm capable. Don't ruin my fucking career before it's started.* Jess remained composed and in control.

'Please, take a seat,' Doug ordered.

Jess eyed the ashtray with a pile of cigarette butts, the picture of Doug's wife and son in an old wooden frame, and the pot of chewed pencils. Fixing her dress and sitting, she said, 'Thank you.' Her heart was pounding, and it felt like it would explode in her chest.

'So,' Doug began, 'about your request. The documentary.'

Remaining silent, Jess desperately tried to act calm. Inside, it felt like her body was on fire.

'You really wanna do this?' he asked.

'I... Yeah... Yes, I do. More than anything.' *Oh, shut up,* she told herself. *Let him speak; you're sounding desperate.* 'Have you heard back from the owner?'

'I'm coming to that.' Doug looked down at the desk, shuffling a pile of papers. After a moment, his eyes fixed on her. 'I think it's been difficult for you. Coming straight from university, entering the real world of work.'

It felt as if her body was deflating, shrinking in front of him, and any second now, she'd evaporate into a pool of water that Doug Hargreaves would wipe up with a mop. She imagined her hands outstretched as her body lowered into quicksand, and Jess Turner would never be seen again. Her mind raced, imagining his next sentence. *Jess, we've had enough of you. We can't afford to keep you on. It's not you, it's me. I shouldn't have given you the job. It was too early. You weren't ready. Get out of here and never come back; that's the best thing for you. Never, ever, I mean ever, write another word again. Not even to type a single letter, an exclamation point, or a question mark, you hear me? Be gone with you now, my child. Don't darken my world again.*

Doug inhaled deeply. 'Look, I'm gonna give you a chance.'

Pop, that's the sound of Jess Turner bursting, the pressure all too much. She had visions of spontaneously combusting, Doug removing his wet, sweaty shirt and wrapping it around her to stem the flames.

Open-mouthed, her lips dry, her body in shock, Jess watched his face to see if there were any signs he was winding her up. Nothing. If anything, his eyes appeared to soften, and his usual smirk resembled a sincere, heart-warming smile.

Wonders never cease, Doug Hargreaves. You do have a heart. You do care, Jess thought. As she went to talk, her tongue felt heavy, like a slab of meat that wouldn't move to speak the words. *Picture him naked,* she thought. *Yes, that always works. Yuk.*

'Say something then,' Doug pushed.

'Oh my God! This is... amazing. I won't let you down, I promise.' At this very moment, she felt like she was going to stand up and do cartwheels around the office. However hard it was, she remained seated.

Doug continued. 'I had an email back early this morning. I mentioned nothing of the documentary. The less the new owner knows, the better. The lodge is yours. He's even going to courier over a key later today. I've pulled a favour with the promise of a glowing review on the place.'

'When can I go?'

'Tomorrow morning if you like. No time like the present. I don't see a problem with you starting straight away.'

'I don't know what to say. Wow! Thank you. Thank you so much.' As Jess shook his hand and walked towards the office door, she heard his voice behind her.

'Just be careful. It's your big break. I'm letting you represent the company. Come back to us in one piece.'

That was her main priority. The first sign of danger, and she'd run as far away from the lodge as possible.

5

THURSDAY MORNING

'Oh my goodness! Jess, how did you persuade him?' Ruth stood at the coffee machine, listening to the loud vibration as it chugged. The smell of coffee beans was enticing, invigorating her senses.

Jess was seated at her desk. The nervous energy revealed her anticipation, her legs tapping the floor, fingers drumming the desk, shifting her body in the chair, and still sipping on a coffee she'd made over an hour ago. 'This girl can be persuasive when the chips are down. I can leave tomorrow morning; Doug's agreed to everything.' She watched Ruth's expression change; her eyebrows lifted, and her lip curled at one end, a sure indication of the unease she felt.

'That's... Okay... That's... I'm just worried about you.' The coffee machine finished, and Ruth grabbed her mug, walking a couple of steps to Jess's desk. 'Last night, I had nightmares about the footage. Christ! I was being chased through a field. The heavy breaths behind me, the wet grass soaking my trainers, and I fell. I couldn't get up. You know how it is in dreams. But it was so real.' Placing her mug on Jess's desk, Ruth said, 'What if it's a sign? A warning that—-'

'I'll be fine,' Jess interrupted. 'The footage has gripped social media. Finally, I can produce something to be proud of, that Doug can appreciate and realise my potential.'

'With all due respect, fuck Doug.' Ruth eyed him through his office window. Thankfully, he hadn't heard. Reverting her eyes back to Jess, she continued. 'Do you think he has your best interests at heart? Of course not; you're a number like the rest of us. He doesn't give a shit about you, me, or anyone else here. He'd sack us at the drop of... his trousers when he walks.'

Laughing, Jess said, 'I thought he wore a belt?'

'Well, it obviously ain't big enough. All I see is arse when he passes. Big hairy fucking butt cheeks on display, his trousers clutching the top of his thighs.'

'Sshhh, he'll hear you.'

Leaning into the desk, she whispered, 'All I'm saying is he doesn't care. Don't do it for him to prove your worth. You're better than that, Jess. You're incredible—all you had to deal with at school, the bullying, the girls trying to humiliate you, and how you rose above it. Look at you now. You make me want to get up in the morning and come to work. Your energy is contagious. I don't know what I'd do without you. You've helped me so much. Showed me the ropes. It's probably the only reason I've clung to my job. I admire you more than you'll ever know.'

'Ahh, thanks, Ruth. I appreciate it.'

'It's the truth. So, when you start saying you want to prove yourself, don't ever think of that idiot who claims to run the place. Do it because it's what you want, no one else. Oh, and come back in one piece.'

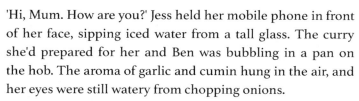

'Hi, Mum. How are you?' Jess held her mobile phone in front of her face, sipping iced water from a tall glass. The curry she'd prepared for her and Ben was bubbling in a pan on the hob. The aroma of garlic and cumin hung in the air, and her eyes were still watery from chopping onions.

'Hey, Jess. I'm good. Your Dad's in the living room; he's dozed off after watching the horse racing. If he thinks I'm going to try and wake him at bedtime, he's another thing coming. Last night it took me nearly ten minutes. I don't know why he keeps falling asleep. He doesn't drink enough water. If he drank half as much as he did beer, he'd be better off. Have you lost weight? You look gaunt. You're fading away, dear.'

Jess smiled, staring for a moment at her mother. Her thick grey hair, always styled to perfection, her deep hazel eyes still dazzling and full of life, and her complexion was always clear and youthful. She looked much younger than her sixty-four years. 'No, I'm the same as when we spoke the other day.' Jess wondered if the apprehension of going to the lodge was starting to show.

'And how's Ben?' Carol asked.

'Good.' Jess took another slug of water and crunched on the ice. 'Yeah, fine, he's coming over this evening. I'm cooking for us.'

'Ooh, lucky boy. What are you doing?'

'I'm cooking a Madras. Ben loves it. It's your recipe. I have Bombay potatoes, chicken, rice, poppadoms, and the naan bread is ready to put in the oven. The full works. You want to smell the kitchen; you'd be proud.'

'I'm already proud. Your Dad and I were just saying earlier, before the bugger fell asleep, how much you've achieved. A new job, a flat, settling down with Ben. You're in a good place.'

'I wouldn't call my relationship with Ben settling down. It's still early.'

'Oh, Jess. You're not getting cold feet, are you?'

'Course not.' She didn't want to tell her mother the real reason. Numerous times, she'd asked Ben to move in with her. They'd been going out for almost a year, and she was anxious to progress and bring things forward. Ben still living with his parents when she rented a flat wasn't her idea of advancement. Bracing herself, she prepared for her next line of conversation. She gripped the side of the table, again her feet tapping on the floor as she went to speak. 'I'm going away for a couple of days with work.'

'Where are you off to?'

'Wake Dad. I want to tell him, too.'

'Hang on a second. He'd sleep through an earthquake. Bob, Bob, Jess is on the phone.' Carol pointed the phone at her husband, Jess's father. 'Bob,' she yelled.

His eyes opened, and he sat up, taking the phone.

'Hey, Dad. You alright?'

'Fine, love. I was napping.'

'Jess has some news,' Carol said.

With his fingers curled, Bob wiped his stubble, his grey hair tossed and unkempt, and his deep blue eyes settled on the phone screen. 'You and Ben are okay?'

'We're fine, Dad.'

'The job is alright?'

'Yes.'

'And Doug's behaving himself?'

'He is, Dad.'

'You know I'll clip the bastard around the ear if he offends you. You're my girl.'

'I'm going away with work. My first major assignment.'

'Where are you off to?' her father asked.

'Doug has given me permission to investigate an unsolved crime.'

Both her parents' expressions seemed to freeze as they digested what Jess said.

'You're not putting yourself in any danger, are you?' Bob asked.

Jess watched her father lean in, trying to dissect what she was saying. Her mother sat, resting her hand on the side of her face.

After explaining the contents of the viral video and the mystery surrounding it, Jess said, 'I'm going to Amersham, a bit of investigative journalism. Doug wants me to report on it, write up an article regarding what happened out there. I'll.. I'll be staying in the lodge. On my own.'

'You are going to be safe, aren't you?' Carol asked.

'Mum, don't worry.' The doorbell chimed from the hall-way. 'I have to go. Love you. I'll call you tomorrow when I'm there. Love you, Dad.'

'Any sign of danger, and you get yourself out of there,' her father advised.

'I have to go,' she whispered.

Again, the doorbell chimed.

'Coming.' Seeing Ben through the front door spy hole in the communal hall filled her with pleasure only he could bring. Opening the door a little too enthusiastically, she kissed him, tasting mint toothpaste, and rested her nose against his smooth skin, breathing in his scent of fresh lemon and a lavish fruity aroma. As she stood back, Jess saw his crisp white shirt, his tight, faded jeans, and polished black boots. 'I'm so glad you're here.'

Smiling, his deep green eyes so tender, Ben answered,

'Me too. What a welcome. Wow! Something smells good. How was work?' he asked.

'Oh, good. I'll tell you all about it inside.'

Jess strolled through the hallway to the kitchen.

Ben followed, complimenting her on the beautiful red dress. Her short blonde hair brushed her shoulders as she walked.

After handing him a glass of red wine, they sat at the breakfast bar.

Eyeing the open laptop, Ben saw the footage Jess was so obsessed with. 'Oh, come on. Enough already. It's beginning to take over your life. Can't you forget about it for five minutes?'

She pushed the lid shut and sipped her wine. 'Sorry. Tonight is about us. Are you hungry?'

'Starving.'

'Good.' She pushed the stool back and stood.

Ben took her hand and guided her back onto the seat. 'I've got this. You've done so much already.'

Her brown eyes widened, maybe through the unease of leaving him for the next couple of nights.

Once Ben removed the bread from the oven and dished up the rice, potatoes, and chicken, they sat, engrossed in conversation. He told Jess all about the upcoming theatre show, the strain of running everything, how he had to keep telling people what to do and how to do it, practically holding their hands, and that he'd wrangled a couple of tickets for him and Jess.

'I'd love that. You know me and theatre shows. When is it?'

Ben spooned a generous amount of rice and potatoes into his mouth and sipped the wine. 'End of the month. I've seen the actors and actresses in rehearsals. Bloody hell, they're good. I don't know how they learn the lines. It's a real skill.'

'Well, they'd ask you the same. How the hell do you start putting a set together? To each their own. How's the food?'

'Beautiful. Thanks, hun.'

Taking a deep breath, she braced herself. 'I have some good news.'

'Oh, has Doug finally kicked the bucket? Horrible old bastard.'

She playfully slapped his hand. 'Don't. He's not that bad. He's given me my first major project. I'm running it completely.'

'Really. Well, that's great news. What is it?'

'It's what we spoke about last night—investigating the footage. The four people vanishing from the lodge in Amersham.' She watched as Ben practically spat the wine into his glass.

'You're not serious. Please, Jess. I didn't think he'd go for it. Please tell me you're winding me up.'

Her skin became hot, and Jess felt her cheeks turn red. 'It means he believes in me. He's funding it. It's exciting. I thought you'd be happy for me.'

Ben leant into the stool, straightening his back. 'Christ, Jess, how can I be? It's dangerous. You don't know what's going on out there. 'Who... Who's going with you?'

After a brief moment, she said, 'Me. Just me.'

'You? And nobody else? You're pulling my leg.'

'No. Doug believes in me. He's letting me take charge.'

'That pompous, arrogant twat. He doesn't believe in anyone. He's fucking laughing behind your back. Sending you on a goose chase so he can mock you and make you look stupid. There isn't a fucking goose. That's about the size of it.'

'I thought you'd be pleased for me. It's all I've ever wanted.'

'So go to a proper firm, report on local crimes. Write amazing articles and be the star I know you already are. Doug doesn't give a shit about you, sending you out there, dollar signs in his eyes because he knows the exposure the video clip has. He doesn't care if you come back, that much is obvious. He's making an idiot out of you without putting your well-being first, and you're falling for it. He's pathetic.'

'He's making an idiot out of me, is he? That's what you think?'

'I... I don't mean—'

'You know what? I'm not dealing with this now. Can you just leave?'

'I'm just trying to—'

'I said get out!'

Ben stood. 'Jess, I'm sorry. I didn't mean to have a go. Can't you wait a couple of weeks until the set is built? I promise if you're still keen to go out there, I'll join you. We'll make a weekend of it. Just the two of us.'

'Get out of my flat.' As Ben grabbed his jacket from the back of the stool and walked along the hallway and onto the street, she felt so guilty telling him to leave, wondering if this was the last time she'd see him.

6

FRIDAY MORNING

Once showered and dressed, Jess slipped into a pair of blue jeans, a thick brown woollen jumper, socks, and comfortable trainers. Through her bedroom window, the sun shone brightly in the clear blue sky with a dusting of clouds, but mid-October often brought a bitter coldness, and the frost was thick on the grass. The table close to her window was iced over, and an ashtray full of cigarette butts was left on top. She was suddenly agitated and had asked the couple upstairs numerous times to empty it. They thought they owned the communal garden and always gave her odd looks when she went out for fresh air. The waft of smoke often seeped into her bedroom in the evening, and she could hear them outside, laughing and mocking her.

After filling her bag with clothes, a couple more jumpers, two pairs of jeans, a black pair of leggings, socks, underwear, and her makeup bag, Jess went down to the kitchen and opened the laptop, pleased to see Doug had emailed her with the address. He'd even written her an encouraging email.

· · ·

Dear Jess.

I wish you all the best, and I look forward to reading your report and watching your docufilm regarding the unsolved mystery. I know how much it means to you and your concerns with progressing in our company.

This is your chance to shine.

Make sure to take care of yourself, and at the first whiff of danger, get yourself home. Although I think you'll be safe, keep the lodge locked at night. The place has gained mass exposure in the last few years, and you don't know what idiots will be hanging around. Call the police if you see any suspicious behaviour.

I know the footage has gone viral and I think it's going to be very interesting, you doing a documentary. Hell, we might even get views. (I'm joking. I know you'll smash it)

If you can be in at the usual time next Wednesday. That should be ample opportunity for you to put something interesting together.

You'll be pleased to know there's Wi-Fi there, and I've provided the password at the bottom of this email.

Good luck, Jess. I'm rooting for you.

Be safe, and see you soon. (Wednesday. 9 am. Don't be late.)

Regards,

Doug Hargreaves.

After reading it a second time, Jess closed the laptop. *Wow, he does have a heart,* she thought.

In the boot of the car, she placed both the large industrial and pocket torch she'd purchased from a hardware store, and once she'd packed a second pair of trainers, laptop, and chargers, the Dictaphone, and all the other equipment needed to document her stay, she slipped into a warm jacket and grabbed the key to the lodge.

After setting the alarm and locking the door to her flat, she said a prayer to herself and closed the main front door. Taking a deep breath, she walked away from the flat and got into her car, fighting the anxiety which quickly encompassed her.

As Jess drove along the A5 towards the M1, she blasted an eighties album from Spotify. The sun reflected on the windscreen, the sky a deep blue, reminding her of the ocean, and the driver's window was cracked open. The cool breeze on her face felt refreshing, lifting her anxiety.

Steering the car onto the M1, she sang, "Girls Just Wanna Have Fun," at the top of her voice, the excitement building, pushing from the pit of her stomach through her body.

Passing the service station and seeing a sign with pictures displaying fast food, burgers, chips, an array of wraps, and cold drinks, Jess realised she hadn't eaten but chose to keep going. It was only an hour's drive, possibly less if the traffic was light, and she could eat once she got there.

She jumped as the phone rang, hoping to see Ben's name displayed on the screen. *I have to call him tonight,* she thought, not wanting the argument to fester. Tapping the answer button on the steering wheel, Jess greeted Ruth with optimism in her voice. 'Morning, how are you?'

'Hey, chick. Good. Have you left yet?'

'On the motorway as we speak. What a glorious day. How's work?' asked Jess.

'Shitty. Oh, Doug has the same grey trousers on, three days in a row. I can see the ketchup mark. Can you believe that?'

Jess laughed. 'I thought it was only me who noticed. It's gross. I had a fight with Ben last night.' Jess went on to tell her friend what happened, how he'd turned up, demanding she forget about the footage and asking her not to go. 'I'm gutted. Just when things were progressing. We haven't had a row for so long.'

'It will blow over. There is Wi-Fi there, right?'

Seeing the sign for Watford, Junction 5, Jess indicated and pulled into the first lane. 'Yes. Doug emailed the code this morning.'

'Great. Call me when you get there.'

'You sound like my mum.'

'I'm worried about you. You don't know the dangers over there. What if you're—-?'

'Nothing's going to happen,' Jess interrupted, her tone firm. 'If I feel I'm in danger, I'll get in the car and drive away. Really, Ruth, there's nothing to worry about.' Jess heard another voice in the background.

'Shit, I've got to run. Doug is on my case; you know how he hates us making calls during office hours. So, you'll be there in an hour. Give or take. Call me. I mean it.'

'I will. Love ya, Ruth.'

'Love ya, chick.'

As the call ended, "Take On Me" played by A-ha, like a sign, filling Jess with courage and determination for anything thrown at her.

～

An icy chill pushed through the window as Jess joined the M25. The articulated lorries caused wind blasts, making the Peugeot rock. Struggling with the steering wheel, she indicated and pulled to the inside lane, watching the speedometer. The stench of diesel was overwhelming, and often, she could smell burning tyres. Coughing, she closed the window, unable to bear it any longer.

After calling her parents again, her mum reading in the living room, and her father sat next to her jotting down the names of the horses he fancied betting on this afternoon, Jess assured them she was safe and managed to avert the many questions by telling them she'd call them tonight.

She thought about Ben. Although she was determined to do this, to visit Amersham, the lodge, and investigate the story behind the footage, she could see his point, too. He was worried and concerned for her safety.

As she drove, her thoughts circled back to the email Doug had sent. One line echoed persistently in her mind.

Although I think you'll be safe, keep the lodge locked at night.

Ahead, the sign displayed Amersham. Junction 18.

Her body tensed as she indicated, taking the slip road to her left.

The A404 leading to Amersham was a welcome sight after the crazy traffic on the M25. Jess marvelled at the fields on either side. Her life was hectic in London, and the commute was usually dull grey buildings, traffic lights, and narrow roads. It was a welcome sight, and she struggled to recall the last time she had been surrounded by so much greenery.

The window was cranked open, and the cloudless sky eased her apprehension. The smell of damp grass and decaying leaves was a welcome transition from the smog and diesel of the bustling London streets.

Jess followed the Amersham Road through Chorleywood and Little Chalfont, taking the A413 past Amersham Hospital and finally seeing a sign for Sheers Woods.

Indicating right, she pulled into a side road and parked near the curb, pleased there were no yellow lines painted along the road, no permit holder only indications, and no other obvious restrictions.

An elderly lady approached a small florist, unlocked a chain, and lifted the red shutter, the noise resembling the screech of a roller coaster coming to a halt at a fairground. Bunches of roses and tulips were displayed in the front window, and other bright flowers were in plant pots. A sign reading "Beth's Bloomin Marvels" was written above the door in bold black letters, and the address and phone number were underneath.

Killing the engine, Jess reached for her mobile phone, pleased to see there was reception. Eying the time, almost 10 am, she knew Ben would be on a break soon. Fighting her pride, she simply texted a heart, pressed send, and watched the phone screen. The word "Delivered" appeared at the bottom, and Jess waited, legs tapping against the pedals, fingers drumming the dashboard. Her lips expanded, and her brown eyes widened as she saw his name appear. Composing herself and wanting to remain calm, Jess answered the call. 'Hi.' *Argh. Too enthusiastic,* she thought.

'Hi,' his smooth, husky voice replied. 'I'm... I... Jess, I'm sorry. I didn't mean to order you around. I'm worried about you. I love you so much.'

Her eyes glazed over. 'I love you too, Ben. I'm sorry as well. I shouldn't have ordered you out of the flat.' After a pause, she said,' I can't remember the last time we argued.'

'Me either. Look, I've been thinking about us, our relationship.'

A knot developed in her stomach, feeling like a fist twisting deep inside, fearing his next words.

Continuing, Ben said, 'We've been together for a year; it's going well. Not just well,' his nervous laugh was evident as he spoke, 'but amazing. I'm crazy about you. I couldn't stop thinking about the argument last night and this morning. I can't concentrate on work. On anything when we're apart. So, I want to move in with you. I can contribute to the rent, or we'll find somewhere better. Whatever you want.'

'Are you—? You're serious? You mean it?' She could hear noise in the background, a woman's voice asking where she should place the boards, and someone using a tool, possibly a hammer, singing to themselves.

'Yes,' he laughed, 'I'm deadly serious.'

'I'd love that,' Jess answered.

'I have to go, but I'll bell you later. Oh, and Jess, keep safe.'

'I will.' After ending the call, she slammed her palms several times on the dashboard, the sudden elation drowning her body. She couldn't remember a time she'd been happier. She closed her eyes, savouring the moment, digesting the conversation, and in her mind, she drifted in the air like a feather caught in a light breeze.

Next, she Googled "Beth's Bloomin Marvels, Amersham." A page loaded with information regarding the business. Beth Harris opened the shop in the late seventies after selling flowers door to door. She had a love of bright colours and beautiful smells and decided to follow her dream by opening a florist. Scrolling down the page, Jess saw Beth as a young woman cutting a ribbon. A local newspaper, the Bucks Herald, had taken photos to mark the occasion. Jess smiled, seeing a vintage Hillman Avenger in the background, her father's first car, and he often spoke about it, comparing all the new models to it. *There's nothing like my old Hillman,* he'd say. *It will go forever.*

Shifting her body, Jess turned, opened her bag, and grabbed the Dictaphone. *No time like the present,* she thought, anxious to get going. The plan was to dictate as much as possible, using the recording device to help with her blog and write notes for the main story. Her phone camera could record interviews, with the idea of capturing as much footage as possible around the lodge.

Where better to start than Beth, the florist owner? Jess wanted to let her settle for a few minutes before bursting into the shop with questions. She'd buy a plant too, as it would help to make a connection.

With her finger on the side button, she began to record her voice speaking loud and clear.

'I'm Jess Turner, and I'm in Amersham, a small town in Bucks or Buckingham, or Buckinghamshire. No. That's not right. Just say Bucks. Okay, let's delete that and start again. I'm Jess Turner, and I'm in Amersham, a small town in Bucks. As I speak, I'm outside a florist, looking along the road that leads to the vast space known as Sheers Woods. It's a name many of you will be familiar with, a name that brings dread, fear, and lots of other emotions when people speak of it. Many believe it's cursed or that an ill fate will befall anyone who enters.

As I sit here, the rolling Chiltern Hills provide a lavish backdrop, alluring to anyone who sees the stunning spectacle, I feel many senses. One of dread, the unknown, another of fear, angst, nervous tension, and also excitement. I'd describe it as a person venturing into Crystal Lake on Friday the 13th, after rumours that a serial killer lurks in the dark underwood. For those unfamiliar, five years ago, a group of friends ventured into the woods and never came out. Their short clip went viral on social media. In regard to its authenticity, many people are divided on its credibility. I'll add a link on my blog for those of you who'd like to view the clip online, and you can judge for yourself. The forest has acres of space with a few cottages surrounded by private land. It's said the owners don't like trespassers and have signs declaring this. My interest will be the lodge where it happened—the very heart of the unsolved mystery where the group of friends disappeared. I'm an investigative journalist, and I've been permitted to stay at the very place before it's reopened to the public. The previous owner, Harold Bennett, sold up after the incident and, by all accounts, is living as a recluse. So, I'm going to exit the car and try conducting my first interview before driving up to Sheers Woods and finding the lodge.'

Jess placed the Dictaphone on the passenger seat, opened the driver's door, and got out, not wanting to spring the device on the unsuspecting woman. She'd grab the Dictaphone if she agreed to the interview. Being polite and sensitive would get her much further.

A strong breeze pushed the chilly air against her body; her cheeks suddenly became numb, and her skin tingled. Behind her, the main road lay empty, enveloped in an eerie silence that seemed to insulate the town.

A baby's cry pierced the stillness, and Jess smiled at the lady pushing the pram, expecting something back. She got nothing, only a stare as if to say, *keep in your world; I'll keep in mine.* Still, Jess wanted to try and engage with her. 'Hi. Do you live here in Amersham? I wondered if I could ask you a couple of questions. I'm reporting on the four missing friends who stayed at the lodge in Sheers Woods.'

The woman nudged against her, knocking Jess back, and crossed over the road.

Inhaling deeply, Jess felt the cold air harsh on her lungs as she turned to Beth's shop. Reaching the door handle, she pushed it downwards, and as she did, a bell rang from above, declaring she was there. Inside the shop, bright petals, long green stems, plants, and neatly arranged bouquets adorned the shelves, tables, and glass cabinets. Jess basked in the sweet smells and aroma of peony, green lily, jasmine, and roses. A black cat scarpered from behind the desk, and she crouched, trying to beckon it to come for a stroke. It disappeared into the back through the hanging divider strands.

A moment later, the lady Jess assumed was the owner, Beth, greeted her with a smile and walked towards her.

'Morning, how can I help you, love?' She struggled to walk and supported her frame with a wooden stick.

Jess had her around the late seventies; her face was adorned with heavy-set wrinkles and dark bags under her eyes, which gave a tired appearance. She smelt of cheap perfume, too sweet and overpowering, and didn't use it sparingly, causing Jess to sneeze.

'Oh, gesundheit,' the lady said.

'Thank you.' Jess needed her onside if she was going to ask questions. 'That small flowerpot behind you. Can I have that?'

'Certainly love. Shall I place it in a bag for you?'

'No, it's fine as it is, but thank you. I saw the sign outside; you must be Beth.'

'Last time I looked.' The sarcasm was followed by a contrived laugh.

'I'm Jess.' She watched Beth produce a card machine, tap in the price, and hand over the device. When she didn't respond, Jess tried again. 'So, how long have you been working here?'

The lady looked up. Something in her eyes, the way the pupils dilated, gave Jess the notion she didn't like small talk.

After Jess tapped her card against the machine, the woman took it back, placed it on the counter, and said, 'Anything else?'

'Er, no. No, that's it.' *Come on, ask her. You can't just leave.* 'Terrible what happened to those youngsters, wasn't it?' Immediately, Jess regretted her words. The atmosphere plunged as if Beth had just heard of a death or her last day on earth was upon her. She appeared to freeze, like a stroke victim, her eyes still and lifeless, her body stiff. After a few seconds, she returned from her daze as if her body was frozen, and she suddenly thawed out.

'I haven't the faintest idea what you're talking about.'

'Really?' asked Jess. 'It supposedly happened at the lodge in the woods. I'm staying up there. On my way to it now. Surely you must—-'

'Get the fuck out. Get out!' she yelled and came walking around the counter, her frame balancing on the wooden stick. 'How fucking dare you bring this to my door.'

Jess backed away, so shocked she felt her legs go weak. 'I... Sorry, I—' With her hand extended behind, pawing for the front door handle, Jess pushed it down, her eyes glued to the old lady. 'Please accept my apology.'

'Turn back before it's too late. You don't want to go up there. It's a hell you could never imagine in your very worst nightmares.' Placing a hand over her mouth and then dropping it by her side, she continued. 'I've said too much. Run while there's still time; don't let them get you.'

Jess stepped back into the street, rushed to the car, and sat in the driver's seat, locking the door and staring in shock at the road ahead.

7

FRIDAY MORNING

The inside of the Peugeot was like an ice box. Jess sat in the driver's seat with the engine off, able to see her breath forming like a dense fog. The simultaneous rush of fear and adrenaline triggered a sudden jerk in her body. In the rear-view mirror, her lips looked a dark purple, and she pressed them together and pulled them, resembling a duck's beak, gently flicking her forefingers over them to bring the colour back.

Beth walking around the counter, screaming at her to get out, and the harsh warning of Jess's life being in danger danced in her mind.

Stunned, she struggled to process the last few minutes. Beth's fierce response to her questions and throwing her out of the shop were testaments to how frightened she was. She'd assumed interviewing the locals about the story would spark debate and encourage calm discussions. The florist's behaviour caught her completely off guard.

What was wrong with her? Jess asked herself. *What was Beth so afraid of? Did she believe the footage was real? Did she know something?* There were so many questions. Gazing through the passenger window, she peeked at the shop, pondering whether to go back inside and tackle her again. She drummed her fingers on the dashboard, her right leg stamping the brakes; the many scenarios played out, not wanting the walking stick wrapped around her neck. *That's the only way I see it ending up,* Jess thought. *Push her too hard, and she'll lose it. But why? She knows something. I'm convinced. The reaction was way over the top.*

Judging how Beth had acted, Jess was unsure if anyone would speak to her.

Frustrated, she brushed her hands through her blond hair and slid them down her face, seeing the strain in her eyes in the rear-view mirror. Beth's final words on leaving the florist played in her mind.

Turn back before it's too late. You don't want to go up there. It's a hell you could never imagine in your very worst nightmares. I've said too much. Run while there's still time, don't let them get you.

Touching the brake with her right foot, Jess started the engine and turned the heating on; warm air pushed through the grills, causing goosebumps on her skin. The digital clock showed 10.22 am. In the time she'd been sitting in the car, no one had passed up or down the street. Buggy woman had long gone, taking the weird look with her as Jess had tried to speak to her.

Reaching for the seatbelt, she clicked it into the holder, contemplating whether to turn back, forget about the footage, and the severe warning about going to the lodge. At this moment, it was the flip of a coin. *Do I? Don't I?* she thought. *I could so easily turn around, go home, meet with Ben over the weekend, and feel safe in his strong arms, far away from any possible harm.*

Pressing the accelerator, Jess pulled the car onto the road

and followed the signs for Sheers Woods. As she drove, adjusting the rear-view mirror, she saw Beth standing in the middle of the road, watching her.

A small white sign to her left on a solid-looking pole planted into the pavement declared the forest was a mile away. Further along on the same side of the road, she saw a petrol station. It looked like a family-run business, as the sign above the door wasn't familiar. "Hannigan's Fuel" painted in large yellow letters with patches of the writing missing and in need of a makeover. A shop stretched across the courtyard, the outside brickwork painted a dull red, again in need of decorating as bubbles had formed and the paint chipped. Three pumps were on the forecourt, two with petrol signs and one displaying diesel. The prices were on a board above each.

With a quick glance at the dashboard, Jess noted that the fuel gauge displayed a quarter of a tank remaining. Not wanting to get stuck in an emergency, she steered the car into the petrol station.

Undoing her seat belt, Jess got out, the severe silence almost distressing as she peered across the road behind her, seeing only trees and shrubs trailing a ditch. The feeling that someone or something was watching was apparent, and Jess quickly rushed to the fuel pump, filling the Peugeot to the brim. The smell of petrol lingered in the atmosphere, the strong, dominant scent so powerful, reminding her of huge meaty trucks, day trips with her parents as a child, and the time they watched drag racing; her mother spent the whole time with ear plugs and nursed a headache for hours afterwards.

Returning the nozzle, she twisted and locked the petrol cap on the car, walked to the shop entrance, and struggled for a moment to pull open the heavy door.

Music played from a speaker, "Road To Hell," by Chris Rea, reminding Jess of her university days, dancing and drinking late into the night. Again, she wondered if the song was some kind of sign. After grabbing sandwiches, oven chips, a packet of chicken Kievs, and pasta, she walked to the alcohol section, grabbing beers and a bottle of Jack Daniel's whiskey. A voice behind startled her. She could feel something touch her hair. Jess swung around.

'Help you?' the guy said, his nose almost touching her cheek and a weird smirk that made her uncomfortable.

'Er... Ye... Yeah. I want to pay for the petrol and these items.'

He looked mid-fifties, with a clean-shaven chiselled face and handsome in a rugged way. But his narrow brown eyes seemed to camouflage something hidden deep within. Jess immediately felt awkward as he gaped at her.

A badge with the name Tom Wilder half clung to his red jumper, and he smelt of petrol, tobacco, and firewood, an overpowering smoky aroma like he'd been burning something. His teeth were pearly white, and his wide grin caused his cheeks to flush.

'Glad you want to pay. I don't like it when people run. Believe me; you don't want me on your arse.' He stepped closer, invading her space as if he got off on her trepidation.

Jess went to speak, but it felt like her tongue was stuck to the roof of her mouth. 'Ex... Excuse... Er...'

'I'm fucking with you. Come on over to the till, and we can settle up. Unless you have another way of paying you'd like me to consider.'

A sense of unease washed through her. She stood,

watching the guy walk around the counter, scan the items, tap the price into the cardholder, and hold it out, beckoning her to come forward.

'Where are you headed?' he asked.

On the spot, like being in a room and everyone pointing their finger, Jess panicked and couldn't control her next words. 'I'm going to the lodge where the friends disappeared five years ago. I'm a journalist, and I'm looking into the story.' The moment they left her mouth, she regretted telling him. His eyes widened as though something inside awakened, like a light switch or a spark igniting a fire. 'What's your take on the story?' she probed.

A door shut behind her, and Jess suspected someone had been listening to the conversation and fled. Spinning around, she looked to the back of the shop, her mind busy, suddenly apprehensive.

The warm, putrid air hit the back of her neck as though on purpose. Jess turned and jerked back as the man handed her the card machine, ignoring her question.

'Press it gently here, and we're done,' he said, being crude as he pointed to the device, his eyes practically crawling over her body.

With shaky hands, Jess tapped her card against it. Handing it back to him, she said, 'Thank you. 'Can I have a receipt?'

Ripping the paper from the card machine, he handed it over.

As she walked out of the shop, she heard the man call out to her.

'It was nice knowing you.'

Jess turned around. 'What do you mean?' Instantly annoyed that she continued engaging with him.

From behind the counter, he placed the card machine

onto its stand. 'Nothing. I'm just saying it was nice knowing you. Good luck.'

Jess went to say something, to ask what he knew, but she felt unsafe; the guy was a grade A creep, and she didn't want to spend a second longer than needed.

As she stepped out of the shop, the man followed, standing in the doorway eating a bag of crisps, watching as she pulled away.

$\sim$

Freak. What a bloody freak. What's his problem? Jess thought, remembering his name, Tom Wilder. Once at the lodge, she'd research more about the florist and petrol station. *What is it with this place?*

She was driving towards the woods, having left the petrol station a few minutes ago, seeing the creep standing by the front door.

Rounding a bend and gripping the steering wheel, the road became steep, and the automatic gears shifted.

The bush was lower here, and tall trees adorned the rolling fields on either side of the road as she approached the forest entrance. The car window was cracked open, and lukewarm heat pushed from the grills. Although the temperature was single digits, the chilly fresh air was invigorating. The smell of burnt wood and pine was evident, and as Jess glimpsed in the wing mirrors, making sure petrol perv Tom hadn't come after her, and seeing the road clear, she finally relaxed, her shoulders slumped, her breathing more regular and the excitement she'd felt earlier had returned.

As she drove, keeping the speed under thirty miles an hour, worrying an animal could roam out onto the road, she couldn't help thinking about the group who'd ventured up here five years ago, having driven this very road, looking out from the camper van at the trees partially blocking the sunlight, blissfully unaware of the fate awaiting them as they edged closer to the woods.

Instantly, the turning was upon her. Jess hit the brakes, and the Peugeot skidded, the wheels desperately trying to grip the road. Flicking the gear into reverse, she touched the accelerator, guided by the rear and wing mirrors, indicated left, and turned the car towards the entrance.

The first thing she noticed was how barren the forest was. There was no sign of life. Nothing, as if everyone had been wiped off the planet. Although cold, Jess imagined families, couples holding hands, a dog running through the wet grass, anything. It was eerie, and she suddenly felt alone.

The landscape stretched as far as she could see, lavish fields extending into the horizon. Lower down, nestled in the valley, the terrain dipped into the earth. Towering oak trees overlooked proudly, their skeletal branches reaching for the sky. Stone walls divided fields where Jess expected to see cows feeding, horses galloping, and sheep seeking warmth. The solitary was a stark contrast to what she'd imagined.

To her right, the narrow gravel road wound along the hillside.

This is it—the start of my adventure.

Gently pressing the accelerator, Jess drove into the forest entrance, under a wooden frame which she guessed stopped larger vehicles coming in off the road. On top hung a sign that read "Welcome to Sheers Woods. Enter at your own risk."

'Enter at your own risk. What's that supposed to mean?' Jess said aloud. 'What a peculiar sign.'

Steering the car to her right, she crawled along the narrow road, tiny stones crunching under the tyres and leaping up, pelting against the metal and the windows. 'Really? This is just great. No wonder there's no one here; it's an assault.' Hitting the brake and fully opening the window, Jess stuck her head out, looking at the rough ground and inhaling the fresh air. With her head back inside the car, she stamped on the accelerator. Clouds of dust swirled, engulfing the vehicle and making her cough.

As she followed the road around a bend, she saw a large, run-down hay barn situated against the hedges. The once sturdy wooden slats desperately clung to each other, bowed and rotten, with extensive gaping holes.

The front door hung off its hinges, the wood long decayed, the red paint dull and fading. The corrugated metal roof was infested with rust patches, and the edges curled upwards due to the elements.

Jess pulled onto the grass and got out of the car. Grabbing her phone, she began filming. First, she captured the backdrop and rolling fields.

'Here I am in Sheers Woods—the start of my documentary. I can't emphasise the thrill of tracing the exact steps the four missing friends took and the opportunity I have to be out here. Over the next couple of days, I'll be filming as much as possible with the intention of putting together a short film. I'll attempt to interview the locals, get their opinions on the story, and write a blog. I've pulled over on the way up here as I want to show you something.' Focusing on the fields, Jess slowly panned the mobile phone around, capturing the run-down barn. 'Something has drawn me to this place. I can't say for sure what it is, but I'm going to go inside and explore. As you can see, it looks derelict. I presume it was used back in the day by farmers to store hay. Now, it casts a dreary presence, left deserted and abandoned. It's sad to look at, almost tragic.'

Grabbing her torch from the boot, she placed it in her back pocket. With the mobile phone in her left hand, she used her right hand to ease the barn door back, noticing its cold, splintered, and rough surface. The hinges screeched as the rotten wood scraped on the ground. 'Okay, I'm inside. The windows along the front are cracked, allowing sufficient lighting. I'd describe the smell as musty and stale, much like deteriorating wood. It's unpleasant. Also, the scent of decaying straw hangs in the air. There is... wait, there's something on the walls. Hang on, let me grab the torch.' Moving further inside the barn, Jess lifted the mobile phone, capturing weird symbols painted on the wood. 'I'm... trying to make out these symbols.' She placed her hand on the wall, touching the first picture. 'This is... it looks like a chalice or goblet. I think it's filled with blood. It's tipped on its side, a red liquid spilling over the edge. There's another one next to it. This one is a cross with a loop at the top. Wait, there's something written underneath.' Shining the light, Jess wiped away the dust and read the words. 'Ankh. Life and immortality. These are... These are symbols depicting eternal life. So, was this place used by a cult to practice their beliefs of life ever after? Did they believe their rituals would give them everlasting life?' Jess continued walking along the barn, filming everything. 'This one is an eternal loop, I think. Possibly symbolising the continuous cycle. This one next to it is a heart, infused with what I would guess are blood droplets. Wait, there's writing underneath.' Holding the torchlight closer, she read the words. 'The essence of life resides in the blood.' Shining the torch along the wall, she peered at the other symbols. 'This one's a dagger, and there are more words underneath. Extracting the life force leads to eternal life. Vein-like patterns. An inverted triangle. These are all symbols depicting immortality. This place was used to practise—'

Behind her, footsteps pounded along the ground. Jess spun around, shining the torch at the wooden door, certain it rocked on its hinges. 'Who's there? Hello? I said who's there? Okay, as you all heard, someone else is in here. I'm going to stop filming as I'm feeling under threat. I'll record later, but for now, I'm going to head to the lodge.' As Jess stopped the recording, she heard something crash behind her. Certain she heard muffled whispers as if a small group had gathered and were waiting, hidden in the shadows, she backed out of the barn and stood by the car. Once she'd taken a few pictures, she got into the driver's seat and pulled away.

She'd been driving for a few minutes, and the road was getting steeper but smoother now. Ankle-high grass cushioned the tyres, whipping against the bumper, and the stones seemed to disappear.

Doug said in the email to follow the road to your right for around a mile, but be warned, it gets steep, so be careful. As you get to the top, you'll see the lodge. The views are fantastic, and you'll be completely secluded.

Great, she thought. *At least there's Wi-Fi.* Jess spun the steering wheel as a crow squawked, causing her to pull into a ditch. 'Christ! You frightened the shit out of me. Hello there, a sign of life. Wow!'

Suddenly, more crows joined, the trees appeared to

shake, and the noise was almost deafening. It sounded like a warning, as if they knew something. Pulling away, she gently eased the vehicle around a sharp bend, hearing the wheels spinning with the steep incline. At the top, she yanked the handbrake and got out of the car.

She could finally see the lodge in the distance.

8

FRIDAY MORNING

L arge potholes caused Jess to continuously swerve. The tyres made a popping noise as they crunched over the rough surface. The stones had returned in force, and she worried the tyres would burst, not knowing where to start if she had a flat. 'The Jack first, I think,' she said, placing fingers out as she recalled the task. 'The spare tyre is in the boot; I know that. Place the jack under the car, lift car with jack, undo the bolts with the spanner. Off. New one on. Tighten the bolts. Piece of cake. Or call Ben,' she laughed to herself.

A warmth filled her body at the memory of her father, showing her basic plumbing skills when she was a child, the robust machine to bend the pipe, the cutters, and soldering. Her favourite part was welding the pipes with fittings and holding the flame close until the solder melted and made the joint. He would get Jess to change tap washers, fix leaks around the house, and show her how to repair boilers. That part she loved the most, seeing how all the components worked together to produce heating and hot water. Sometimes, she'd sit for hours in her father's garage, the smell of oil, paint, and strong chemicals as he repaired his motor-bike, narrating everything he was doing. She always appreciated the life lessons that she'd take into her adulthood.

Jess was an only child. Her mother had complications after the birth and almost lost her life, but growing up was never lonely. Her parents were incredible and never once made her feel like she was alone.

Up ahead, a picturesque stone bridge emerged, blending seamlessly with its rustic surroundings. The bridge was adorned with weathered stones covered in moss, which served as both a parapet and pathway leading over a stream directly to the lodge.

Pulling the handbrake, Jess opened the driver's door and stood out, the sound of water flowing underneath a welcome comfort as clear water caressed the rocks. Inhaling, the cold air almost burnt her lungs, the view incredible from where she stood. Rows of fields seemed to stretch for miles, divided by rock walls. Behind them, enormous trees provided a sheltered, practically remote feeling in the backdrop. In the distance, she could see the edge of the town and a few houses scattered along the hills. Situated deep in the valley, a lone cottage stood, and Jess wondered if it was deserted by how isolated the area seemed.

To the right was a beautiful lake. The water glistening at the sun's reflection. She spotted another cottage on the other side of the water, but it was too far to see any characteristics.

She turned towards the lodge. The old stony bridge was the only way to get there. Where she stood appeared to be the highest point, and past the lodge, the road dipped back down, continuing all the way around the forest.

A crooked sign stood at the edge of the bridge, its pole planted in the grass, "No heavy vehicles" written in black on a white background. 'Heavy vehicles. A bit random. Does that include my car? Try lifting it. I'd say it's heavy.'

She thought about Doug and wondered if he was mocking her, half expecting Jess to turn up to work Monday morning with her tail between her legs, his eyes full of sarcasm, his face showing a deep satisfaction.

I knew you'd be back. We had a small wager in the office; everyone put in a tenner, winner takes all. I said Monday morning. Don't worry about it, Jess Turner. Now go and make the coffee and empty the dishwasher, good girl. You'll learn one day that you're not cut out for this line of work.

She imagined him leaning over, his fists on the desk, that tedious smirk, the body odour, still wearing the ketchup-stained grey trousers, his slick black hair almost glued to his scalp.

Backing away from the bridge, Jess sat in the driver's seat, released the handbrake, and gently tapped on the accelerator. The stones danced under the tyres, the window open, the cold air whipping against her skin, courageously pushing through the apprehension. 'I have this,' she assured herself. 'I have this.'

As the Peugeot rolled off the bridge and onto the grassy path on the other side, she hit the brakes, a plume of dust swirling around the vehicle. Brimming with eagerness, Jess slapped the dashboard. *Yes. I'm here.* The dust settled, and as she peered at the lodge, standing remote, its isolation suddenly became very real.

She swallowed the lump in her throat as reality hit and saturated her body, the haunting image of the four friends clinging to the air like ghosts, their voices whispering in the breeze as if pleading with Jess to release their souls.

∽

The veins were visible on her hands as Jess clasped the steering wheel, parking the car by the side of the lodge.

Turning off the engine and reaching into the glove compartment, she grabbed the lodge key secured in an envelope. Jess stepped out, closing the driver's door. The clunking sound seemed to echo through the forest as if announcing she was here, its eyes glancing and almost piercing holes in her body.

Standing beneath the dazzling sun, wisps of cloud enhancing the deep blue sky, she stared at the lodge, overwhelmed by its elegance. She didn't know what to expect. The footage had shown the inside, but it was grainy; the clip often jumped and went out of focus. Maybe expecting a rundown old cabin, a glorified barn, or an abandoned shack that had been spruced up and rushed to get ready. But this? This was spectacular.

The robust front door faced towards the bridge, and the lodge ran lengthways, stretching to the back of Sheers Woods. Jess strolled around it, taking everything in. It had two floors; its shell was thick, stained brown oak with large windows comparable to a lake house in a thriller movie. The black-pitched triangular roof had Velux windows cut into it so you could gaze at the stars from your bed, and the tall flue for a wood burner poked out towards the back. Security lights were strategically placed along the front and side of the lodge, hanging on nails, and Jess could only imagine how it looked at night. Trees aligned the back of the lodge, just behind the road leading further around the hill, and to her left, a low rock wall separated the area from the other fields. A bed of flowers and plants ran around the property, and although the grass was wet, it didn't look soggy. As she walked along its length, the fresh earth smelled of dead leaves, algae, and decaying plants.

Situated in the far corner of the grounds was a brick structure, which Jess presumed was an old well. She gazed at the area of grass, almost seeing the inflatable ball being pushed into the air, before realising she was standing in the same spot as the friends had done five years ago.

'What happened to you all?' Jess asked aloud, almost expecting the wind to carry the answer. The trees behind the lodge prompted a chilling memory. The figure standing, watching.

Walking back to the car, she grabbed her bag from the passenger seat, placed the torch in the boot, and stood at the front door, easing the key into the lock, gently twisting and opening it.

Closing the front door behind her, Jess leant against the smooth wood and looked over the place.

The living room was extensive, with a kitchen area and breakfast bar to her left. A large, double-glazed window above the sink provided a view across the valley. The black marble counter looked expensive, with a toaster, kettle, and coffee machine. Under the counter, Jess was pleased to see the washing machine, dishwasher, and, further along, a large grey American-style fridge freezer with an ice machine caught her eye.

From the kitchen, she looked across to the living room and saw a black four-seater sofa facing the front door with an elegant-looking mahogany coffee table perched in front. Its legs were a dark brown and looked stylish and robust. An empty magazine rack rested on top. Next to the sofa was a comfy-looking black armchair, facing forward and nestled against the cream-coloured wall. Behind the sofa, she noticed a bookshelf, hoping there'd be a thriller she could tuck into if she couldn't sleep.

As she eyed the living room, the scene in the footage ran

through her mind, the two men on the sofa, one sitting and the other lying with his legs over the edge, chatting to the women who would have stood near where Jess was. She knew every inch of the clip, every frame, and it felt so familiar, being in the same place where it happened.

To the left side of the front door, a flat-screen TV rested on a wall with a pivot to adjust its position.

Dropping her bag, she walked through the living room, her trainers squeaking on the wooden floor as she stepped into the hallway. A spiral staircase curved to the first floor and was painted black, with murals carved into the design, primarily animals, elephants, giraffes, hippos, and a few angels with bows.

Further along, there were two bedrooms at the back.

She opened the furthest door on the left at the back of the lodge, seeing a plain bedroom, again stunned by the view through the window of the rolling fields and just as thrilled to be standing next to a king-size bed, the mattress resting on a brass frame, solid and durable.

Grabbing the bag from the living room, Jess set it on the bed, removed her folded clothes, and placed them in the chest of drawers behind her.

Reaching into her jeans pocket, she grabbed her mobile phone and tapped the screen, wanting to quickly send a message to her parents, and Ben and Ruth, to let them know she'd arrived safely. The signal bar was empty, with the words "No Service" written in the right corner. 'Damn it. What a great start. There's Wi-Fi. I'll find the router and tap in the code.' Back into the living room, phone in hand, and finding the router on a shelf under the TV, Jess crouched, finding the code and tapping in the digits.

Nothing.

No connection.

'Come on, don't do this. Maybe I've entered it wrong.' Again, Jess tapped the digits, slow and precise.

Nothing.

'You have to be kidding me. Why? I've tapped the digits correctly.' After photographing the code and spreading her thumb and forefinger on the screen to blow up the picture, she tapped in the code a few more times, each time with the same outcome. No connection.

Suddenly lightheaded, her eyes glazed over as she realised she couldn't contact Doug to ask about the Wi-Fi code, thinking, *If anything happens to me here, no one would know until it's too late.*

9

FRIDAY MORNING

The Wi-Fi not working was a huge problem—a game changer of the highest order. Jess needed to research and keep in contact with the outside world while reporting from the lodge. The headlines were already playing out in her mind.

Jess Turner disappears while staying in a secluded lodge deep in the forest, which people are dubbing The lodge bodge. Cab-in and gone. Turner round and go back. Jess found dead in bed in glorified shed.

She tapped the phone screen, again seeing "No Service" in the right-hand corner. After entering the Wi-Fi password a few more times, Jess slung her phone onto the sofa, watching it bounce on the soft cushions.

Back in the bedroom, she grabbed the Dictaphone from her bag, tested it, and moved to the kitchen, sitting on one of the tall chairs by the breakfast bar to begin recording.

'So, Jess Turner here, following up on the viral clip. It was a heck of a journey, and here's me thinking it would all run smoothly. On the way out here, a few weird things happened. First, I went to interview a shop owner, hoping to get her take on things. I won't reveal her name as it's not fair, and she's obviously frightened. I expected to learn her thoughts on the footage, but she freaked, not wanting to talk to me, basically throwing me out. A second altercation happened on the road leading to the forest, but the less said about that, the better. I was made to feel extremely uncomfortable, and at one stage, I think someone was watching me through a gap in the door. And the weird barn with the ancient symbols. That was slightly scary. It's apparent some kind of ritual or sacrifice happened there. I got it on video. As I turned the recording off, I'm certain I heard muffled whispers.'

Jess stopped the voice recorder for a moment to take a breather, glancing out the window at the barren fields. *Why is it so quiet?* She continued to dictate. 'Sheers Woods and the vast forest is not something I expected. I know it's mid-October, but I thought there'd be more people here. No, sorry, that's wrong, someone, anyone. A sign of life. It's as if I'm cut off from the world. Weird, I know, but it's how I feel. Anyway, I'm here now, safe. I was hoping to do some work on the laptop and research for my story. It seems there's no Wi-Fi, so I'm trapped here, unable to talk to anybody or reach the outside world. I'm going to take a walk, do some filming on my phone, and see what's around, maybe a clue or something that may give answers to this viral mystery. The chances of finding anything are slim, but there may be someone as interested as I am in the story and willing to talk.' Easing off the chair, she walked to the window. 'As I stand here, the sun gleaming through the window, I see a cottage on the horizon, and the lake to my right is quite breathtaking. I'm going to film, starting with the inside of the lodge, and then take a walk outside.'

After switching off the Dictaphone, she placed it in her

pocket. The voice notes would make writing the blog much easier and help her stay organised.

The en suite bathroom was basic, with a matching white bath, sink, and toilet. After brushing her teeth, she splashed water on her face and wiped her mouth with a towel she'd brought from the flat. Then, she grabbed her mobile phone from the sofa in the living room, deciding to try the Wi-Fi password before going out. Again, Jess crouched by the router. 'Come on, please work.'

Nothing.

Holding the phone in front of her, she pressed the record button and pointed the camera over the living room.

'Welcome to Sheers Lodge. The interior is quite stunning with all the modern facilities you'd need: a washing machine, dishwasher, microwave, and even an American-style fridge. For those of you familiar with the viral clip of the four friends who went missing, this is the place they disappeared from—the last time they were seen. I'll give a quick tour before filming the outside of Sheers Lodge. Although it's been replaced, the sofa from the footage is brown, this one's black, it's in much the same position as the old one, towards the back of the living room. Even the black armchair is in the same spot beside the sofa and against the wall. The only other thing I can see that's different is the front door—which has a glass panel fitted. It's through the front door that we see a person with their face blurred out, running into the lodge, followed by frantic voices. As you can see, towards the back of the lodge, there are two bedrooms on either side of the hallway. It's from back there the screams were heard as the camera holder raced into the living room and the clip finished.'

Pausing the recording, Jess opened the front door, pointing the camera to the space at the front of the lodge,

careful not to film her car. 'The camper van would have
been parked somewhere there. Obviously, it's gone now. I
presume it was towed away, possibly by the person or
persons responsible for their disappearance. I did some
research, but it's impossible to locate without the registra-
tion plate, which we never saw. As they pulled away,
the tyres burst, and they raced back into the lodge.'
Swinging the phone camera around, Jess pointed to an area
of grass by the side of the lodge. 'Right there is where the
group threw an inflatable ball to one another, and behind
the lodge, we'll go there now, is where the creepy shadow
appeared as if hiding, watching them.' With the video
running, she walked along the side of the lodge, the stones
grinding under her trainers weirdly satisfying, and stood by
the edge of the road. Although cold, the sun was intense, the
icy breeze lashing against her body. 'Okay. Roughly where
I'm standing is where the shadow appeared.' Tall oak trees
stood close together, almost concealing the area of wood-
land behind. Dry, shrivelled leaves decorated the ground,
resembling tight claws, and bushes swayed in the wind.

Jess panned the area with the phone, recording every
movement. 'On social media, many say it was photo-
shopped; others believe it was supernatural, an entity or
demon of sorts. And lots say it was complete bullshit. Me, I
think it happened exactly how the viral clip played out. I
believe so much of what I see on social media. I
guess it's why I'm here; I love a conspiracy theory. I feel
under no illusion that the four friends met a terrible fate
five years ago and that someone or something stalked them
and is responsible for their disappearance. And yes, I
believe they were taken from the lodge, as the clip suggests.
But I will try my best to go into this with an open mind. I
will film as much as possible and try to piece the puzzle

together. Right, I'm going to take a stroll across the bridge and follow the road leading to the entrance.'

As she walked along the side of the lodge towards her car, Jess pointed the phone camera to the fields, spreading her fingers on the screen and zooming in on the valley. 'It's vast. There are fields as far as I can see. I didn't realise how extensive it was. But it's quiet. There's literally no one around.' As Jess approached the bridge, something caught her eye in the corner of the screen. Turning the phone slowly, she observed what appeared to be a clothesline—the thick white wire extending between branches. 'If the washing machine fails, I guess I have a backup to dry my clothes.'

The clear, gentle flowing water added tranquility. The rocks resting on the base were visible and so clean they could have just been placed there.

With her mobile phone held out, Jess reached the other side of the bridge and followed the narrow road as it curved around the hill.

She stopped, suddenly startled.

In the distance, around fifty yards from where she stood, she could see something through the gaps in the trees—a figure walking through the forest, wearing what appeared to be a feathered outfit and a strange bird-like mask with a huge beak.

'Okay, that's weird.' Jess zoomed in, trying to get a clearer picture. 'I'm not sure what that's about. The figure appears to be walking towards the hay barn. Excuse me. Why are you dressed like that?' she asked, optimistically hoping they'd remove the mask and talk to her.

Abruptly, the figure stopped and turned towards Jess, remaining still and staring directly at her.

The phone shook in her hand as she filmed, contemplating whether to approach it or return to the lodge. 'What are you doing out here?'

No movement.

'Can I talk to you? I'm filming a documentary about—'

Suddenly, the figure began walking towards her. She turned, charging back through the woods, the video still rolling, filming the ground, twigs snapping under her trainers, erratic breaths as she reached the bridge. Spinning around, focusing the camera through the gaps in the trees, Jess searched, unable to see bird person. 'Where did they go? Shit. That was creepy.' For a moment, she remained still, listening for a rustle of leaves, the sound of a low swinging branch being forced back. Confident the figure had backed away, she raced across the bridge, stopping to catch her breath.

On her right side, a groan cut through the silence.

Straightening her body, Jess lifted the phone and continued to record, seeing the clothesline sway, trembling as if something had just been placed on it.

Pointing the phone, she scanned its length and glimpsed an object dangling.

'What the fuck? This... This wasn't... Someone's just done this.' As she stepped to the end of the clothesline, she saw hair, tangled and knotted, as if ripped from a person's head. Patches of dried blood, stiff and clumpy, clung to the strands. Visions played out of someone being held against their will, an axe or other sharp tool lifted above them, brought down, and bang. Scalped. 'It can't be real. Someone's done this to frighten me.' With her arm extended, pointing the phone and recording the grotesque object, Jess continued narrating. 'It looks real. It appears to be human hair. Why would someone hang it over the clothesline, knowing I'd find it? If it's a joke, it's sick.' She thought about the other scenario. What if it was real? What if someone had just been scalped? The hay barn was a testament to rituals carried out in the past. Maybe the object was left to warn her away? Frighten her into leaving.

Eyes seemed to peer from the bark, the trees watching as if they were about to close in and crush her.

Aware bird person may be following her, Jess stopped the recording, and after taking a few photos, she backed away and rushed to the lodge, closing the front door and locking it.

With her face pressed against the glass and making sure bird person hadn't followed her to the lodge, Jess turned and leant against the front door, flicking through the last few photos she'd taken. The hair was disturbing. Slung over the clothesline. The dried blood. It was placed there in the time she'd crossed the bridge, saw the strange figure walking through the woods, and made her way back to the lodge. A matter of minutes. Had someone seen her arrive? Were they watching her? Were they out there now?

After observing the video recording and ensuring she'd captured everything, she tried the Wi-Fi, carefully entering the code.

Still nothing.

As she stepped away from the front door, a floorboard gave way, the crunching noise intense as her left foot went through the gap, and she fell backward onto the floor, twisting her ankle. Resting her elbows on the floor, her back arched, she took a breather, reaching both hands under her left leg and gently lifting. Her jeans were ripped, the broken board had grazed her skin, but her foot was out. Bringing her left knee to her chest, she rolled her foot, thankful the pain wasn't too harsh.

Knowing a swollen ankle would hinder her investigation, Jess decided to take a warm bath to ease the pain. She could use the Dictaphone to narrate the recent findings at the same time.

In the bathroom, she ran the taps, yellow water spilling from the mixer spout. 'Yuk, it looks like piss. That's disgusting.' After a minute, it cleared, and she fitted the bath plug, grabbed her toiletries from her bag, and poured shower gel into the bath. The notes of lavender and coconut were comforting as Jess removed her clothes, throwing the torn, bloodstained jeans onto the floor.

Steam filled the bathroom, and condensation covered the mirror. As she stepped into the bath, she opened the window and slowly eased her body into the hot water.

Lying back, she closed her eyes, wondering if her parents were trying to ring. She'd promised them a phone call on arrival.

Gripping the edge of the bath, she leant over and grabbed the phone from her jeans, stunned to see it had gone two-thirty. The winter nights drew in fast, and soon it would be dark.

"No Service" remained displayed in the corner of the screen.

Placing her phone on the floor and grabbing the Dictaphone, Jess continued to narrate.

'Something a little concerning happened while I was filming outside. I have footage of a person, at least I think it was a person, wearing a feathered outfit and bird-like mask. They seemed to be making their way to the hay barn. I also have pictures and a video recording of what... what appeared to be human hair hanging over the clothesline. Someone is either pissing around, winding me up, or—'

The sound of running and gravel crunching outside the lodge interrupted her narration. Grabbing the edge of the bath, her body still, motionless, she waited, feeling her lips quiver. Slowly, she stood, hearing the whooshing sound of water under her, her body cold as she pushed her face out the window, the icy wind lapping her skin. 'He... hello? Is someone out there?' The silence was disturbing, the valley deep below void of life. Soon, the sun would set, bringing with it only darkness. She stared into the horizon, her breaths short and sharp. Reaching for the handle, she pulled the window, the noise comparable to a fridge door closing, like trapping the wind with your foot. Ripping the handle down and locking the window, the satisfaction of hearing the loud clunk aided her unease. Her addled mind caused doubt. *Did I lock the front door? I can't remember. What about upstairs? Were there windows or doors left open?* She hadn't been up there and couldn't be sure. What she was certain about was that someone was running along the gravel outside. The scrape of footwear in the stones, the footsteps racing.

Leaning over, she reached for the large white towel and dried her body, wrapping it around herself. Opening the bathroom door, she walked into the bedroom and put on a fresh pair of knickers, black leggings, which would be more comfortable, the warm jumper from earlier, and sliders for her feet.

Turning her ankle, she was pleased the hot bath had eased the pain.

Tapping the phone screen, checking for a signal now a force of habit, Jess placed it into the pocket of her leggings and put the Dictaphone on the bed.

In the hallway, she peered at the front door. Closed. The sigh was heavy as it left her mouth.

After looking through the windows in the living room and kitchen, and ensuring they were locked, she was confident whoever was outside had gone. *Maybe it was a fox,* she thought. *Keep it together. I'll go into town, make my calls, and come back here. Hopefully, the Wi-Fi will work later.*

It would get cold as the evening set in, and seeing radiators hanging on the wall, she thought, *there has to be a boiler somewhere. I'll look for it when I get back.*

Grabbing the car keys from the kitchen worktop, she opened the front door. A horrifying screech spilled from her mouth as she looked at her car.

All four tyres were slashed.

10

FRIDAY EVENING

'This can't... It... This... Who would do this?' Anger charged through her veins, and her heart almost leapt into her throat.

Jess planned on driving to town, contacting everyone to let them know she was okay. Possibly conducting a few interviews. It was out of the question now.

Balling her fists, nails digging into her skin, she raced around the side of the lodge. As she reached the bathroom window, she turned, seeing the stones were disturbed. Moving closer, she knelt, pawing at the ground. *Are these fresh footprints? Was someone out here moments ago, maybe watching as I bathed?* Only for the deflated tyres, Jess would question her thoughts, wondering if she was being paranoid. A shiver pulsed through the middle of her back as she imagined the person out here, slashing the tyres, creeping to the window, and running. *Would they come back? Would they try to get in next time?* Suddenly, she recalled bird person. How she'd spotted the figure walking towards the hay barn and how, after seeing her, it followed.

But for how long? Had they intended on frightening her? Or did they walk up the narrow road, slash the tyres and flee?

So many questions were forming in her mind. The anger transposed to fear as she stood by the bathroom window. The palms of her hands felt clammy, and her legs weakened. Slowly backing away, she looked over the horizon. Bushes and shrubs as far as the eye could see. So green and lush. Above, a crow squawked, the noise unsettling, almost intrusive of her space. The tall trees in the distance lined like soldiers, as if watching, creating murky shadows that blanketed the forest in a threatening poise.

Below, deep in the valley, profound shadows cast their embrace.

Over by the car, Jess checked all four tyres. The saggy, almost sponge-like rubber appeared to fold over on itself. 'Arsehole.' Turning, she rushed over the bridge, along the road, and down to where she'd seen the figure earlier. 'Hello? I know it was you. I have you on camera.' Jess scanned the woods, searching for the figure. The place seemed deserted. 'Hello? Thanks for slashing the tyres, by the way. Very frigging mature. Arsehole. Come out and show yourself. Hello?'

Branches stirred as the sound of wings flapped and birds flew from a tree close to where she stood.

After waiting a few moments, she walked back towards the lodge. It was cold, beginning to get dark, and she had to occupy her mind; there was no choice. She was stuck here. The slashed tyres stopped her from driving, and the lack of Wi-Fi and reception prevented her from talking to anyone.

Inside the lodge through the kitchen window, the red sky far off in the distance was eye-catching, but the darkness clawed.

On the living room wall, Jess saw a thermostat hidden behind the bookshelf and turned it to maximum, hearing a booming noise coming from one of the cupboards. 'Yes. Heating. One consolation.' The radiator began warming up, and she pressed her hands on the grill, appreciating the heat.

Grabbing the remote control from the coffee table, she turned on the TV and sat on the sofa, the white noise booming through the speaker. As she pressed through the different channels, only a black screen displayed, abruptly remembering the non-existent Wi-Fi and wanting to hurl the device across the living room.

Although she'd only seen Ben last night, she missed him so much. Their nights were mainly spent cuddled into one another, binge-watching the latest Netflix or Amazon series and sipping wine.

If it wasn't beginning to get dark, she'd attempt to walk along the road until she found someone. The cottage in the valley was her best bet. It had to be occupied, surely.

Easing off the sofa, Jess walked to the fridge, grabbing a bottle of beer and a sandwich she'd purchased from the petrol station. She thought about stamping on it, hoping the sandwich container would act like a voodoo doll and the man behind the counter would wince in agony.

Back on the sofa, she twisted the beer cap and opened the sandwich, thinking about earlier, petrol perv and how uncomfortable he'd made her feel. While driving away, she saw his face in the rear-view mirror, knowing she was coming here.

Once she'd eaten the ham and cheese sandwich, she scrunched the plastic cover and placed it beside her, sipping the ice-cold beer. It felt refreshing, and right now, she could easily sink a few of them to ease the tension of being stranded out here.

Tomorrow, I'll venture out. At least then, I can make calls and start to put the docufilm together, chat with the locals, get their perspective, and write up a blog.

After finishing the beer, she placed the empty bottle on the floor. Her eyes felt heavy, her lids began to close, and Jess fell asleep, tossing and turning on the sofa. Her dreams were so vivid. She'd driven up to the petrol station, and after a brief argument, the doors locked, the windows bolted as if by themselves, and petrol perv came running towards her from behind the counter wielding a chainsaw. His horrific grin was the last thing Jess saw as she woke.

'Where am—?' Shaking off the drowsiness, her eyes focused on the living room and the blackness through the kitchen window. Jess grabbed her phone and tapped the screen, seeing it was almost 7 pm. She'd been asleep for a couple of hours.

Standing, her feet numb, pins and needles tingling her skin, she grabbed a glass from the cupboard and filled it with water from the kitchen sink.

Her body jolted as the area outside the lodge was drenched in light. The glass dropped from her hand, shattering over the tiled kitchen floor, and she knelt, sweeping the large pieces into a pile.

As Jess remained on her knees, she could hear her heart pumping in her ears, fearing the strange figure she'd seen earlier had returned.

The outside lights went off.

Slowly, she stood, gripping the worktop and straightening her legs.

Backing away from the window, she began recording on

her phone, needing to document every possible threat. The only sound was the heavy pants coming from her mouth. Through the window, she could see specs in the distance scattered along the hills, imagining the town so alive on a Friday night. She pictured couples getting ready for a meal out, friends meeting at the local pub, families eating or watching telly together, unaware she was here in the lodge, stranded with no one to help. Slowly lifting her hand, Jess grabbed the front door handle, yanking it down to make sure it was locked. She leant against the side wall, waiting, trying desperately to listen—dead silence, like she was locked in a soundproof room, her ears tingled with quiet. It wasn't natural. Living in London, there were always sounds: vehicles pushing along the road, footsteps and voices from the flat above, laughter from the communal garden, dogs barking outside and people talking on mobile phones as they passed her window. Sounds were everywhere, and it didn't stop. Out here, the constant stillness was almost deafening.

Okay, what now? she thought. *I can't stay by the door all night. I think they've gone. Whoever was outside has—*

The lights burst into life. Through the front door glass, Jess could see the narrow road leading to the bridge, the bushes opposite, and the deflated tyres.

The adrenaline coursed through her veins, her mind so noisy and perplexed.

With her left arm extended, she turned the key, the clunk almost unbearably loud, broadcasting to anyone hiding that she was coming. The groaning sound was intense as she pulled the front door back and stepped outside. It was so cold; the air hit her hard, her face suddenly sore, and her body shuddered. Her breath seemed to stumble from her mouth as if her lungs were being crushed. Aided by the security lights, she walked from the lodge towards the car.

Someone was there.

Standing on the bridge.

In her peripheral vision, she saw the silhouette. He was around twenty yards away and appeared to be pawing at the stones.

Apprehension replaced dread, and Jess needed to take charge. 'What the hell are you doing? Hey, I'm talking to you. I'm recording you. I'll show it to the police. Do you hear me?' Her voice became louder, more dominant. 'You need to leave.' Still pawing at the stones, Jess watched the man turn towards her. He was around five foot ten, maybe seventeen or eighteen, dressed in a jumper and jeans. His hair was messy, and he appeared to wear dark glasses. As Jess spoke, she noticed his head tilt sideways as if listening to where the voice was coming from. 'Do you hear me?' she asked.

Instantly, he started running towards her. His hands reached out as though feeling for obstacles.

In complete panic, she stood and rushed towards the lodge, dropping her phone, fear pushing through her body, praying she didn't stumble. As she reached the front door, closing it behind her, his hand stopped it.

With as much strength as she could muster, Jess turned, trying to force the door closed, but the guy was strong and didn't seem like he'd give up.

'Go away. What is wrong with you? Leave me the fuck alone, you arsehole.' With her left hand on the door, she reached forward, her right hand slapping his face and grabbing the glasses. As they dropped to the ground, Jess saw his eyes. They'd been gorged out of the sockets and stitched. She'd never seen anything so horrific. Slits for eyes, like sharp knife cuts. His face was scarred and harsh, his skin a weird yellow colour from lack of sunlight. 'What's happened to you?' she cried out. 'Why are you doing this? I'm begging you, leave me alone.'

As he tried to speak, only mumbling sounds coming from his mouth, Jess saw it. His tongue had been removed. The shock was instantaneous, the strength draining from her body as she dropped to the ground, knees sliding along the floor as she continued pushing. Again, she screamed, 'What's happened to you?'

Suddenly, he threw a notepad at her, let go of the door, and backed away, running into the night.

The stillness rang in her ears, a sudden shock to her system, and Jess got off the floor and grabbed the notepad. The writing was in pencil, scrawly, amateurish, as though a toddler had gone berserk with a crayon.

You must leave now.

Or what happened to the others will happen to you.

11

FRIDAY EVENING

B right headlights appeared at the bridge, and Jess, standing by the front door, leant her body out, still clutching the notepad, and gazed along the road. The security lights still shone from the lodge as the vehicle's headlights backed off.

Picking her phone up from the ground, she tapped the screen and continued recording.

'The person who called to the lodge has run off—a vehicle appeared by the bridge. I don't know if he got into it. I have to see what the hell is going on out here. If something happens to me and you find this recording, show it to the police. Tell them who I am. Jess Turner. I'm under threat. My fucking... tyres have been slashed. I was chased by a... a giant frigging bird earlier, I found human hair draped over the clothesline, and now someone has given me a message that it's not safe to be here. This place is crazy.' As she reached the bridge, she saw the vehicle reversing along the road, a transit van picking up speed, a figure in the driver's seat, but the headlights made it difficult to notice the van's colour or the driver's features. Jess couldn't tell if the young man was in the back. Holding her phone at arm's length, the glare of the headlights bright on the screen, Jess called out, 'What have you done to him? Stop and talk if you're so brave. Hey, stop.'

The vehicle disappeared around a bend, and suddenly, her surroundings became silent.

With only her phone torch attempting to cut through the darkness, Jess walked back along the road towards the lodge, struggling to push the image of the visitor out of her mind: his desperation in warning her, the eagerness to help. *Where had he gone?* she thought. *Was the van driver after him? Had he escaped?*

The front door to the lodge was open, and Jess wondered if someone had got inside. Quickly pushing the thought to the back of her mind, she lifted the car keys from the breakfast bar, locked the front door, and went back outside, opening the boot and grabbing the torch, shining the light to the bushes on her right and along the path, the cold air hash on her face. As she walked in the opposite direction of the bridge, filming everything, the smell of pine was evident, the dry leaves crunching under her trainers weirdly satisfying, and distant smoke wafted in her direction.

Although dark and with the apparent danger of being so exposed, she needed to find someone who'd help. As long as she remained isolated in the lodge, the threat of being stranded became more real.

The security lights went out, and the area around the lodge was soaked in darkness, only her torchlight illuminating her surroundings. She kept walking, her mind plagued by the young man she'd seen at the lodge. The notebook he'd thrown at her. Although blind, he'd heard her car pulling up and walked out here to give her the message. It was like he'd escaped from somewhere, held against his will. His face was dry and scaly, his skin starved of light.

She'd heard stories like this in the news recently: A mother and father had kept their daughter locked away for years. But this, they'd cut his eyes out and removed his tongue. Was it because he'd escaped before? The more Jess thought, the more horrified she became.

The message ran through her head again.

You must leave now, or what happened to the others will happen to you.

Does he mean the footage? Jess thought.

Slowly, she walked along the dirt road, the lodge just behind her. The bushes stopped as she rounded the path which led along the hills. The vast space was so open, exposing her to predators lurking in the shadows.

As she peered across the valley, only bleakness was visible. Above her, the half-moon shone deep in the night sky. Stars glowed and seemed to wink as if to guide her.

Bushes rattled in the wind, and the trees seemed to sway like drunks on a street corner. In the distance, an animal's screech startled her.

Through a gap in the hedges, a light glowed beyond the valley, a dot on the horizon, like a lighthouse.

It had to be the cottage she'd seen earlier.

Suddenly, she paused, looking for the vehicle lights she'd seen minutes ago. The driver had stopped at the bridge as if threatening her, trying to be intimidating, waiting, and reversing along the road. So why hadn't she seen headlights leading around the forest? There'd be something, a glow through the bushes, trees gleaming in the distance as the vehicle crawled away from the lodge. Unless... they were still here. The driver may have parked and got out. Watching her. Waiting.

A snapping sound came from the field beside her. Jess pointed the torch. The phone screen shook in her hand as it recorded. 'Hello? Is someone there?' Like an animal in the headlights, unsure of where to turn, her heart almost hopping in her chest as she struggled with the anticipation. *I have to get back to the lodge,* she told herself. *I need to barricade myself inside. It's not safe out here.*

From her left side, a whisper clung to the sharp breeze.

'We're coming for you.'

She shrieked, backing away, too frightened to question the voice. Her legs went, and she stumbled backwards onto the ground, the phone and torch landing beside her. Jess rolled onto her side, the stones rough on her hands as she pushed herself off the ground, slipping and almost falling again. Spinning around, facing the lodge, she crouched, placed the phone in her pocket, grabbed the torch, and began running along the path. The torchlight flickered in front of her, hopeless in this blackened void. The wind whipped against her ears, stinging the skin, white noise, again reminding her of the viral clip. She jumped. Her heart seemed to stop for a moment as the lights sprung to life by the lodge. Reaching the front door, she fished the keys from her leggings, her hands shaking uncontrollably as she tried to find the lock. Footsteps pounded along the path. The keys dropped onto the ground, and Jess screeched, unable to look behind her. Bending down, the footsteps almost on top of her, she grabbed the keys, rammed them into the lock, and opened the front door, slamming it behind her and locking herself inside.

As Jess turned, her right leg went through the same gap, and her body fell sideways against the floorboards. Resting for a moment, she placed the palms of her hands on the floor and under her right leg, lifting her foot out of the hole. As she did, it hit against something—an object hidden under the floor.

'What the heck is that?' she said aloud. With the torchlight pointing under the floor, she crawled onto her stomach, reaching her right hand between the gap, her fingers spread, fishing around for the object. She touched the soft paper, realising it was an envelope, and removed it from under the floor.

On the front of the envelope, written in black pen, were three words.

Our weekend away.

Jess held it in front of her and opened it, seeing a small hard drive.

Her body went cold, knowing what could be on it. Was this the breakthrough she needed? Would this answer all her questions? The excitement rushed through her body, and for a split second, she forgot about the threat she was under.

Quickly, she stood and walked to the bedroom.

The hard drive may give the answers Jess sought.

Alternatively, it could expose the imminent terror, revealing the truth behind the disappearance of the four friends.

And the immediate danger to Jess of what may lie ahead.

Sitting on the floor with her back pressed against the bedroom door, she loaded the hard drive into the side of the laptop and clicked play.

12

FRIDAY EVENING. JESS VIEWS THE FOOTAGE FROM FIVE YEARS AGO

'There's a petrol station. I have to pull over. We're almost out.' The driver turned around, clutching the steering wheel, seeing the camera pointing at her. 'Don't you ever get tired of recording? Jeez, Matt, give us five minutes of privacy.'

Jess noticed their accents were possibly Australian or New Zealand and wondered whether they lived in the UK or were here on holiday.

'My subscribers are going to love it,' Matt laughed. 'Raw footage, going to a lodge in the woods. They say it's haunted, you know. What could be more intriguing? So here we are, my girlfriend Emma is driving, and I'm with my best mate Danny and his girlfriend Maria.'

'It's not haunted. Who told you that shit?' Maria dragged hard on a joint, like her life depended on it, as if trying to suck a thick milkshake through the eye of a needle, the smoke filling the camper van, then she passed it across to Danny, who sat next to her, his legs crossed under him, evidently enjoying the hit. Pushing the window open, he sat back down. The noise of the road became more apparent, and the smoke cleared. 'Oh, that warm breeze drifting through the window. It's so... invigorating. Who the hell says it's haunted?' Danny asked in a raspy voice. The smoke seemed to catch in his throat, causing him to cough. Passing the joint back to Maria, he lay down on the soft cushions.

Slowly, Matt focused the camera on Danny and zoomed in. 'Christ! You have severe crow's feet. I never noticed. You need to get some cream for that.'

'Piss off,' Danny laughed. 'A face for the radio, huh? Go on, you can say it.' With one arm resting behind his head, Danny kicked at the lens. 'Who says it's haunted? Please put that thing down. I feel uncomfortable with a camera focused on me twenty-four-seven. All my flaws are exposed to the world.'

'I read it on the internet,' Matt stated, ignoring his instructions.

'It must be true then,' Maria answered, again dragging on the joint and scrunching it out on a piece of cardboard.

'It's true. I think it's a witch. It's said you can hear her screaming late at night through the valley. If you see her, you're supposed to die like an hour later or something. Perhaps it's instantly. I can't remember.'

'Bullshit,' said Danny. 'Jeez, you believe everything you read. It's complete crap.'

'Okay, I'm pulling in here,' Emma declared, steering the camper van beside one of the pumps. Opening the driver's door, she stood on the forecourt. The sun blazed down, and the soft breeze from the fields seemed a welcome relief as she stood, arms out as if embracing nature.

The door slid open, and Matt had the camera trained on her. 'So, tell everyone what you're looking forward to.'

Grabbing the nozzle, she began filling the vehicle with

petrol. 'Rest and relaxation. Plenty of it. I can't wait to just chill and unwind.'

As Jess watched the recording, seeing her standing by the camper van, the haze from the heat rising on the forecourt, the smell of petrol seemed almost seductive as Emma sniffed hard and laughed into the camera. She looked tall, around five foot seven, with shoulder-length black hair and sparkling green eyes. She wore a white top with flowers etched into the material, denim shorts, and black ankle boots.

Matt passed the camera to his friend Danny, who was still lying on the cushions and moaning about having to record him.

Matt came into view, standing beside Emma as she filled the camper van with petrol. He was taller. Maybe six feet, with cropped blonde hair, brown eyes, and a light stubble. He was medium build and wore a black T-shirt, red shorts, and sliders.

'I hate holding this thing,' said Danny. 'Anyway, no one will remember you once the witch gets you. You've had it, mate.'

'Is it recording, you dick?' asked Matt as he approached the window.

'Yes, go on. Make it quick. I have an important meeting with sleep.'

Standing by the side door, he began speaking. 'I'm Matt Adams, and we're in Amersham, Bucks, heading to a lodge for a much-needed break. I'm documenting our stay for my YouTube channel, *The Chilling Floor*, which I'll upload in a few days.'

'Get you,' Danny laughed. 'Subtle plug somewhere in there. Now you have two subscribers.'

Bending forward with his middle finger up, Matt continued. 'The lodge is deep in the forest, so I doubt we'll get a reception. It's ropey as it is. There are rumours about the woods. Many believe it's haunted.'

Emma laughed with a tinge of sarcasm as she replaced the nozzle, and Matt seemed to blush as though embarrassed.

'Anyway, I'll be recording loads of footage, which I'll upload when I have the chance. Wish us luck.'

In the background, Jess could hear the others as they shouted goodbye.

There were no blurred-out images or dubbed voices. It was genuine, raw, and she couldn't stop watching.

The laptop screen went blank as Jess clicked pause, her skin tingling with excitement. It felt like she was at the premiere of a film, an intimate screening, a meet and greet with the cast. She'd seen the footage so many times before, familiar with every move, every cough and spit, the dialogue engraved in her brain. But this, it felt exclusive, the director's cut, like she was the only person in the world with backstage passes, seeing the four of them in a new light, getting to know them and their possible harrowing story. Although Jess sometimes doubted the authenticity of the short recording on the internet, the newfound footage could hold the answers. It may also be an extremely difficult watch.

'What's wrong?' Matt asked, the camera fixed on his girlfriend.

'Nothing. Let's just go.'

'Emma. Did something happen? Talk to me?'

'It's nothing. Can we get out of here?' She walked around the front of the vehicle, opened the driver's door, started the engine, and pulled away, a thick cloud of exhaust fumes spewing from behind the camper van.

The camera jumped, unsteady, as Matt tried to focus on their surroundings. 'Slow down. We're not in a rush,' he said.

Danny's leg was visible as he lay on the pillows. Maria was giggling to herself and looked completely stoned. Pointing the camera between them, Matt zeroed in. Danny was slim, with a long, lean body stretched along cushions. His hair was deep black, cropped short, and he had heavy-set wrinkles on his face, thin lips, and dark brown eyes. Although geeky-looking, Jess thought he was attractive.

Maria had long, perfectly straight blonde hair that appeared to glow, like a model in a shampoo ad. Her eyes were bright green and sparkled, her lips full as though she'd had them filled but not overly, and Jess thought she wouldn't look out of place on a catwalk.

The camera pointed at Emma, her short black hair resting on her shoulders.

'So, are you going to tell us what happened in there?' Matt asked.

'He's a fucking... creep. Jesus! What's his problem?' Emma exclaimed as she shifted the gears, the crunching noise harsh as the vehicle continued pumping fumes from the exhaust.

'Who's a creep?' Matt swung the camera to the window opposite. The bushes went by so fast that the picture became momentarily blurry.

'The guy in... in the petrol station. He was asking weird, personal questions. Where was I headed? Was I alone? Did I want company? No, I fucking don't, jerk.' Turning around, flashing a look into the lens and back on the road, she continued. 'He came up to me, all in my face like, I could smell his rank breath, that grin, urgh! Disgusting. I felt someone watching me.'

'Watching you?' Matt asked.

'Uh-huh. When I turned around, a door closed. I'm certain I saw a figure for a split second. Someone was there.'

'Do you want to go back? Me and Danny will sort 'em out, hey Danny?'

'Yeah,' his deep voice muffled through the cushions as he lay on his stomach, trying to get comfortable. 'You go, I'll hold the camera,' Danny suggested.

As Matt swung the camera, struggling to find the off switch to end the recording, Jess glimpsed a vehicle behind the camper van for a split second before the screen went blank.

Leaning against the bedroom door, Jess paused the recording and stood, stretching her arms over her head, and rolling her shoulders. A stress knot had developed in the middle of her back, and she turned her body to either side, trying to rid the pain.

The daunting sense of being trapped hit her hard, and panic washed over her body.

Opening the bedroom door, she walked to the living room. The extreme silence was almost raucous. Leaning her face to the glass, she looked out through the front door, the bleakness encompassing her surroundings. Certain no one was out there, she stepped to the kitchen window, the lights in the distance providing relief. Ensuring the handle was fully locked in the downward position, Jess grabbed another glass of water, careful not to drop this one, and walked back into the bedroom. Leaning against the cold wooden door, she grabbed the laptop. The sense of anticipation gripped tight as she thought about the footage she'd found. Matt had made a documentary, and whatever happened before the edited version was loaded to social media, it seemed Jess was about to find out.

Why had the recording been hidden under the floor?

What happened while they'd stayed in the lodge?

Where the hell were they now?

As Jess braced herself and clicked play, the security lights flicked into motion, and something hit the bedroom window. She jumped, bringing her knees to her chin, stunned into silence. Fear caused her eyes to blur, and it felt like her oxygen was cut, as if her airways were blocked. She swallowed hard. After a minute, she stood, slowly dipping into her pocket, grabbing her phone, and started recording. Staring at the window, she eased one leg in front of the other, tiptoeing across the room, the lights beyond the valley, almost sensual, alluring. With her right arm extended, pressing the button on the handle and forcing it up, a vein throbbing in the side of her neck, she opened the window, the screech severe, like nails down a chalkboard grating every one of her senses.

With her body leaning over the window frame, Jess pointed the torch and camera to the ground outside the lodge.

Someone had thrown an inflatable ball at the window.

She gasped, almost dropping the mobile phone as she closed the window, tugging the handle and hearing the clunk as it locked. Jess gulped hard, tossing the phone and torch on the bed, and moved into the bathroom, throwing water on her face, splashing it over the mirror above her head and onto the tiled floor. Cupping her hand under the tap, she slurped cold water. Wetting her cheeks and cooling her warm skin, she looked at her reflection. Her short blond hair was damp with sweat, her skin parched, and the bags under her eyes were more evident. It looked like she'd aged ten years.

Moving to the hallway, she grabbed a broom from the boiler cupboard, turning it upside down, and walked to the bedroom window. Opening it and leaning her body out, she jabbed the handle towards the ground, trying to deflate the ball, but it was gone.

Hurling the broom on the bedroom floor, Jess shut and locked the window, grabbed the phone off the bed, and continued to record. She closed the bedroom door and sat, her back pushed against it, reversing the screen, and recording herself.

'Okay. I have most of it on film. I'm trapped. It's going to be a long night, but I will get through this. Whoever, or whatever is doing this, they won't beat me. I'm stronger than they think. I now understand what Matt, Emma, Danny, and Maria, I think those are their names, went through five years ago, and believe more than ever that something is going on out here. It's so dark outside. I daren't go out for fear of being attacked. So much has happened since arriving at the lodge. I'm scared, I admit. But I came here to make a documentary and to write a blog, and nothing is going to deter me from that. As soon as the Wi-Fi works, I'll load the pictures and video clips onto a file and email them to myself. I'm worried my phone will be taken and all this will be lost. Tomorrow, when it's bright, I'll—'

As the security lights powered on, Jess reversed the screen, pointing it at the window. 'I think someone's outside,' she whispered. Keeping her voice as low as possible, she continued. 'I don't know whether to open the front door and approach them. Shit. How many scary films do you watch

and end up shouting at the TV when someone does something stupid, like hearing a noise and racing towards it? Or
you think someone's in the cupboard, and the first thing you
do is force open the doors. I don't want to be that person.
But I don't know what else to do. I promised to film as much
as possible. I know it's stupid going out there. I have to see
how this plays out. The lights are still on outside. Oh, Christ!
What do I do?' The camera remained pointed at the
bedroom window, Jess filming everything. She waited, sat
on the floor against the bedroom door, the seconds dragging, her arm outstretched, fingers aching from holding the
phone, her heart thumping, resonating in her ears.

Suddenly, a figure came rushing at the window.

Jess yelped, her feet sliding against the floor as she
pushed backwards. As she stood, loud thumps pounded
against the window, and she thought the glass would break.
Then, he appeared. The young lad who'd called over earlier
and handed her the note. The dark glasses were gone, his
mouth open as he tried to shout for help.

'Oh my God! Wait.' Jess saw his arm. His hand had been
removed, and blood squirted from the stump. His panicked,
stricken state caused him to leap like a wild animal.

Tossing the phone on the bed and unlocking the
window, Jess reached out and tried to hold him, but his addled state of mind prevented her from calming him down.

Turning, he faced the woods and fell on the ground,
leaving his blood smeared over the glass.

13

FRIDAY EVENING

After passing out, Jess lay unconscious on the cold floor and abruptly opened her eyes, the torch glaring beside her. Glancing around the bedroom, her lips were wet with saliva, her head ached, and her mind was disorientated. For a moment, she'd forgotten where she was, how she'd ended up on the floor, alone, tired, and with no memory of the past few minutes.

Getting to her feet and feeling woozy, the room began spinning, and she reached for the window ledge, steadying herself. Her body spasmed, seeing the broom on the floor by her feet and recalling the scene only moments ago as she'd leant over the window ledge, trying to burst the inflatable ball. Then the security lights switched on, the figure racing to the window.

Mucus dribbled from her nose down to her lips, and she wiped it with the back of her hand, sniffing hard, the brain fog beginning to clear.

The chilly air surged through the window, the lights on the hill gleamed in the distance, and Jess braced herself, grabbing the torch off the floor and leaning over the window frame.

The body was gone.

'Where did he go? I saw him collapse. They'd cut off his hand, butchered him, and left him beside the lodge.' Her body hung over the frame, the pain sharp on her ribs as she waved the torch over the ground. The inflatable ball had blown a few feet along the grass, but the body had been removed.

Rushing to the kitchen, she grabbed the bottle of whiskey from the fridge, cracked open the cap, and took a swig. It felt severe, the harsh taste burning her throat. She swallowed hard. With every breath came a groan of fear deep within her lungs. Again, she put the bottle to her lips and drank. The buzz felt good. She was lightheaded, an adrenaline rush coursed through her veins, and Jess kept swigging. The sharp, sweet taste on her tongue, the warmth as it worked down her throat, the undeniable rush.

After taking another swig, she crept to the bedroom and peered over the window ledge. Only the inflatable ball rolled in the breeze. As she closed the window and locked it, she could still see the smeared blood on the glass.

Oh Christ, that poor guy, she thought. *What have they done to him?*

She sat on the floor, leaning against the bedroom door, tackling her conscience, and needing to go and look for him. It was madness. She knew it. However much she wanted to continue the documentary tonight, it was too dangerous. As soon as she opened the front door and stepped out into the darkness, the chances of being attacked were imminent.

Bracing herself for what may come next and desperate for answers to aid her escape, her eyes flicked to the window before she clicked play.

The camera panned to the lodge, and the clear blue sky overhead gave a calm, soothing feeling.

'This is amazing,' Matt said as he filmed the others grabbing their bags and exiting the camper van. 'So, we're finally here. It's certainly quiet.'

'Too quiet,' Maria said as she placed her arms through the straps of her bag and stretched. 'It's stunning, though, isn't it?' Swinging around to the camera, her eyes still glazed over from the joint, her words somewhat slurry, she said, 'Thanks for organising this, Matt. It'll be amazing.'

'No problem. It's exciting—four days to chill and relax with no one bothering us.'

The camera panned on Emma, the driver, as she walked over to Matt, dropped her bag, and cuddled him. 'I'd love a nap,' she said as she stepped back. 'The drive was exhausting.'

'We can do that,' Matt stated. 'We're free to do what we want. It's our holiday. If you want to sleep, let's sleep.'

Turning towards the lodge, seeming overwhelmed as she took it in, Emma remarked, 'It's huge. I didn't expect it to be this big. I saw it online, but the pictures didn't do it justice.' Peering out over the valley below, with the back of her hand over her eyes and shielding the sun, she remarked, 'Smell that fresh air, wow! It's so invigorating, and look at the view. Unreal.'

'It's certainly a picture,' Matt added.

Pointing towards the cottage, she said, 'I wonder if someone lives down there.'

'They must do.' The camera slowly turned with Matt, panning over to the cottage in the valley. 'I think I can see smoke from the chimney.'

'Why someone would choose to live so far from civilisation is beyond me. Matt, are you going to record everything? I feel like I'm on Love Island or Big Brother.'

'Not everything,' he laughed.

'Good,' Emma said. 'Well, join me in the bedroom then. And leave the camera behind for five minutes.'

'Five minutes? You're being generous.'

'You said it,' Emma answered with sarcasm in her voice. 'Camera off now,' she ordered.

The screen went blank for a few seconds and continued with Matt standing in the kitchen by the window, his arms outstretched and the camera pointing at his face. 'I'm Matt Adams; welcome to my YouTube channel, The Chilling Floor. I'm with my girlfriend Emma, best friend Danny, and his girlfriend, Maria.'

'My girlfriend for the moment,' Danny called from the sofa in the living room.

The camera panned on Maria. 'Hey.' She playfully slapped him on the arm. 'It can be easily arranged.'

The picture trained back on Matt, his smile revealing perfect white teeth.

'We've been friends since our stay in a residential care facility. Basically, our parents were fuck-ups and didn't want anything to do with us. So there we were. Lost in the system. We stayed in hostels for a while, working wherever possible until we had enough money to come to the UK.'

'Really, Matt. Do you have to tell them our whole life story?' Emma sniped.

Matt ignored the comment. 'I've been dating Emma for... a few years now, isn't that right, Emma?'

The camera rotated to Emma, standing in the kitchen corner, wearing a cream-coloured dressing gown and her black hair wrapped in a white towel.

'There or thereabouts. I can't see it lasting another minute if you don't turn that bloody thing off.'

Disregarding the sarcasm, Matt turned the camera back on himself. 'We're here deep in a forest in Amersham, Bucks, which is shrouded in mystery. I only found out right before we booked this trip. People have seen things lurking in the shadows. Weird chanting sounds can be heard and growling coming from the woods. Others have seen orbs and strange lights through the trees. It's said that if you venture into the woods late at night, you'll never return. We're staying in a lodge, deep in these very woods, and I'm determined to find out what's going on here. You can see the fields stretching over a valley through the window behind me. The sun is shining, and I can't think of a better place I'd rather be. But the forest is rife with rumours, stories of something roaming the woods late at night, and I'm setting up a camera, intent on recording as much as possible to see if I can capture any footage of this... this thing. It's not documented on the internet as, apparently, the locals won't talk about it. There isn't much on social media, but I stumbled on a couple of forums, the darker kind, where people posted their opinions. Everything from demons to witches, entities, paranormal shadows, and cults has been suggested. I even saw one comment talking about humanoid monsters such as Bigfoot or Sasquatch, as it's also commonly known. Okay, that should do it for the moment. I'll record more later.'

Swigging a can of beer, lying horizontal on the sofa in the living room, Danny called out, 'You don't believe that shit. That there's something here. The woods are haunted, do you? It's crap.'

'I don't know. But the forums I found on this place

suggest otherwise. Some reckon there's a demented family who prey on people who stay here.'

'Bullshit. What utter crap,' Maria said as she moved next to Emma.

Matt placed the camera on the kitchen worktop, leaving it recording, and walked across the living room, sitting on the sofa. 'It's not. If you read the forums, you'd think differently. People are convinced. I'd show you only there's no reception. I thought there was Wi-Fi up here.'

'Matt, I'm not spending the only few days I have listening to you talk shit about this place, freaking us all out, recording our every move. Please, hun. I want to enjoy this place. Come on.' Emma left the kitchen and went into the bedroom at the back of the lodge.

The bedroom where Jess was staying now.

'I think it adds intrigue. I'm all for you recording,' Danny said as he swigged more beer.

'Emma's right,' Maria stated, joining the men on the sofa. 'It's beginning to freak us out. You should have told us before you booked it.'

Danny leant across, placing his arm around her. 'I'm here. I'm not going to let anything happen to you.'

'Is it true? For real?' Maria asked. 'Has something been seen in these woods?'

'Of course it's not real. We'd have heard something about it on the news. Matt likes to scare us. He's making this shit up.'

'How many followers do you have on YouTube, Matt?' Maria asked.

'Er... Erm... almost fifty. But that's beside the point. If this recording goes viral, I can start using ads on my platform, get sponsors, and make big money. I'm convinced there's something out here.'

Maria looked between the two men: the fear evident on her face. The blood seemed to drain from her body, her fingers tapping on her lap, and she shifted on the sofa. 'What do you think is out here?'

'Surely you're not falling for it?' Danny expressed. 'You know what Matt's like.'

'I am here, you know. All I'm saying is keep the doors and windows locked at night, and whatever you do, don't venture out alone.'

For a moment, the camera went blank.

The sound of laughter filtered through the laptop speaker as the picture returned. They were in a restaurant.

Maria sat next to her boyfriend, Danny. She wore a black plunging V-neck top. Her blonde hair was held in a high ponytail, her tanned skin seemed to glisten, and a butterfly tattoo was visible on her shoulder.

Danny wore a white shirt and sported a light stubble. His cropped black hair was wet with gel, and he didn't notice the camera pointing at him immediately. 'Matt. What are you doing? Come on, Bro, we'll get kicked out.'

'For what?' answered Matt. 'It's not a cinema.'

'Maybe it's plagiarism,' Maria pointed out. 'They may have a copyright infringement in place and sue the arse off you. They might think you're out to steal a super-secret recipe.'

'It would serve you right,' Emma said, sounding agitated.

The camera scanned the restaurant, showing couples deep in conversation, staff balancing trays of food and drink, walking between tables, chefs rolling dough, making pizza and garlic bread, and Dean Martin's "That's Amore" played softly through the corner speakers.

Emma was visible, elbow leaning on the table and her

head resting on her hand. Her black hair was held back with a band, her complexion glowed, and she looked relaxed. 'I'm starving. The smell of garlic is so appetising. What are you all going for? The meat feast pizza looks good.' She took a sip of sparkling water.

Danny and Maria shared a bottle of red wine, and Matt had a glass of beer on the table in front of him.

'I'm going to start with the dough balls,' Maria announced.

Seeing the camera pointing straight at her, Emma said, 'Put the bloody thing away. I swear, I'm going to go home. Pillock.'

There was a brief pause. It was much later. Maria looked tired, and her cheeks were bright red from the wine. Danny was slumped on the seat next to her. Their voices were loud and boisterous, and they were debating who was the better action star—Arnie or Sly.

'Arnie's made the better films,' Matt insisted. 'Commando, The Terminator, Predator.'

'I remember that film. Wasn't there a monster in the woods?' Emma looked at Danny and Maria, the sudden silence revealing their unease. The side of Emma's face enlarged as Matt zoomed in, her troubled expression clear to see. Her hand covered the screen for a second, and she laughed. 'So what? You all think there's a predator in the woods where we're staying, is that it? I can't believe you're all swallowing Matt's story.'

Danny and Maria remained silent as if their opinion may cause trouble. They didn't appear to need the hassle.

'Here, take this. Film everything.' Passing the camera to Danny, Matt stood. 'Only one way to find out.'

'What?' asked Emma, tugging at his arm. 'What are you doing? Sit down. I mean it, Matt, sit down now.'

'Excuse me!' he shouted. The restaurant went completely quiet. The voices muted, the staff appeared to freeze on the stop, and the chefs looked out from the kitchen. Matt blushed, his voice slurred from too much beer. 'My friends and I are staying at a lodge in Sheers Woods. Is it true? The rumours, I mean. Is there something... something up there?'

No one answered.

'You, my friend.' Matt pointed to a man sitting at the next table. 'How long have you lived here?'

The man looked embarrassed at the question, pushing his specs further up the bridge of his nose. Pulling at the collar of his suit jacket, he went to speak, but it seemed the woman sitting opposite kicked him under the table. 'A... A few years. I've lived here for a few years. I... I don't know what you're talking about.'

'No one has heard anything about it,' the woman answered. Her black hair was tightly permed, her lips pursed, as she played with a button on her green jacket. 'Turn the camera off, or we'll call the police.'

The camera swung to Emma, who sat, looking mortified. A red rash had developed on her neck, and she covered her face with her hands.

Continuing, Matt tried to win their trust. 'I don't mean to scare any of you. I was hoping to film the locals and get their take on the story. That's all. I'm sorry if I offended anyone.' Matt glimpsed at the lens. His lips widened, and his eyebrows raised high on his forehead as if embarrassed.

'No one wants to talk about it,' a voice answered from a table near the kitchen.

Turning the camera, Danny focused on the man sitting by himself, drinking a neat whiskey. He was completely bald, and his head was almost too oval. He had a drinker's face, blotchy red cheeks filled with veins, and a deep purple-coloured nose too big for his face. His dark blue shirt was creased as if it had been lying on the floor for weeks.

'I didn't mean to cause any aggravation,' Matt offered.

'Tomorrow night. It's a... a full moon. It's when they strike. You're all in danger. The best thing you can do is get as far the fuck away from here as possible. Drive out of Sheers Woods and never look back.'

Slumping back on his chair, back straight and eyebrows knotted, Matt looked apologetic.

A woman's voice called from beside where they sat, but the camera was focused on Matt.

'The worst mistake you all made was coming here. You need to get out while you still can. Get away from the lodge, and don't ever come back here.'

Emma placed her hand in Matt's, her voice low and controlled. 'We need to leave. I told you, didn't I? I warned you not to say anything.'

'I'm sorry. Christ,' he whispered, 'I didn't think it would cause this much commotion.'

A waiter came from nowhere, covering the lens with his hand, and said, 'Come on. It's time to go.'

Silence resonated through the camper van.

With the camera panned on his face, Matt began speaking. 'Well, that was weird. And what did he mean about a full moon tomorrow night?'

'Are you for real?' Emma shouted from the driver's seat. 'We've just been hurled out of a restaurant due to your stupid fucking documentary, and what does he do? Carries on recording. I've seen it all now.'

Danny and Maria remained silent.

Matt's face went scarlet as he appeared too embarrassed to look at anyone.

Suddenly, Maria burst into laughter, followed by Danny.

'Wow! That's just great,' Emma stated. 'What's better than coming on a break with one idiot? Three of them. And you are both encouraging him. I give up.'

'You have to admit it was funny,' Maria declared. 'Poor Matt's face was a picture. I bet you wanted the ground to open and swallow you whole.'

'You could say that,' replied Matt. 'What was their problem?'

'Er, they didn't want a bloody camera shoved in their faces,' answered Emma. 'Maybe that small problem.'

Danny shifted on the floor and lay down on the cushions. 'I've eaten way too much. I guess we're having a barbecue tomorrow night. It looks like we're banned from Amersham.'

The four laughed as Matt turned the camera to Emma, her body leaning forward in the driver's seat as she watched the road.

'It's weird though, guys, don't you think?' Maria pressed her body against the camper van, shifting her head from one shoulder to the other and stretching. 'They do seem to be hiding something.'

'Or they're frightened,' Emma added. 'I've never seen locals so... together, as one, as if they're keeping a secret. It was so weird.'

'What was weird was Matt paying the bill. That was weird,' Danny added.

'Oh yeah. In the rush to get out, I forgot we didn't split it. Thanks for reminding me. You can all cook the food tomorrow for the barbecue. Hey, I'm sorry I ruined the night,' he offered.

'You didn't,' Danny assured him. 'It was——'

'There's that prick's place. Look, he's still open.' The light from the petrol station glowed, illuminating the forecourt. Jabbing the brakes, Emma slowed the camper van.

'What did he say to you?' Maria asked.

'He was awful. A proper fucking creep. Made me feel so uncomfortable. You know, when it feels like you're being perved over.' Pulling the vehicle to a halt, she leant her body across the seat and screamed out of the window. 'You fucking prick!' Jabbing the accelerator, she drew away.

'Wait. Oh my God. Did you see that?' Matt shouted. He was pointing the camera to the left side of the petrol station and leapt forward. The camera went blurry as he placed it close to the window.

'What?' Emma shouted. 'What did you see?'

'Danny, Maria, did you see that?' The lens honed on their faces: the shock evident as they seemed to wait in anticipation for what Matt had seen.

'What, mate? I didn't see anything?' Danny replied.

'You're scaring us. What was it?' Maria asked.

'There... There was... a van. A black... A black van.' Matt was trying to catch his breath. The trauma seemed to cause his speech to slur, and he spoke as though he'd been running. 'I think someone was loading a fucking body into it.'

14

FRIDAY NIGHT

Seclusion shrouded the bedroom as Jess hit the pause button and stared at the laptop screen. The shock of hearing Matt's account of what he'd seen at the petrol station was slowly digesting, mulling around in her head.

While previously researching the lodge and the friends' disappearance, she'd also seen the forums where people had suggested something lurking in the woods.

Her fingers rested on the laptop keys, eyes still and unfocused.

Through the bedroom window, the lights sprinkled across the hills, blinking in the distance. At this moment, she wanted to run. To get as far away from the lodge as possible. It wasn't safe. That much was obvious. Opening the front door and running would only lead her into the arms of whatever was out there. Fighting the tiredness, knowing sleep would leave her vulnerable, the only thing she could do was watch the footage and hope it gave her the means to escape. If the group found a way out, the answer would possibly lie on the hard drive.

As Jess stood by the window, a noise came from upstairs —a shuffling sound on the ceiling above her head. She spun around, facing the bedroom door.

Something was up there.

Tiptoeing to the bed, she grabbed her mobile phone and continued recording.

'I think someone's in the lodge,' she whispered. 'I don't know what to do. As yet, I haven't checked upstairs. This is ludicrous. Anyone could be hiding up there. I... I have to go see.' With the phone lens pointing at the bedroom door, Jess crept across the floor, the boards groaning under her feet. 'If someone's up there, I'll hide. It's my only option. Shit, this is crazy.' Easing the bedroom door open, she peeked into the hallway.

Another sound from above. The creaking noise appeared to scratch at the walls.

Jess waited, debating whether to climb the stairs or hide. The noise seemed to stop.

'I'm going to go up there,' she said in a calm, controlled voice, the phone lens focusing on the TV screen as white noise filled the corner of the living room.

In the kitchen, she opened the cutlery drawer and grabbed a large knife, debating whether to go to the fridge and take another swig of whiskey to help get through the night. She decided against it, knowing a drunken stupor would only add to her problems if someone got inside the lodge.

After turning the TV off, the sharp knife jutting from her pocket, she waited at the bottom of the stairs, gripping the railing, her left hand touching the cold, smooth texture. The metal stairs squeaked, the whine seemed to fill the lodge, and she imagined the bolts loosening and plummeting to the ground below. As she crept to the first floor, trying to keep as silent as possible, she knew if someone were upstairs, they'd be alerted.

The stairs twisted back on themselves as she reached the first floor, turning the lights on, her arm extended, filming the upstairs hallway. Beside her, a large window hinted at an incredible view over the fields, though obscured by the darkness.

It was late, and there were fewer lights than earlier on the hills.

Further along the hallway, a beautiful skylight gave an outstanding glimpse above the lodge. The half-moon encompassed by glistening beads helped ease the tension.

As Jess continued recording, she steered the phone to the end of the upstairs hallway.

A door budged.

She stumbled back, grabbing the railing to steady herself. 'Is someone there? This isn't funny. I need you to leave. I'm going to call the police.'

A clunk. The door on the far left appeared to shift on its hinges.

The raucous squeal echoed through the first floor, grating on every nerve in her body.

'I have to check,' she whispered. 'If only for peace of mind. I know it's stupidity, but what choice do I have? I need to know if—'

Another creak.

It sounded as though the floorboards were dipping.

With a deep breath, suddenly lightheaded, her heart punching in her chest, she rushed along the hallway to the back left bedroom, yanked on the door handle, and pushed it back hard, hearing it bounce against the wall. Pawing for the light switch, she flicked it on, and a dim glow filled the room. The window was open, with a curtain resembling a phantom flapping in the breeze. The room felt like it had never experienced heat.

Charging across the room, Jess grabbed the handle, closed the window, and locked it.

Eyeing the large bed, a white mattress lying neatly on top, folded in one corner, the plain walls, and a window displaying only gloom outside, her suspicions were satisfied. The room appeared empty.

Her eyes were drawn to the space under the bed. Visions of her crouching and an arm reaching out, grabbing her wrist, and pulling her under warped her thoughts. Switching off the light, she closed the bedroom door.

Next, she checked the bedroom opposite—two comfy-looking single beds with light sheets under grey quilts. Again, the white-painted walls were completely bare, and although the heating was on, the room was freezing.

The window was locked.

Along the hallway towards the stairs, a bathroom with a matching white basin and pedestal, a close-coupled toilet, and an electric shower over a plain white bath. The window was closed, and Jess tugged at the handle to ensure it was locked.

Finally, next to the bathroom on her right, another bedroom. After quickly checking the window was locked, she backed out and closed the door.

Quickly, she turned and charged down the stairs, dashing along the hallway and slamming the bedroom door behind her.

Placing the knife on the floor, she sat in silence, her emotions drained, expecting someone to kick the bedroom door in at any moment, the fear of holding them back and being stranded in the lodge overpowering her. She dug her nails into her skin, frustration swamping her every thought.

Panic rose from her stomach, and Jess began gasping for breath, the palpitations strong, like a drum booming in her ears. After a couple of minutes, it passed, and she lay on the floor, shoulders against the bedroom door, and tried desperately to relax.

Grabbing her phone and turning the volume down, she watched the recent video clips she'd taken and flicked through the pictures. The ancient symbols engraved on the wall of the hay barn, the hair slung over the clothesline, the strange figure walking through the woods. Already, she had so much material. So much to verify something going on here.

The hard drive was proof the four friends had stayed at the lodge. She needed to guard it with her life, and when she left Sheers Lodge, people would finally believe the story.

And hopefully, a light would be shed on the mystery of their disappearance.

Satisfied she was alone in the lodge; Jess grabbed the phone and continued recording. Reversing the screen, she gazed at her image, troubled by her appearance.

'I look like shit,' she whispered. 'My hair is wet, and I have beads of sweat on my brow. Christ! I even have bags under my eyes from tiredness. Don't be alarmed. I apologise in advance, but I defy anyone to go through this and still look presentable. Anyway, I don't have professional lighting, makeup staff, or sound technicians. It's just me. If I don't sound optimistic or upbeat, it's because I'm scared. I'm completely terrified. I have two options. Well, one really. Running into the night or staying put, hiding in the bedroom, in the hope of making it through the night. I wish it were a live stream on YouTube or TikTok, and then I could put up a poll, ask for your thoughts, and let you help me choose. I probably wouldn't listen anyway. I know something's out there. As soon as I leave the lodge, they'll come for me. I've found a hard drive. It shows the four friends who vanished from here five years ago. If... When I get out of here, I'll bring it to the police, and we'll hopefully get the answers we need. I don't know where they are or if what's happening to me, happened to them. I'm going to stop recording now as I need answers. It may be the only way for me to find out if they escaped. Possibly the only way I will as well.'

Jess turned off the video camera, opened the laptop, and hit play.

15

'Pull over Emma!' Matt shouted.

'What? Where?'

'Here. Just pull over here.'

Only a corner of the camper van was visible, but Jess could clearly hear their voices.

'It's not a good idea, Matt. I'm scared.' Maria's voice was weak and strained.

'I've got to see what was inside the van. Danny, will you come with me?'

'It's dangerous, Bro. I don't want to be caught in any shit going down. Are you sure you saw a body?'

'Someone was holding a blanket. The shape resembled a body. I'm positive. Emma was shouting out of the window. We were all laughing. I looked to the side of the petrol station, and there was a man standing by a van. Whatever he was holding, he loaded it into the back. I know it sounds mad, but I saw it.'

'So, let's call the police,' Emma insisted.

'I haven't got a signal. Have any of you? That's a no, then. I have to see what he loaded into the van.'

'Okay, I'll come with you.' Danny offered.

'Emma, Maria, are you coming?' asked Matt. He picked up the camera, directing it at his girlfriend in the driver's seat. Her expression was one of horror and confusion. Her eyes were still as though she were in a daze, and the colour seemed to drain from her face.

'No. I'm not going. Are you mad?'

'I'm with you, Emma. We'll stay in the van where it's safe,' Maria pressed. 'You two can be heroes if you like. Don't involve us.'

'Fine,' Matt insisted. 'Please understand, I've got to do this. If there is someone in the back of the van, they may need our help. Keep the camper van locked. If anyone comes, spin around and drive back into town.'

Turning to face the front, it appeared Emma was considering what to do. After a few seconds, she turned back. 'A lot of good that's going to do. You saw them in the restaurant. The locals are too frightened to talk. There's something going on here. I say we head back to the lodge.'

'Keep the doors locked. We'll be back in a minute.' The camera wobbled and became blurry for a second. The side door opened, and Matt stepped out, focusing on the petrol station around fifty yards behind them.

Emma had pulled the vehicle beside the ditch. Along the road, the only light was the neon sign.

Danny stepped out, closed the side door, and they walked back along the road.

Jess could hear their heavy breathing. The anticipation seeped through the laptop speaker. The more she watched, the more intrigued she became.

After pausing the recording for a moment, she turned her body, bringing her legs to the side to get more comfortable and pressed play.

The picture was erratic as Matt and Danny walked towards the petrol station.

The lens scanned the bleak fields stretching on their right, the thick bushes across the road visible by the moonlight, and back to the camper van. The hazard lights blinked in the distance.

As they approached, Matt seemed to duck behind a wall, capturing the ground momentarily.

'Can you see anyone?' Danny asked.

'Hang on, let me focus this thing. I'll zoom in on the shop. No, I can't see anyone.' The front doors were closed, the lights were on, and Matt slowly recorded along the length of the shop, seeing the coffee machine through the glass, the shelves stacked with crisps: sweets, chocolates, a couple of sandwiches in plastic containers, and a glass cabinet displaying doughnuts. 'Okay, there's no one behind the counter. As far as I can tell, there doesn't seem to be any CCTV cameras, but I can't be sure. I say we go now.'

'Fuck, this is insane. Come on then,' Danny said, his voice tinged with uncertainty.

The camera captured the black van parked to the left side of the petrol station. The lights were off, and the doors closed.

'Have you got any signal?' Matt asked.

'Nothing. You?'

'Nothing. Keep watching the inside of the shop. Tell me if you see anyone. I have the camera trained on the van. We may need this footage as evidence.'

'This is crazy. I don't feel comfortable, Bro. Let's just get out of here.'

'Danny, we have to help.'

They passed the petrol pumps to their right side, the air

and water machine on their left with an "Out of order" sign written in black pen on a discoloured piece of cardboard.

'Wait,' Danny said as they approached the transit van.

'What?'

'I saw a door open towards the back of the shop. No one's there.'

'What do you mean?' As Matt turned, the camera followed and focused on the back of the shop, zooming in to the toilet sign and another room to the right marked "Staff only."

'I mean, the toilet door opened, but no one came out.'

'You think we're being watched?' asked Matt, again steering the lens along the length of the shop and back to the toilet door.

'I think... I... We need to leave, Bro. I don't have a good feeling about this.'

'No shit,' Matt stated. 'What gives you that impression? The fact I saw a body being loaded into the back of the van. Yeah, I don't feel too comfortable either, funny enough.'

'You're such a prick.'

'I can't see anyone standing at the toilet door. Are you sure it hasn't been open all the time?'

'Positive,' Danny urged. 'I've had some wine, but I know what I saw. The door opened. No one came out. So, I think someone is watching us.'

In a hushed voice, Matt stated, 'Emma said the same thing earlier. She came out of the shop; certain she was being watched.'

The camera trailed to the back of the van around twenty yards from where the two men stood.

Matt stepped towards it, the camera unsteady and his breaths choppy, possibly through apprehension. His right hand reached for the handle, visible in the corner of the screen, and he tugged it. 'It's locked. Shit.'

The camera dropped.

A loud crack resounded through the speaker, and Jess gripped the sides of the laptop, her heart almost in her throat. The van's back tyre was visible as Matt grabbed the camera.

'Can you see through the window?' asked Danny.

As Matt picked the camera up, he stepped closer to the van, his hand visible as he cupped it to the glass. 'No, it's too dark. I can't see shit.'

Suddenly, the engine turned over and roared to life. Exhaust fumes filled the air, and the van reversed, the back edge hitting Danny's shoulder and knocking him sideways. The tyres spun, churning gravel and spraying dust into their faces.

As the van pulled away from the petrol station, Matt grabbed Danny.

'Are you alright?'

'Yeah. The crazy fucker tried to run me over.'

The picture jumped and became blurry as they ran towards the parked camper van.

'For the... shit, I'm so unfit. For the record, we tried to open the van doors. A man was waiting in the driver's seat and drove off. Danny was hit, but he's not injured. There's definitely something wrong here. I have it on camera. Should we follow the van, Danny?'

His friend sounded fitter; his breaths more controlled. 'I can see the van lights along the road. I don't know. Did you see anything through the glass?'

'Nothing. It was too dark.'

'If you're certain you saw a body being loaded into the van, we should go back to town,' Danny insisted. 'Report it.'

'Are you crazy? They won't get involved. You saw them at the restaurant. We were practically kicked out for asking questions. They're too frightened. We have no reception out here. We have to follow it. It's our only choice.'

The side door of the camper van opened. Again, the camera rested on the floor of the vehicle.

The two men spoke together, trying to explain what happened: the toilet door opening, the feeling of being watched, approaching the van doors, the driver reversing, hitting Danny, and pulling away.

'Then we need to drive back to town,' Emma suggested, 'and call the police.'

'I can't be absolutely sure,' Matt said. 'What if it was all innocent? I can't prove there was a body in the back. If we report it and I got it wrong, I'll look like a right twat.'

'There's only one way to find out?' Danny suggested. 'We need to follow it. See where it goes.'

'For Christ's sake!' Emma groaned.

Picking up the camera, Matt pointed it to the front as Emma started the engine, flicking on the full lights and pulling away.

'Drive faster,' Matt shouted. 'Step on it.'

'I can't drive any faster. Do you know how old this thing is?'

'We're going to lose them.' Matt trained the camera on Maria as she linked Danny. 'Are you okay?' he asked.

'I... I want to go home. I don't feel safe here. Can we just leave?'

'Nothing's going to happen. Once we stay together, we're safe,' Danny assured her. 'If Matt saw a body being loaded into the van, we need to help.'

As Maria sat rooted in the corner of the vehicle, Matt steered the camera to the front.

'Can you see the van, Emma?'

'No. there's no lights ahead. This is such a stupid idea. What am I supposed to do if I catch up with it? Ram them off the road? Scream for them to stop and politely ask what they're doing with a body in the back of the van? Come on, Matt.'

The road narrowed, and the glare of the full lights filled the air. The eerie silence was haunting.

'I can see lights just ahead,' Emma shouted.

'Please,' Maria insisted. 'Can't we just go back to the lodge?'

'Maria, hun, I'm not going to do anything stupid,' Emma promised. 'At the first sign of danger, we'll leave. Fuck this place. Stop worrying, okay? I won't put us at risk. Wait.'

'What?' Danny asked.

Emma slowed the camper van, almost stopping. 'The van is turning off.'

'Okay. So keep following,' Danny insisted.

'You don't get it. It's turned into Sheers Woods.'

16

FRIDAY NIGHT

As Jess paused the clip, Emma's words mulled over in her mind.

You don't get it. It's turned into Sheers Woods.

Jess stood, shaking her legs to rid the cramp, expecting to see the young man from earlier running towards the window.

Outside, only a couple of lights remained, gleaming in the distance along the hills, the fields swallowed in blackness. The half-moon shaped like a smiling emoji glowed bright in the night sky.

The display on her mobile phone showed almost 11 pm. Jess ached through fatigue and pined for sleep. Her body was drained of energy, and it felt as though she'd been dragged through the fields, beaten, and left to die.

Although the heating was on, it seemed to make no difference to the temperature of the lodge.

Removing her top and leggings, she threw them on the back of a chair by the dressing table.

After brushing her teeth in the bathroom, she pulled the

quilt back, tucked her tired body under the sheet, and closed her eyes.

Images of her mother and father swarmed her head, envisioning their agitation in trying to contact her, knowing they'd be worried she hadn't called.

Ben, her boyfriend, would have been frustrated he couldn't get through.

Ruth, her best friend, asked Jess to call when she arrived.

She thought about the footage. The last people who'd visited the lodge had disappeared.

Was she next?

Why had there been only a snippet of the recording online? How come the rest of the footage hadn't been loaded, hidden in an envelope under the floorboards of the lodge?

Where were they now?

Her brain was addled with questions, and however much Jess wanted to keep watching, her eyes were sore, her body beyond tired.

But she dare not sleep. Drifting into a slumber, surrendering to fatigue, made her vulnerable and defenceless. Jess had to keep awake.

With her body pressed against the headboard, the blanket pulled to her neck, and her feet stamping on the soft mattress, Jess tried desperately to get warm.

As her eyelids grew heavy, her breathing slowed, and tiredness encompassed her. Shutting her eyes, she fell into a brief moment of repose before jolting awake, blinking hard and focusing on the room.

Grabbing her mouth, she tugged her bottom lip and gently patted her cheeks.

Again, her eyes began closing, and she dozed off.

Something woke her.

Turning onto her side, she jabbed the phone screen.The display showed it was just gone 1 am. She blinked at the darkness, the room slowly coming into focus.

Bang.

It sounded like someone was thumping on the front door.

Bang.

Bang.

Air caught in her throat, and Jess struggled to breathe as strange gurgling sounds emitted from her mouth. Her body was suddenly rigid, paralysed with fear.

The security lights around the side of the lodge were off. There was time. She could open the window and flee into the woods. Jess contemplated it.

Bang.

Bang.

Bang.

Momentarily, it felt like her breath had stopped. As though her lungs were empty, and she couldn't fill them.

Swiping the mobile off the dressing table, she crept to the bedroom door. This time, she didn't narrate for fear of being heard.

Holding the phone in front of her, she eased down the bedroom door handle and pulled it back. Her lips widened, biting on her tongue, eyebrows raised, anticipating a groan from the hinges and being heard.

Too fearful of stepping into the hallway, she turned on the record function, poked the phone out, grabbed her wrist to steady her hand, and tried to film the front door.

A click, followed by the light going off in the living room.

Someone was pounding on the front door from inside the lodge.

17

A FEW HOURS EARLIER.

'I 'll be there in a couple of hours. Can you hear me? Hello, Toby. The reception's terrible. Hello?' Alice Harper jabbed a button on the steering wheel, ending the call. She was driving along the A355 towards Beaconsfield, heading to Birmingham to stay with her boyfriend for the weekend. She hadn't seen Toby for a couple of weeks, and although she hated driving in the dark, she looked forward to spending time with him.

Tapping the radio tuner on the dashboard, she attempted to tune into a local station. Music wasn't her thing. While driving, she preferred talk shows. It felt comforting. As though someone else was in the car keeping her company.

She watched in the rear-view mirror as a motorbike rounded a bend behind her, pulled close to the bumper, and at the last second, it swerved around her, the rider turning and giving her the V sign.

'Oh, up yours, arsehole. You don't own the road. What's wrong with some people?' Tapping the brakes, she glared at her reflection, flicking a hand through her long auburn hair. Her lips were still swollen after having them filled yesterday. Toby hadn't seen them yet, and she worried what he'd think.

They'd been going out for a few months after meeting at a bar in Chelsea, London. Toby was down on a rugby tour, and Alice was out with a few friends.

After gaining the courage, he started chatting with her at the bar, meeting his teammates for breakfast the following morning after going back to her place, excited to tell them he'd gone home with a model.

Alice liked him. There were no airs and graces. He cared about family and listened. That was his greatest attribute. He listened to what she had to say and took an interest in her life.

The glare from behind caused her to swerve. A vehicle approached, flashing its full beams. As she pulled over to the left, so did the driver behind.

'Go on, overtake.' Pulling up the handbrake, she undid her seatbelt and turned, signing for the driver to keep going. 'I know I'm driving slow. Just pass me.'

The lights behind went off.

'Fine, stay there,' she insisted. 'But you're on your own.' Indicating, she pulled onto the road, watching in the wing mirror as the lights returned and the vehicle pulled out behind her. 'Christ's sake! Just overtake me.'

The vehicle was around thirty yards behind her, gaining momentum.

Adjusting the rear-view mirror to ease the glare, Alice continued driving slowly, trying to force the car behind to overtake. Gently jerking the steering wheel, she pulled her car into the ditch, the tyres mounting a grass verge and dust spraying over the windscreen. She slammed the brakes, the steering wheel jolting in her hands, and sat, watching the driver pull in behind her.

'What is wrong with you? Are you mad?' Winding the window down, she placed her arm out, swiping the air with her hand to persuade the driver to go.

Again, the lights went off. The driver's door opened, and a man got out and walked towards her.

Abruptly, she closed the window and locked the doors, tapping the accelerator and stalling the car. She saw him crouching by the window, shouting beside her driver's door.

'You have a brake light out. I'm sorry if I startled you, but it's dangerous.'

The tension eased from her shoulders, her fingers released the steering wheel, dropping to her lap, and Alice undid her seatbelt and opened the car door. 'I'm... Wow! Sorry. I must seem so rude. I thought... Well, you never know,' she said, her voice breaking slightly.

'Come. Let me show you,' he insisted.

Alice got out and followed him behind the car. The sudden threat disappeared. The guy seemed concerned for her, like a father figure. Something in his voice displayed genuine concern. He seemed aware of her susceptibility, and his mannerism put her at ease as if he were apologising for helping.

'This one. This is the one that's broken. Here. I'll show you.' Quickly, he got into the driver's seat, pulled away, and hit the brakes.

'It's okay now,' Alice shouted. 'You must have a magic touch. They're both lighting up.'

'Strange,' he said as he joined her on the road. 'It was definitely out while I was behind you.' Suddenly, he kicked the backlight so hard that the glass shattered. 'It's out now.'

As Alice turned, he grabbed her, placing a cloth over her mouth and loading her into the boot.

A few minutes later, an off-duty police officer still in uniform pulled up behind Alice's abandoned vehicle.

She stepped out, grabbed cones from the boot, and placed them on the road. Then, she removed her mobile phone and made a call. The signal bar flickered, the ringtone weak. 'Hey. Where are you? Okay. Hurry up. There's some glass on the road, but nothing I can't handle. Okay, see you in a minute.' Ending the call, she grabbed Alice's phone from the car, removed the SIM card, and dumped it in a bin bag along with the glass and debris she had swept off the road.

As the pick-up truck pulled over, the driver jumped out. 'Hey, officer. What happened?'

'It's Louise. I'm off duty.'

'I'm winding you up,' the guy responded. 'Anyone come by?'

'Not a soul. You know what to do with the vehicle. It can never be found.'

'You saying I can't do my job?'

'I know you can.' Louise watched the pick-up truck pull away, towing Alice Harper's car. She cleared the cones off the road and headed home without alerting anyone about what had happened on the A355.

18

SATURDAY MORNING

Easing her arm back, fingers tight around the mobile phone as it recorded the dark living room, Jess squeezed her eyes tight, stinging in their sockets, and braced for the sudden pounding along the floor. Only moments ago, someone was banging on the front door. And then the living room lights went out.

The pain was severe in her stomach. It felt like her intestines were twisting inside her body.

Leaning against the bedroom door, head back and eyes almost piercing the ceiling, Jess waited. Her heartbeat punched through her ears, her body shaking, and she worried she'd pass out again. Panic worked through every vein, and she forcefully gulped air, trying to remain conscious. *Please. Don't let me faint. Think of happy times. Brighton Beach. The sun warming my body, and the sound of waves crashing against the shore. Don't faint. You—*

A handle shifted.

The front door opened.

Again, Jess squeezed her eyes tight, her hands pressed

together, sandwiching the phone, her fingertips touching her nostrils.

As she turned and leant her body into the hallway, the security lights glared through the open front door.

On three, she said to herself. *One. Two. Go.* Charging into the living room, leaving the lights off, she slammed the front door, pleased to feel the key in the lock. Twisting it, she backed away, seeing a shadow through the kitchen window. She kept stepping backwards, eyes glued to the front door. Anticipating someone grabbing her from behind, she reached back, swiping at the space. In the hallway, Jess pawed at the wooden frame, edged into the bedroom, and closed the door.

Throwing the phone on the bed, she tipped the chest of drawers on its side. The crash caused ringing in her ears as it hit the floor. The harsh snapping sound denoted something broke. It was the least of her worries. With her foot against the wall, body arched, she heaved the large object in front of the door.

Reaching for the handle, she pulled hard, satisfied it would give her enough time to escape through the window if someone came back.

With a huge sigh, releasing some of the tension, Jess placed her head in her hands, unable to believe what was happening. First came a chuckle, which quickly turned to tears. Wiping her eyes, she straightened her body, stretching her neck, adamant this wouldn't beat her.

Grabbing her phone, she turned the lights out, got into bed, and leant against the headboard.

As a child, when her father would read her bedtime stories, he'd always finish with his own one, Jess's favourite about a local Bogeyman who used to drive an ice-cream van. Children would rush to the vehicle asking for screwballs, ninety-nines, oysters, or funny feet, seeing the creepy old man who'd spring from behind the counter and try and catch them. When her father would leave the room, Jess would lie for ages, imagining what he looked like and how, if he came after her, she'd escape. Pulling the blanket over her head and curling into the fetal position was her solace. A way for the Bogeyman to leave. Her shield of protection against his evil clutches.

But now, her only defence was fight or flight.

As she stared at the wall, she found her mind suddenly empty. Numb. Unable to process thoughts and too weary to digest the craziness of the last few hours.

So she gazed into the darkness, still, impassive. Every so often, she'd find herself drifting, so she'd slap her face and stamp her feet on the mattress.

Please don't sleep. I can't go to—

Through the bedroom window, the security lights sprung on.

A scraping noise penetrated from outside. It seemed to come from directly behind her, right beside the lodge.

Pushing the blankets away, she stepped out of bed, got on her hands and knees, and crawled to the bedroom window.

The first thing she saw was a figure, bandages wrapped tightly around their face.

'Oh my God,' Jess whispered, slamming her hand to her mouth.

The person turned, parting the bandages so they could see her. Then, they continued to drag a large sack along the grass.

∼

It felt like she'd been standing by the window for hours, observing the figure as it pulled the sack into the woods. She tried to think, to string a sentence together and come up with something, anything to explain the recent events. The trauma was too much. It felt like her mind had snapped, the remnants of a cruel nightmare, and any second, she'd wake up safe and sound in her flat.

The glass was cold against her forehead, the security lights had long gone out, and Jess pushed away from the window and fell face-first onto the bed.

Light pushed through the window as Jess woke. For a split second, she expected the alarm to go off, denoting it was time to get ready for work.

Reality hit.

She was lying flat, the blanket cold and damp under her body.

Turning, she saw the chest of drawers on its side, placed against the bedroom door.

The last thing she remembered was her trance-like state, almost hypnotised, staring through the window at the bleakness beyond the lodge.

Grabbing the phone, she tapped the screen. It was almost 8 am.

She'd fallen asleep for a few hours. Out cold. In one way, it was a blessing. Her tired state would hinder the decisions she had to make. Fatigue would play havoc with her mind.

Getting off the bed, she went over to the window, remembering only a few hours ago how she'd seen someone dragging a sack towards the woods. *It had to be his body,* she thought. The young lad who'd warned her to leave. He'd stood, banging the window with his bloody stump. Jess could see the bloodstains still smeared on the glass.

Through the window, mist clung to the tips of the grass, and a gloopy fog seemed to clutch the air, patches hovering just above the ground. She suddenly felt smothered as she tried to search for the lights on the hill.

As she grabbed her top and leggings from the back of the chair and put them on, someone thumped the glass. She jumped so hard she could almost feel her lungs rattle. Feeling disorientated, she peered at the figure by the window.

'Are you going to leave me out here all day?' Ruth asked, with a puzzled frown on her face, her arms out and palms facing upwards. 'I've been knocking on the door for ages.' Looking at the chest of drawers against the bedroom door, she asked, 'Why have you barricaded yourself inside? I thought we were friends.'

'Oh my goodness! Ruth. Sorry. One second.' The relief was instant. Jess could feel it drain from her body. As Ruth walked away from the window and towards the front of the lodge, Jess felt a sense of urgency as she heaved the furniture away from the door. The sound of crunching wood filled the room, and she knew the whole thing would collapse if she tried to lift it.

Opening the bedroom door, she rushed through the living room, seeing Ruth's face pushed against the glass as she twisted the key. 'Am I glad to see you.'

'You look like shit. And what happened to the tyres?'

'Quick. Get inside.' As Ruth stepped past her and into the living room, Jess scanned the area, making sure they were alone. She closed the front door, locking it, and turned to her friend. 'There's... The... So much has happened. It's so fucked up.'

'What do you mean? Calm down. What's happened?'

Walking to the fridge, Jess reached for the whisky bottle, removed the cap, and slugged the alcohol, grimacing as it worked down her throat.

'I mean Sheers Woods. Want a drop?'

'No. God no. It's early.'

Taking another gulp, Jess placed the bottle back in the fridge and continued. 'There's something twisted, deranged going on here.'

'What, Jess?'

'I've found... footage. The real footage of the friends who went missing. You know, the viral video I came out here to investigate.' She told her about the florist, the man at the petrol station, the barn with the ancient symbols, the figure dressed as a bird walking through the woods and how they'd followed her, hair hanging on the clothesline, her visitor last night, and later, seeing him pounding on the window with his bloody stump. 'They removed his hand. There was so much blood. It's still on the window.'

'Wait. Slow down. Slow down.' Ruth struggled to take everything in. Her friend was talking so fast and behaving erratically. 'Where is he now?'

'He's... Er... A bandage.'

'Huh?'

'Someone was in here last night. The lights went out.'

'Could it have been a power cut?' Ruth asked.

'No. No, I heard the light switching off. Later, there was a dragging sound outside the bedroom window. I saw them. Wearing a bandage around their head to disguise them-selves. They were dragging... dragging a sack along the grass.'

Standing by the breakfast bar, Ruth's eyes glazed over and her body became rigid as she tried to process everything. After a moment, she said, 'I think we should leave.'

Wiping the stress from her eyes, Jess looked through the kitchen window. The fog was still heavy in the air, choking the view of the fields. Turning to her friend, she stated, 'I have it all recorded. Most of it, anyway. There's no time to show you now, but I have pictures and videos. Enough to put together a short documentary and report the findings to the police. I'd still like to stop in Amersham. See if anyone will talk.'

'Okay,' Ruth said. 'Go and get your stuff. Hurry.' Removing her mobile phone from her handbag, she frowned at the screen. 'Do we have a signal anywhere?'

'No. Nothing. The Wi-Fi hasn't worked since I got here.' In the bedroom, Jess got a fresh jumper and leggings, slipped on a pair of socks and trainers, grabbed her laptop, recording equipment, clothes, and toiletries, and shoved them all in a bag.

Ruth joined her, helping to pack everything.

After a final check, Jess said, 'Right. Let's go.' Locking the front door, she threw the keys on the outside step.

As they walked through the mist, Ruth's car was gone.

19

A FEW HOURS EARLIER

'Let me out. Please. I can get money—anything you need. I'm begging you. Let me out.' Alice tried to separate her hands, but they were bound with rope, as were her ankles. Her head throbbed—the result of the cloth doused in strong chemicals being placed over her nose and mouth.

The boot stank of petrol, and the stench seemed to strip away at her insides. Leaning forward, fighting the cramp in her stomach, she tried to push her head against the boot, only making the ache worse.

Earlier, she'd been driving along the A355, excited about spending the weekend with her boyfriend, Toby. Lights had flashed behind her. She'd pulled over. The next thing she recalled was the driver smashing the lights, and everything went dark.

'Hey. Can you hear me? I said let me out. Hey.' Tears stung her cheeks, and she sniffed hard. It felt like her head would explode with the pain.

Her body rattled with the rough terrain, and she feared the driver would crash or push the car into water. Her mind raced with possible scenarios. Sinking, stuck inside the boot with no way out. She was claustrophobic, unable to use lifts or go into confined spaces. This was her worst nightmare, and she had to find a way out. 'Please. I'm begging you. I can't fucking breathe.' Raising her voice, she screamed, 'Let me out!' Her cheeks felt swollen, her skin burned, and again, she tried to open the boot with her head.

The vehicle travelled at great speed, and the sharp bends and potholes flung her around like a rag doll.

As it slowed to a stop, she thought about feeling for something to use as a weapon. With her hands and feet tied, it was hopeless.

The engine died, and as the boot opened, the cloth was again placed over her mouth to knock her out.

Now, regaining consciousness, she sat on the cold ground and blinked hard, her eyes wet and sticky, the severe ache working across her forehead. A radio played in the distance, only the sound of muffled voices and ad breaks with catchy jingles. Suddenly aware of the gag around her mouth, her hands and feet still tied with the rope, she screeched. A pathetic sound spilled from her lips, and she urinated through fear. The relief was intense as Alice shifted, the liquid stinging under her legs.

A door slammed.

Silence.

Then voices, faint, distant, resonated from above.

Blinking hard, trying to focus, Alice stared at only darkness, attempting to part her hands. The rope was so tight, and the more she moved them, the hasher the burns on her wrists.

The hatch opened above, the bright lights intense. Then a voice.

'What have we here? Hello. I'll be your guide for the next day or so.'

Stretching her neck and tilting her head back, she saw him—the guy from the road still wearing the same red jumper and blue jeans. He pointed a phone camera at her as if recording. Again, muffled screeches spilled from her lips. She peered around, realising she was held in a basement. The walls resembled a cave, with dark grey stones, sharp, and it smelt musty and damp.

Tom Wilder spoke in a calm, relaxed tone. 'So you're the new fish. You should feel honoured. You do look scared, mind. But then, you have every reason. We'll let you rest first and then bring you to the usual place. It's exciting. There's quite a few attending.'

The basement door slammed shut, and Alice sobbed into the sleeve of her top.

20

SATURDAY MORNING

'No. This can't be happening.' Ruth stood, looking at the empty space where she'd parked her car.

'They've done it. They've towed it away.' Jess raced to the bridge, searching for the vehicle, but the thick mist made it difficult to see more than a few yards. 'Fuckers. They've towed it away. They must have done it while we were packing in the bedroom. Can you believe this shit?'

Still staring at the vacant space where she'd parked her car, unable to drag her eyes away, Ruth shouted, 'Do you see anything?'

'Nothing,' Jess joined her friend, observing the stunned look on her face, and placed an arm around her. The realisation of Sheers Woods had hit hard.

'I can't believe it. I only got it a few weeks ago. Shit. What the hell, Jess? This is mental.'

'The focus has to be on our safety. Let's dump my gear inside the lodge. We need to make a run for it. It's early morning. We have a better chance while it's light. There's bound to be someone who can help. We can try the cottage in the valley.'

After Jess grabbed the key from the step, she unlocked the front door, and they carried her stuff to the bedroom. Opening her bag, she grabbed the hard drive and placed it in her pocket. The feeling of being back in the lodge was daunting. There was no way she could spend another night here. They had to leave now. If they could make it to the road, they could flag someone down.

There had to be a way out of here.

Outside the lodge, the mist that had plagued the horizon began clearing, making way for magnificent light.

Although damp, the air was fresh, pure, and felt almost untouched. The grass swept out like a carpet, blanketing the muddy undergrowth, and the sky was a spectacle of blue with soft white clouds drifting in the atmosphere.

Once Ruth came out of the lodge, Jess locked the front door.

'You ready?' Ruth asked as she looked towards the bridge. She fixed the collar of her coat and looked down at her ankle boots. 'I wish I'd worn trainers. I didn't expect... you know.'

'Yeah. Let's get going. I say we walk away from the bridge. It seems less foggy that way. It should lead around to the cottage. There's nothing on the way up here. Only that hay barn I told you about.'

Linking arms, they followed the road past the lodge and around the hills. The grass was wild and cumbersome, and the stones were sharp on their feet. Thick branches hung over the hedges and sprung in the breeze like a child on a trampoline.

Recalling the voice she'd heard last night while walking this route, Jess needed a distraction. 'Sorry about the car.'

'It's not your fault. Oh, I haven't spoken to your parents, but Ben rang last night. I told him I hadn't heard from you. He was worried. He said he tried several times. You'll probably have loads of missed calls. I said I was coming out here this morning, and I'd get you to call him when I got here.'

Their phones still showed no signal.

The bushes were more overgrown as they reached the bend. Nettles slapped against their forearms, and thorns pricked their skin.

The road became steeper the further they walked, and Ruth slipped a couple of times, Jess linking her arm so she didn't fall.

Every so often, they checked behind to see if they could see anyone.

'Why is it so quiet?' Ruth asked. 'It's as if people know not to come in here.'

An unsettling notion crossed Jess's mind. 'What if they're stopped?'

'How do you mean?'

'I mean a roadblock. Who's going to question someone in a high-vis jacket with cones blocking the entrance?'

Ruth processed the suggestion. 'Well, I got in here.' She paused for a moment. 'And you.'

As the women looked around them, the terrifying concept hit hard.

They were trapped.

'Look, there has to be a way out,' Jess said, trying to sound optimistic. The relentless stress wreaked havoc on her nerves, and her body felt exhausted. She had to remain positive. 'We need to keep moving.'

Stunned into silence, Ruth tried to digest the situation

they were in. Her mind was addled with the possibility of being trapped. Hunted. The air became heavy, and a knot seemed to grind from the pit of her stomach. 'Did they escape? The friends. Did they make it?'

'I... I don't know. I haven't watched the entire clip. Maybe the answer is right in front of us.'

They reached a fork in the road. The path on their left led through the grass and down into the valley. They could see the cottage in the distance. To the right, it swept around the forest.

'Which way?' asked Jess.

'I say we keep moving. Hopefully, we'll find another way out and get onto the main road.'

'Okay,' Jess answered. 'I think you're right. Christ! It feels like Jack and David on the moors. Beware the moon.'

'Yeah,' said Ruth. 'Let's hope we don't hear any strange howling.'

'Shit,' Jess said.

'What?'

'The footage. While the group were out at a restaurant in Amersham, Matt asked the guests their opinion on Sheers Woods and if they believed something was going on out here. One of the guests mentioned something about a full moon. He said tomorrow night was a full moon. It's when they strike. He went on to suggest they were in danger.'

After a moment, Ruth said, 'It's when they strike. What did he mean? When who strikes?'

'I... I don't know.'

'Is it a full moon tonight?' Ruth asked.

'Let's hope not.'

As they followed the narrow road, steering their bodies around overhung branches and avoiding the intertwining roots in the soil, Ruth questioned Jess about the footage she'd found. She listened intently, wondering if they walked this route, hoping to find a way out.

The more she heard, the more freaked out she became.

As they rounded a bend, Ruth stopped to adjust her boots.

Jess saw it first. 'Ruth. Er, Ruth.'

'Yeah. What's up?' Her attention shifted to where Jess pointed, seeing a figure standing around a hundred yards along the road. The person wore jeans and a long trench coat, their head and face concealed with a bandage. They stood, brandishing what appeared to be a machete, staring in their direction as if they were waiting.

'It's the... the person who was outside my bedroom window. I saw them dragging a sack along the grass. They turned and saw me watching. It's the same person.'

'I say we go back.' Ruth suddenly felt unsteady. She turned, feeling her legs go weak.

'Wherever we go, they'll block off our route.' Jess stared the figure down, realising it was a stupid thing to do. The person stood statuesque, carving a menacing silhouette in the distance. 'Let's cut through the grass. The cottage is that way. If we run, we can be there in a few minutes. Come on. Let's go.'

The women linked arms, trampling the wet grass, their footwear damp and soggy from the mist, silent only for their sharp breaths as they desperately tried to find a way out.

They glimpsed behind, hoping they weren't being followed. It didn't appear as though they were being pursued.

As they ran through the trees towards the cottage, the smell of damp bark strong in their lungs, they saw a man standing over a graveyard. He was tall and slim, wearing a hat, a checkered shirt, and grubby-looking jeans. He had a shovel in his hand, and it looked like he was tending to the grave.

They stopped, facing each other with newfound optimism.

'Oh, thank God!' Jess shouted, bending forward to recover.

Ruth was panting heavily next to her.

'Excuse me!' Jess shouted. 'My friend has had her car stolen. Someone is standing along the path with a weapon. A... A machete or something. We're being threatened and need your help.'

The man straightened his back, almost in slow motion, and turned, staring at the two women. His eyes were practically closed, possibly from the natural light, and his mouth locked open as if in shock. He appeared in his early seventies, maybe older, with deep wrinkles lining his face.

'How can I assist?' he asked, his voice deep and husky as if talking was a struggle. He dropped the shovel and moved closer to the women.

'My name is Jess Turner. This is my friend Ruth. We're staying in the lodge at the top of the hill. Do you have a phone we could use?'

'No. But there is one at the cottage.'

Turning, Jess looked over the valley. 'There? That's where you live?'

'Yes.' His mouth appeared to fold over on itself as he grimaced. 'Why do you need a phone?'

Jess explained they were stranded in the lodge, without Wi-Fi or signal. She didn't want to go into the story. 'We're in danger. Please, can you help us?'

'Danger, you say. There's nothing dangerous about Sheers Woods. I've lived and worked here all my life. Never seen or heard anything suspicious or untoward.' He looked between Jess and Ruth. 'But if you're adamant you need help, go back to the lodge. I'll make a call.'

'Can you do it now?' asked Ruth, the eagerness evident in her tone.

The man picked up the shovel. 'After I've finished here, I'll ring the police and let them know what's happened. Have you out in no time.'

'Call them now,' Ruth said sternly. 'What the?—'

'Thank you,' Jess interrupted, grabbing Ruth by the arm, and slowly heading back to the lodge.

Joe Egan continued digging. Every so often, he looked up, watching as the women walked along the road towards the lodge. When they were out of sight, he wiped his brow, straightened his back, and strolled back to the cottage.

Turning on the outside tap, he washed the mud from the shovel and laid it on the ground. Removing his dirty boots, he opened the front door and walked through the hallway and into the living room. The vintage telephone, with an elegant circular disk for dialling, sat on a small table in the corner.

He thought about the women who'd approached him. The desperation on their faces, their voices strained.

As Joe crouched by the phone, his knees cracked, his back hurt, and it felt like his body was giving up. He didn't know how much longer he could tend the graves.

Joe's parents had bought a small plot of land in Sheers Woods and had the cottage built from scratch. They'd farmed animals, predominantly cattle. It was financially demanding, and when Joe's parents died, he found it more economically viable to sell the stock and move away from agriculture.

The cemetery was managed by a small, private company, and they'd asked Joe if he'd tend the graves. The money was dire, but it kept him fit and active. The last thing he wanted was for his body to cease up.

As Joe reached forward, their voices seemed to fill the living room.

We're being threatened and need your help. Can you do it now? Call them now.

Tugging the phone, he pulled the cord out of its socket and placed it in a drawer.

Footsteps charged along the hallway, and the sound of jumping irritated him. Joe turned, seeing his son, Andrew, the smirk on his face, the wide eyes looking to the floor, his crusty lips curled at one end, and his dirty fingernails scratching his scabby chin, a sure sign of guilt. Andrew continued jumping, clapping his hands together. His tight Y-Fronts were stained yellow at the front, his body bony and pale, ribs visible through his skin. As he rubbed his bald head and scratched at the wisps of grey hair at the sides, flakes fell to the floor.

'Go and put some clothes on, you imbecile,' Joe demanded. 'What have you been doing while I've been out?'

His wild brown eyes edged sideways and back on his father.

'I asked you a question?'

'Noth... nothing,' he said, his voice gravelly with phlegm. Andrew grimaced as he backed out of the living room, realising his father's annoyance and seeing his face turn red. His heavy eyebrows dropped low on his face, and his eyes narrowed into horizontal lines.

'You better not have done anything. Do you hear?' Joe

charged out of the living room, grabbing his son by the throat, hearing him wheeze. Andrew's rank breath was putrid and stale, like rotten cabbage left in a pan and infested with bacteria. His chapped lips parted, revealing blackened teeth. Joe watched his son shake his head, his eyes so wide it looked like they'd burst.

'Nothing,' he said with a strained voice. 'I... I mean it. Honest. I didn't do anything. Only listened. Nothing else. I... I like the noise.' Mucus sprayed from his nostrils as he spoke, feeling the relief as his father let go of his throat. Rocking on the spot, Andrew sneered to himself.

Standing back, Joe looked at his pathetic son, eying him up and down. 'Go and get some bloody clothes on. How many times do I have to tell you? And change those pants. You've had them on for days. You're revolting.'

As Andrew leant against the wall, bending his wrists forward and covering his face, Joe walked to the back of the cottage, hearing the muffled cries from the basement underneath him.

21

SATURDAY AFTERNOON

Once inside the lodge, Jess slammed the front door, and the women hugged.

Ruth could see the stress on her friend's face: her pale complexion, bloodshot eyes, and dilated pupils. 'It's okay. Help is on its way. We'll be out of here before you know it.'

Wiping her teary eyes, Jess was determined not to break down. Swallowing the lump in her throat, she sighed heavily. 'Thank you for this. You don't know how much I appreciate it.'

'You'd do the same for me.'

After Jess checked her phone signal and again tried the Wi-Fi code, she stood by the kitchen window. The mist had completely cleared, and the view of the hills lifted the claustrophobic feeling that earlier seemed to choke her. Her mind wrestled with the haunting visions of the young lad banging on her bedroom window and the figure concealed with a bandage blocking the road. Turning to Ruth, she asked, 'Should we cross the bridge and head for the entrance?'

'I don't think it's a good idea. It's safer to wait here.'

'I don't hear any sirens. How long has it been since we spoke to him?'

'A half hour, maybe more,' Ruth stated. 'They'll come.'

'What if he hasn't made the call? Maybe he forgot. He didn't seem to think there was anything suspicious about this place.' Turning to Ruth, she asked, 'Don't you think that's weird?'

'Maybe he doesn't realise the sense of urgency. He's probably stuck in his ways. Working on his clock.'

Turning back and looking out the window, Jess said, 'Or maybe he doesn't intend to make the call.'

For the next hour, they waited. Ruth by the front door, Jess by the window, listening for a siren in the distance.

They heard nothing.

While they waited, Jess continued to dictate, relaying the story of them trying to escape, seeing the person on the road disguised with a bandage, and finishing with the gravedigger and them pleading for help.

She filmed the woods through the kitchen window, and she and Ruth talked about their fears and the need to escape, trapped like animals inside the lodge.

'Okay,' Ruth said when she'd given up hope and began pacing the living room floor, 'here's our options. One, we try and make it to the main entrance.'

'They'll block it off. It's too dangerous. Like you said, it's safer to wait here. Later, we'll have a better opportunity to keep hidden when it's dark. Oh, Christ! This is madness. How are we going to get out of here? What's the second option?'

'We remain here, keep everything locked. Where did you get to when watching the footage you found?'

'Er, Matt saw what he thought was a body being

loaded into a van. It was at the petrol station on the way up here. They got out and approached the vehicle, but it pulled away. When they followed it, the driver pulled in here. To Sheers Woods.'

'Shit,' Ruth stated.

'I know.'

Playing with her jacket button to distract herself, Ruth said, 'It doesn't look like he's made the call. Maybe he's—'

'In on it,' Jess interrupted.

Reality struck as the women's icy stares locked together.

'I say we lock ourselves in the bedroom, watch the rest of the footage, and hopefully find a way out. If they made it, we will too. The answer must lie on this hard drive. When it gets dark, we either run for it, or there's another alternative,' Jess proposed.

'What other alternative?'

'We break into the cottage and make the call ourselves.'

22

SATURDAY AFTERNOON. JESS AND RUTH
VIEW THE FOOTAGE FROM FIVE YEARS AGO

The next scene showed Matt stepping away from the camera. He wore a red T-shirt and black boxer shorts. His face looked swollen from sleep, and crease marks ran down his left cheek. 'I have to whisper as the others are asleep,' Matt stated. 'I think they're getting pissed off with all the filming.' He glanced to the side, looking to the stairs and back to the camera. 'I wouldn't blame them really. So, last night was eventful. I'm still convinced a body was loaded into the van. I don't have it on film, which is a bummer, but I've got the van as it pulled away. I'm sure it was the same man Emma spoke about. Danny is... hang on.' He turned again, looking towards the back of the lodge. 'Danny is sure someone was watching as we walked over to the van. Anyway, we followed it, and Emma saw it turn into Sheers Woods. That's when the camera battery ran out. We waited on the road for a minute or so and pulled in after it. We could see the van's lights fading into the vast space, which means he brought the body here. Maybe you all think I'm crazy, but I know what I saw. Later, I'll suggest a hike and convince Emma, Danny, and Maria to look for it. They still don't believe me and think I'm having them on or my mind is playing tricks. Whatever. We have no Wi-Fi and no reception to call for help. The locals are reluctant to talk and seem to be harbouring some... some fucking secret. I need to back off from filming as the others, Emma in particular, are getting pissed off. I might be able to do it on the sly. I'll see. But something is going on here. I can feel it. Something isn't... shit.'

The screen jumped as Emma walked down the stairs.

The picture returned with the group outside, throwing the inflatable ball to each other. The four were dressed for the hot weather with T-shirts and shorts. The camera rested at eye level a few feet from where they stood in the grass. The corner of the lodge was visible.

As the inflatable ball was tossed between the four of them, Danny pretended to poke the lit cigarette into it.

'Don't, you arsehole,' Maria sniped. 'What's wrong with you?'

'I'm joking. Come on, I'm hungry. Are we going to eat?'

'That was really something last night,' Emma said as she slapped the ball towards Maria.

'What?' Matt asked.

'You know what. First, you practically get us thrown out of the restaurant, and then you make up some half-arsed story about a body being loaded into a van.'

'I didn't sleep well last night,' Maria announced as she hit the ball to Danny. Her clenched fists and straight, tense body indicated her aggravated state.

'I believe him,' Danny said. 'Why make that shit up?'

'For views. It's pathetic,' Maria pointed out. 'If it carries on, I'm going home. I mean it.'

'I'll second that.' Emma forcefully punched the ball at Matt, hitting him on the head. 'You deserved that. Twat.'

'Okay. I'll drop it. What are we eating tonight?' asked Matt.

'I say we have a barbecue. We have loads of meat, burger buns, coleslaw, and salad. I don't want to chance going out into town again. Not after last night.' Again, Emma smashed the ball at her boyfriend, who managed to duck out of the way. 'Matt can cook after the shit he's put us through. It's only fair.'

'Er... I bought the food last night,' Matt expressed.

Catching the ball, Emma ran at her boyfriend, extending her leg and trying to trip him up. 'Do you want to sleep in the camper van?'

'No.'

'Good. Then you're doing the barbecue.' She grabbed at his shorts, and Matt turned, the two of them kissing.

As they walked back inside the lodge, Jess and Ruth could clearly see a figure, someone or something, standing by the trees. They paused the recording and zoomed in, unable to make out any features. It wasn't any clearer than the short clip loaded online.

But they were watching.

It seemed like late evening. The camera pointed to the kitchen window. The sun was starting to disappear behind the hills, and it was slightly darker than earlier when the four had thrown the inflatable ball at the side of the lodge.

It cut for a moment and then showed Danny crouching near the front door, his right side visible. 'Are you positive this is the right password, Bro?'

'Yes,' Matt said. 'I got an email before we came here confirming the booking. It included the password and where to find the barbecue with instructions of lighting it and shit.'

'Ooh, strike match on box. Hold match to firelighter. Watch coals burn. Add food. Eat food.'

'You're a prick,' Matt laughed.

They jumped as the door knocked.

'Who the fuck is that?' Matt asked, grabbing the camera and pointing it towards the door.

'I don't know. Maybe the owner checking the place out, making sure we haven't smashed it up. Do we answer?'

'We have to. They know we're here. Our van's outside.' The camera swung around the room as Matt steadied it and appeared to rest it on his shoulder.

With his face pressed against the door, Danny spoke through the side gap. 'Who is it? Hello? Who's there?'

'What are they saying?' asked Matt.

'I don't know. I can't hear anyone. Who's there?'

'Don't open it,' Matt ordered.

'Bro, someone knocked on the door. We have to open it.' The lock clunked, and a faint creak echoed as Danny pulled the front door towards him.

Matt zoomed in, filming his friend as he stepped outside.

'Well? Who's there? Danny? Danny?' Placing the camera on the floor, Matt followed.

There were voices faint in the distance. Danny said someone had knocked on the door and that they couldn't have vanished. Matt asked him to keep his voice down and not freak out the girls. The two men returned moments later, the sounds indicating that they had closed and locked the front door.

Grabbing the camera and turning it on his face, Matt clearly looked worried. His eyes were wide open and flicking around the lodge. His voice was hushed. 'So, you heard that, right? Someone knocked on the front door. When we answered, they were gone. I don't like it. Maybe we should just pack up and leave.'

'Are you serious?' Danny asked as he sat on the sofa.

'I said keep your voice down,' Matt insisted.

'It's your fault, Bro. Filling their heads with shit. Talking about fucking witches, demons, bodies in the back of fucking vans. If we leave, it's on you.'

'Look, I apologised to Emma. I'm not going to mention it again.'

'It's a little late for that, Bro. You've already planted the seeds in their heads. You're scaring them with this crap. You need to give it a—'

The glass pounded next to where Danny sat. He jumped off the sofa and faced the window.

The screen was obscured momentarily, and it looked like Matt almost dropped the camera. As the screen blanked out, a loud, shuffling sound was heard as he said, 'Shit. I'm gonna end up breaking this.'

'What's going on?' Maria asked from the back bedroom.

Again, pounding noises on the living room window.

Danny opened the front door. Matt followed, steering the camera on a skinny-looking lad around sixteen or seventeen.

Jess gasped, recognising him. There were no dark glasses, his eyes looked normal, and she could hear him speak.

'Please. You need to leave here. Go. Now. Or they'll come for you.'

Matt and Danny stood, obviously shocked and unable to answer him.

The lad rushed past the camper van and across the

bridge, disappearing along the dirt road with the camera trained on him.

The following clip rolled with Matt and Danny. Their flustered state became apparent as they paced across the floor, pushing their hands through their hair and clenching their fists.

The camera appeared to rest on the kitchen worktop with a full view of the living room.

'Keep quiet, you hear me? The girls can't know anything about this. Don't mention it. Absolutely nothing. They're already freaking out. Are you listening to me?' Matt hissed.

'I got it. Nothing.' Strolling to the living room window, Danny pressed his face to the glass, looking out. 'What the fuck was his problem? Did you see his face? His skin. It looked like... like he'd been locked away and starved of light. Man, that was some freaky shit.' In a hushed voice, he whispered, 'Matt, his warning, what does he mean?'

'Who was at the door?' Maria stood in the hallway wearing shorts and a skimpy T-shirt, blinking the sleep from her eyes.

'No one,' Matt insisted.

'Well, there was. I could hear his voice. What did he want?'

'He was looking for someone,' Danny interrupted. 'He had the wrong address. It's nothing to worry about.'

As Maria walked back into the bedroom, a hand went over the camera, and it turned off.

It was later, and the sun was dipping low behind the hills.

They'd started a campfire. The sound of crackling wood was invigorating and added to the eerie atmosphere.

Matt had a guitar and was sitting against a tree.

Danny and Maria were cooking on the barbecue; the smoke was heavy in the air.

'You were supposed to be doing this, Matt. Don't ignore me. Yeah, you only hear what you want to hear. Unreal,' Maria stated, throwing a bap at his head.

Emma was crouched next to Matt, sipping on a can of beer.

They all looked content, and if they were worrying about the previous incidents, it didn't show on their faces.

The camera appeared to rest on the decking at the side of the lodge, close enough to hear their conversation.

Emma looked at the lens and back to Matt. 'You haven't got it recording again, surely?'

'Oh, chill out. I can edit anything if you don't look your best.'

'What are you saying?' Emma asked with levity in her voice. 'I don't always look my best, is that it, huh?' She poked at his ribs, climbed on top of him, and twisted a knob on the guitar, sending it out of tune. 'Say sorry. Go on, apologise.'

Lying back, holding the guitar at arm's length, Matt said, 'Okay, I'm sorry. You always look beautiful.'

'Good boy.'

'To me, anyway,' he added.

'Right.' Emma twisted another knob. 'Take it back.'

'Okay, I take it back. Jeez.'

After re-tuning the instrument, Matt poked at the barbecue, appearing to check if the food was cooked. He sat back down, strumming the guitar, his fingers soft on the strings, and began singing Wonderwall by Oasis as Danny and Maria handed them burgers, sausages, and salad. They all sat and ate, drinking beer and wine, and laughed together.

The tape continued to roll. They finished eating, and again, Matt picked up the guitar.

'Shush. Wait a second. Did you hear that?' Maria looked behind her into the fields.

'Hear what?' asked Matt, placing the guitar on the grass beside him.

'Listen,' Maria ordered. 'I heard something.'

An intense snapping sound came from behind them, like a thick piece of wood cracking over someone's knee.

Emma stood. 'Someone's there.'

'It's probably an animal. We're in the forest, you know,' Matt suggested as he stood and joined Emma, swigging on a beer. They looked out over the fields, their fingers intertwining.

'Do you know an animal that makes that noise?' asked Danny, remaining on the ground.

Maria shifted closer to her boyfriend. 'I say we go back inside. Have a game of cards. It's safer in there. I'm getting more freaked out by the minute.'

'Babe,' said Danny, placing his arm around Maria, 'nothing's going to happen. You're safe.'

A scream bellowed from the valley.

Danny dropped a beer over his T-shirt. He jumped to his feet, helping Maria up.

Grabbing a torch by his feet and shining it into the fields, Matt said, 'What the fuck was that?' The others remained silent, and Matt raised his voice. 'I can't see anyone. Hello? Where are you?'

'Someone's in trouble,' Maria said, moving from one foot to the other. 'It sounded like a woman screaming.' Pulling a mobile phone from her pocket, she looked at the screen. 'Still no reception. Christ! What is it with this place?'

'I don't have any either,' Emma declared.

'I say we jump in the van and get help?' Matt suggested. 'Amersham is only a couple of miles away.'

'Someone help me; I'm begging you.'

The four of them stood, too afraid to move. Suddenly, Danny said, 'We... We have to help her. She's in trouble.' Turning towards the voice, he yelled, 'Where are you?'

The place was silent. Only their breaths and the crackling of wood as they appeared to consider their next move.

The torch shook in Matt's hand, the light dancing along the ground, through the bushes, and back into the bleak fields. 'Can you tell us where you are? Hello? We're going to help! Just tell us—'

They all stepped away as another chilling scream ripped through the air.

'Can we just leave this place?' Maria asked.

Emma joined her, placing her hands on her shoulders. 'Look, we're going to get help. We'll drive the camper van into town and call the police.'

Charging out of view, Matt returned seconds later with the keys and tossed them to Emma. Then he clutched the camera, continuing to film everything.

After turning the key, the engine churned over several times, and smoke billowed into the air. 'Yes,' Emma shouted, thumping the steering wheel. 'This thing is temperamental at the best of times. Right, everyone pile in and lock the doors. We'll drive to town and get help.'

The others joined her, and she rolled the camper van along the grass at the front of the lodge.

The picture was erratic, jumping between faces as Matt recorded from the back.

As Emma pulled away, the tyres burst.

The side door opened, and Matt spilled out of the van. 'What the fuck? The tyres. They've fucking burst the tyres.'

Danny and Maria joined him.

A second later, Emma opened the driver's door, her fist closed and biting on her knuckles. 'What happened?' she yelled.

'They've burst the tyres,' answered Danny. 'We have to leave here now.' Turning to Matt, he said, 'You were right about this place. Something's going on.'

'Er, guys. Guys.' Maria pointed towards the fields. 'There's someone coming. We need to get back inside the lodge.'

As Matt and Danny turned to where Maria pointed, a bright torchlight shone on their faces.

The picture jerked left and right as the four entered the lodge and locked the front door.

'Check upstairs is locked. Go, go, go,' Matt shouted. 'I'll do down here.'

Emma and Maria were stood together by the front door.

'Are we going to be able to leave?' Maria whispered. 'Are we?'

It looked like Matt was searching for the off switch as he placed the camera on the breakfast bar.

'No, leave it on, Matt,' Emma insisted. 'If they break in, we need everything recorded. These fuckers can't get away with it.'

'Check the Wi-Fi again,' Matt ordered as he walked over to the two women, the three of them bunched together. You could feel the tension as their bodies shook. 'I'm going to make sure everywhere is locked. Check the Wi-Fi!' Matt shouted.

Emma grabbed the camera, filming as Matt turned and

rushed to the kitchen window, pulling down the handle, then over to the living room window by the sofa, doing the same, and disappeared along the hall towards the back bedrooms.

The camera slowly panned around to Emma's face as Maria announced she'd check the Wi-Fi.

'I... This is Emma Hunter, and I fear we're under attack. Jeez, I can't even fathom my words or understand what's happening as I speak. I, with my boyfriend Matt and friends Maria and Danny, have come away for... for a last-minute break. But... something is going on out here. There's fucking someone... or something trying to harm us. We were at the restaurant and it's obvious the locals are harbouring a secret. No one wanted to talk. They were scared. Matt saw something. He bel... believes it was a body being loaded into a van. A few minutes ago, someone was screaming for help, and as we tried to leave, our tyres burst. If we're attacked, or worse, we don't get out alive, I want everyone to see what's happening to us.'

'It's no good. I can't log in,' Maria said as the camera pointed at her.

Danny came rushing down the stairs, almost tripping. 'Everywhere's locked. I say we make a run for it while we still have a chance.'

A door slammed at the back of the lodge. The camera shook in Emma's hand, and the three of them looked at Matt.

'We need to make sure no fucker gets in here tonight,' Matt ordered. 'Our lives depend on it.'

Ferocious banging noises resounded. Someone was at the front door. It felt like an axe against wood. Bringing his hand to his lips, Matt ushered the others to keep silent. Again, the smashing noises ripped through the dimness as the front door shuddered with the weight of the pounding. With a sudden act of bravery, Matt waited, pulled the door open, and looked out. 'There's no one there.' Slamming the door, he rushed over to the kitchen and pulled open the drawer. The sound was intense, like glass smashing, as he rummaged through the cutlery drawer, pulling out a handful of large knives.

Again, Danny announced, 'I'm... I'm going to make a run for it. I can do it.'

'No. It's not safe.' Pointing the knives to the floor, Matt joined the others and handed them out.

'Oh, God! This is insane,' Maria said. 'I can't stab anyone.'

'Maria, if these fucks get inside, you have no choice. It's you or them. Are you listening to me? Maria?'

She nodded, her face contorted as she lifted the knife, feeling the sharp point. 'Oh God!' Emma placed the camera on the breakfast bar, focusing the lens on the front door.

Danny moved closer to Matt, his voice broken and hoarse. 'I can make it. You stay here?'

'Are you mad?' asked Matt.

'Look.' Danny walked to the window in the living room, cupping his hands and face to the glass, then over to the window in the kitchen. 'I think they've gone for the moment. Otherwise, they'd be banging on the door and trying to get inside. I can make it to the main road. I'll flag for help.'

'And if you're attacked?'

'It's better if it's just the one of us attacked. Maria won't make it. You can see the state she's in. She has a better chance locked up here.'

'I don't like it, Danny. It's too risky.'

'I have to try, Bro. I'll get to the road and flag someone down. Then we can get the hell away from here.'

Hearing their conversation, Maria stepped closer. 'Danny. I'm begging you, don't go. Don't try to be a hero. Please listen.'

Placing his arms around her waist, he kissed her on the mouth. 'I'm going to get us help. I'm fit; I can make it. We'll be out of here before you know it. I love you so much, Maria.'

Pulling him close, she placed her hands on his face and kissed him hard. 'I don't want you to go out there.'

'When we're home,' he whispered, 'we'll get married. Just how we planned.'

'You promise me?' she muttered.

'I promise.'

As Danny stepped to the front door, Matt slowly unlocked it, poking his head out. The camera recorded their every move.

'It looks clear,' Matt announced. 'I'm going to ask again, although I know you won't listen. Please don't do this.'

With an arm around Matt's shoulder, he said, 'We have no choice.'

Once Danny had left, Matt slammed the front door and locked it. He grabbed the camera and walked to the kitchen window. 'He has to make it to the main road.' Turning towards Emma and Maria, standing by the front door and holding each other tight, Matt said, 'He's going to make it. We have to be strong. He'll reach the main road before you know it.'

'And if he doesn't?' Maria snapped. 'You knew something was up here.' Saliva sprayed from her mouth as she spoke. 'You've brought this on us.'

'Maria, come on. It's not Matt's fault,' Emma pleaded.

'Your fucking... overactive imagination. Your stories. You told us something wasn't right here.'

'And I'm right,' Matt proclaimed.

'Stop, Matt,' Emma ordered. 'You're not helping. Let's all take a breath and try to remain calm.'

'You spoke of conspiracies and the rumours about Sheers Woods before booking this place,' Maria pointed out. 'You read it on forums. Why the fuck didn't you tell us until we were here? It's your fault. If something happens to Danny, it's on you.'

'Okay. We all need to chill,' Emma pushed. 'Nothing is—'

Maria charged towards the front door, unlocking it.

'It's not a good idea,' Matt shouted.

'I'm going after him.' Maria yelled.

'Please, Maria,' Emma begged. 'Please get a grip. He'll be back before you know it.'

Maria faced the door, and Emma grabbed her wrist.

'Let go,' Maria screamed. 'I said let go.' As she stepped out through the open door, a figure raced at her. She lifted the knife, plunging it straight into Danny's neck.

23

SATURDAY AFTERNOON

'I need Andrew to go up there.' Tom Wilder removed the bandages around his head and face, feeling instant relief, and watched as Joe stood by the front door of the cottage and swept the mud from the shovel into a drain.

The tap ran, splashing over the rough ground, and he pushed the dirty water away from where he stood with gentle strokes of the yard brush.

'He's getting dressed,' Joe said without looking up.

'They're going to cause a massive problem. Give him a radio and send him up there. I haven't got time to deal with them now. But I will. Believe me. He needs to keep an eye on them. Louise has set up cones by the main entrance. No one is going to question a police officer.'

'So, you got another one? I hear her in the basement.'

'Yeah, last night. Louise cleaned it up. The car was towed away, and it'll be destroyed like the others. We've been watching this one for a while. It's easy money.'

'It's a bit close to home, don't you think? You practically took her from up the road. It's dangerous.'

'You worry too much, old man, that's your problem.'

Joe rested the broom against the front door. 'When is it going to stop?' Looking at Tom's face, he saw the creases from the tight bandages he now held in a ball and recalled the time Tom dropped Andrew home after work with an idea for a new business venture.

Andrew had learning difficulties. He'd been a hindrance to his father since birth. He was born with a brain defect that limited his ability to learn and affected his social skills. Joe had little patience for his son and often beat him senseless out of frustration or locked him in his room for hours at a time, listening to the whining noises that frequently carried into the night.

Joe's wife left when Andrew was young after threatening to call the authorities. At least that's what Joe told people.

Mildred had been missing for years, and when people asked, he told them his wife had moved abroad to start a new life.

While working at the petrol station, Andrew had befriended Tom Wilder, and they'd become close. Conversation, mainly on Tom's part, eased the long shifts and sheer boredom.

One night, when Andrew was restless, he told Tom about his mother. How she'd disappeared years ago, and just after she'd left, he saw his father digging a grave late at night.

Tom was always striving to make money.

Underground organ trading had thrived in the shadows for years, driven by the desperation of those in need and the allure of immense profits. Buyers sought these illicit transactions to secure life-saving organs, often paying exorbitant sums ranging from tens of thousands to millions of pounds, depending on the organ's rarity and the urgency of the procedure.

Tom Wilder wanted in on it. To traffic organs. That was where the big money was. But it was too risky. Hiding bodies after mutilation was difficult, and there was no way he could let them live for fear of being exposed.

He had to find a way to dump the bodies without them ever being found.

The conversation with Andrew had given Tom the vision needed.

Joe Egan. Andrew's father. He was a gravedigger. It was perfect.

While dropping Andrew home one night, Tom spoke with Joe and made him an offer he had no choice but to take. He told him Andrew had shown him where his mum was buried in the cemetery behind the cottage. If Joe refused, he'd make one phone call and have him banged up for the rest of his life.

Joe had to help.

'I asked you when is it going to stop?'

'Are you mad?' Tom responded. 'You must be. How much money have I made you? This is the thanks I get.'

'We were almost ruined five years ago after that clip circulated. Even then, you didn't stop straight away. The coverage this place got. Thankfully, we had Louise and a couple of other officers on our side. Otherwise, we were finished. The people coming here snooping around, the thrill seekers and kids daring each other to come into Sheers Woods after dark. You said you'd stop. Let the dust settle. It took a while for you to come to your senses and see the risk. We all went back to normal. Now you bring this shit to my door again.'

'Don't forget what I have on you, old man. Your wife, Mildred.'

Looking out over the fields towards the graveyard, the old, crumpled headstones, the withered flowers, the long grass leaning with the breeze, Joe said, 'I can't keep hiding them.'

At the back of the cottage, Alice Harper lay in darkness on the cold floor of the basement, feeling hopeless and pathetic. Although she'd managed to work the gag loose from her mouth, her hands and feet were still tied with rope. The severe ache in her head had worsened, and she was so drained and weak.

Earlier, she'd heard shuffling sounds on the ceiling, someone jumping around, and then the hatch lifted. The light had strained her eyes, and she'd blinked, seeing a man standing, looking down at her and grinning. She'd begged for him to release her. Her screams filled the basement. He'd climbed down the stairs, approached her, and licked her right cheek. Then the hatch slammed shut.

Blinking, she tried to focus on her surroundings, seeing only darkness. The footsteps on the ceiling had gone, her skin still damp from his tongue, and she was losing hope.

'Let me out of here. I beg you. Hello? Can anyone hear me? Let me out. Please, someone help me.'

The smell of decay, rotting timber, and crumbling mortar filled her lungs. Further along the basement, water leaked from a corroded pipe.

Drip.

Drip.

Drip.

With her hands raised, the rope cutting into her wrists, she turned on her side, wriggling along the ground like a snake. Bringing her knees to her chest, she kicked out, sliding a couple of inches away from the hatch.

The basement was large and appeared to stretch the length of the back room, possibly further.

The drips were louder as she moved further along the ground. The cracked concrete floor scratched at her skin, cutting her arm, and ripping her clothes.

'Can anyone hear me? I'm locked in the basement. Help. Can someone help me?' Tears spilled from her eyes, her nose ran, and she needed the toilet. An ache worked through the top, slowly becoming a migraine. Any moment now, she'd vomit. There was no way of wiping her face. As she lay on her side, trying to hold her head up, the strain severe on her neck, she reached her arms out, pawing at the space in front.

Her eyes burnt, trying to focus as she blinked, unable to see anything.

Then something shuffled towards her and grabbed her hair.

24

SATURDAY AFTERNOON

'Pause it. Pause the clip, Jess. I'm sorry. I need time to digest... Christ! What they went through. She... She stabbed him. Oh shit, this is too much.' Getting to her feet, Ruth stood by the bedroom door, her hands covering her face, processing the horror they'd seen.

Jess stood and held her friend, pulling her close. 'Look. We're going to make it. Don't fold on me now. I need you to be brave.' Leaning back, she saw Ruth's eyes water, tears rolling down her face.

'I'm trying. It's all so... sick. What is going on?' As Ruth turned and glared out of the bedroom window, she saw a figure through the trees, watching them. 'Get down,' she yelled.

The women dropped to the ground, resting on their knees.

'What did you see?' Jess asked. The room spun momentarily as an adrenaline rush coursed through her body. Her skin tingled, and her heart punched hard.

In a hushed voice, Ruth said, 'Someone is out there. They're watching the lodge.'

'What do they look like?'

'I didn't get a good look, but I saw a type of bird mask, I think.'

'Bird person.'

'Huh?' Ruth asked.

'When I arrived here, I walked towards the hay barn. I saw a weird figure through the trees. They were wearing a bird mask and a strange, feathered outfit. I need to take a look.' As Jess straightened her legs, Ruth pulled her back down.

'Are you mad? They'll see you. We have to hide.'

Crouching, Jess nodded. 'Upstairs. Follow me and keep low.'

On their hands and knees, they left the bedroom and crawled along the hallway and up the stairs. On the first floor, they stood and walked to the large window on their right.

'Can you see anything?' asked Ruth.

Waves of grass bowed in the wind, branches swayed, and leaves blew along the ground. The bright sky that had earlier lifted their mood was now drenched in thick clouds. Shifting to the left of the window, Jess looked across the fields. 'I see it. It's still there.'

'What are they doing?'

'Just standing, staring at the lodge. It's definitely the same figure I saw yesterday morning. They have a large bag by their feet.'

'Can they see you?'

'I... I don't think so. They're watching my bedroom window.'

'Should we make a run for it?'

'I don't know. They'll most certainly have weapons. It's too risky.' Jess zoomed in and took a photo.

Click.

Click.

'What are they doing now?'

Click.

'Still watching the lodge.'

Click.

'What if they try and get inside?'

Click.

'Then we hide. Wait. Hold up.' Placing the phone back in her pocket, Jess watched as bird person reached down to the bag, opened it, and strolled to the lodge. 'Shit. They're going to try and get in. Quickly. Follow me.'

Ruth's knees felt like they'd buckle. Wiping the sweat from her brow, she followed her friend along the upstairs hallway and into the last bedroom on the left.

'Duck down on the other side of the bed,' Jess instructed. 'Keep hidden. I'll wait by the door. If I hear anything, join me, and we'll jump them.'

'This beats a Saturday brunch in London any day of the week. Nothing like a trip to the countryside. I can't begin to tell you how much I'm enjoying myself.'

As Ruth walked across the floor and hid behind the bed, Jess said, 'Yeah, but I don't like the neighbours. I think it will lose a couple of stars on Tripadvisor.'

'Anything?' Ruth asked.

'No. Nothing. I can't hear anyone downstairs.' Her hands were sore from pressing onto the wooden floor, and her knees felt hot and swollen. 'We know there's at least two of them,' Jess surmised. 'Bird person and the one who stopped us along the road disguised with a bandage.'

'And the old man?'

'Yeah. He's likely involved. We have to find a way to get to the cottage. If we can make the phone call, we can—'

'What's wrong?' asked Ruth.

'I can hear something?' Jess whispered.

'What?'

'Wait a second. It sounds like, I don't know, a tapping noise. Like they're banging something.'

They remained in position, Jess crouching by the opened bedroom door, Ruth behind the bed. They waited, listening for the sound of broken glass, a door opening, anything that would indicate bird person was inside the lodge.

It began to get dark. The heavy clouds smothered the sky, casting a suffocating veil over the landscape.

'I have to go downstairs. Wait here, Ruth. Keep hidden.'

'I'm coming with you.'

As they walked along the upstairs hallway, listening intently for any sounds, they reached the top of the stairs and made their way to the ground floor.

Jess eased down the steps, the clunking of her trainers intense, and felt Ruth's arm on her shoulder. Reaching the ground floor, she turned left, peering along the hallway to the back bedrooms. 'If there's someone in here, we have a knife. We'll use it. I swear.' Diverting from the hallway, Jess charged along the living room and grabbed the front door handle. 'It's jammed. I can't open it.'

'Here, let me try. No, it's stuck,' Ruth declared through gritted teeth. 'They've rammed something against the handle. I can't pull it down.'

Racing to the kitchen window, Jess tried to push it open. 'It won't budge. They've nailed it shut. We're locked in.'

25

SATURDAY AFTERNOON

'Hello? Who's down here?' Stretching her arms out, Alice swiped at the darkness. Due to her confused state, she couldn't tell how long ago it had happened. Minutes or maybe hours, but something had touched her hair. Through her sobs, she mumbled, 'Is someone else down here?' Her teeth chattered. The dank, cold basement gnawed at her bones, and she fell forward onto her elbows, banging on the ground. Desperate to escape, she tried to force her hands apart, but the rope only cut into her skin.

'Timmy? Where's Timmy?' a soft, gentle voice asked.

Falling against the rough stone wall, Alice began shuffling on her knees and edged back towards the hatch. 'Who are you? Who the fuck are you? Why are you down here?'

'Where's Timmy?' the soft voice asked again.

'Who the hell is Timmy?' Suddenly, Alice heard scurrying as the person moved out of her space and along the basement floor. The noise stopped. Alice blinked, desperate to find a way out. 'You people are sick,' she screamed. 'Do you hear me? Let me out of here. I can get you money. My father will transfer it instantly. I beg you, let me out of here.' Lifting her head, she tried to listen for sounds. The crack of the reverse light cover seemed to reverberate around the basement, ricocheting off the walls. Her mind was suddenly noisy, his grin as he turned to her and held the cloth over her mouth. *Why did I get out of the car?* She thought. *What a stupid, stupid mistake. I'm always so astute.*

Vomit surged through her body and sat in her mouth, dribbling from her lips and down her clothes. Wiping her vomit with the back of her hands, she swallowed it, closed her eyes, and fought the severe headache that threatened to consume her.

Panic drowned her body. Her chest tightened, breaths fast and awkward. 'I can't die here. I need to get out. Someone let me out,' she yelled. A boisterous scream ripped from her lungs, and her ears hurt.

Footsteps pounded on the basement ceiling.

Pushing her body against the rough wall, the sharp stones digging into her back, she braced herself, body taut, as the basement hatch opened.

'What have we here?' Tom Wilder asked. 'I hope you're comfortable. It's going to be an eventful night. You shouldn't get so stressed. You'll use up all your energy.'

'What do you want?' Alice hissed. 'Money? My father can transfer cash instantly. It will only take a few moments. Please, let me call him, and we can sort this out.'

Climbing down the stairs, Tom gripped the hammer tight in his right hand.

The blow to the side of her head knocked her unconscious.

～

'Andrew, can you hear me? Andrew, come in?' Releasing the side button of the radio, Tom listened to static and turned the volume down. 'Andrew, are you there?' A mumbling sound pushed through the speaker, and Tom struggled to understand what was being said. 'Take the mask off, you idiot.'

'Sorry. I... I didn't realise.'

'Have you done what I asked?'

'Yes. All... All the windows are... are secure.'

'And the front door?' Tom asked. 'Did you wedge the handle?'

'I wedged it. It's wedged. I did very good.'

'Okay. Well done.'

'I couldn't do the... the top windows. They might... might jump.'

'They won't jump. Listen, stay near the lodge. Make sure you watch them and don't let them escape. Everything's starting soon. I'm going to bring the girl up shortly. It's going to be great. So many people are coming. Stay put and wait until you hear from me. Oh, and put the mask back on in case they see you through a window. Over and out.'

'Is it ready?' Tom asked, as he opened the front door of the cottage, watching Joe turn off the outside tap.

'It's ready. I'll ask again. How long do you intend to keep this up?'

'Is the hole big enough?' Tom pushed, ignoring the question.

'Yes,' Joe growled.

'Okay. I'm bringing the girl up. They'll be arriving soon.

Andrew's watching the lodge. I'll have to deal with them after. Are you coming?'

'No. It gets too... out of hand. You don't know what you're messing with. That shit freaks me out. I don't want any part of it.'

'You're going soft in your old age. That's your problem.'

'Soft?' Joe grabbed the shovel, which leant against the cottage wall, and lifted it, ready to take a swipe. 'Is that how you see me?'

'Whoa. Okay, old man. I'm sorry. I'm just kidding around.' He watched as Joe threw the shovel, listening to it bounce on the ground. Then, he clenched his fists, dark yellow saliva dribbling from his mouth to his stubbled chin.

Wiping it, Joe said, 'Don't ever say I'm soft. After what I've just done.'

'Yeah. Was that really necessary?'

'There was no choice. The young lad was a liability. He escaped before. It could have ruined us, racing up there, and warning the four friends the last time the lodge was open. I had to teach him a lesson he wouldn't forget.'

'Yeah,' Tom said. 'Removing his sight. His tongue. That's some lesson.'

'And then, only last night, he does it again,' Joe proclaimed. 'Well, it's the last time. I trusted him. It's dealt with.'

'But chopping his hand off, leaving him to bleed to death. It's brutal, Joe.'

'Then brutal it is. Timmy didn't learn the last time. He never learnt. He will now,' Joe sniped. 'You don't know what I've done for that boy.'

'You kept him locked in the basement for years.'

'I fed him. Looked after him. That's the thanks I get!' Joe shouted, his voice strained. 'You remember the time Timmy

walked in late one night without knocking and saw an oper-
ation being carried out. When he finally calmed down, he
threatened to call the police and tell them what happened
here. I had to keep him locked up. There was no choice.
That boy was never right. I did what I had to do.'

'How are you going to tell Andrew?'

'What?' Joe asked.

'That you've murdered his son?'

26

SATURDAY AFTERNOON

'Can you see anyone outside?' Ruth had just checked the rooms upstairs. Although she could open the windows, jumping from the first floor was out of the question. Downstairs, all the windows were nailed shut.

'Wait, let me see.' Crouched by the kitchen window, Jess slowly stood and peered across the fields. Her hands were trembling, her face hot and flushed. 'Er, I can't see anyone. This is ridiculous.' Jess rushed to the front door and wrestled with the handle, desperately trying to work the obstruction loose. 'I feel sick. We're trapped in here. I have to get out. I can't do this anymore. I have to get out, Ruth.' With her right foot on the door, she tried to force the handle down, worried it would break. 'It's no use. It's stuck.'

'Look, is there another way out of here?'

'No. Unless we jump from an upstairs room, but it's too dangerous.' Again, she tried to yank the door handle down. 'Come on, open.'

'Stop. It's not going to open. We need to be smarter than them. It's what they'll expect. Okay, so we may open the front door, but they'll be waiting for us. We'll fall straight into their trap.'

Turning to her friend, Jess shouted,' So what do you suggest?' She saw Ruth's expression change to one of shock. Her lips quivered, and her eyes bulged.

'You need to keep calm. Panicking won't help. We do the exact opposite of what they expect.'

'Which is?'

'They'll want to see us running around, possibly smashing a window or screaming. They'll get off on it. We remain here and out of sight. They won't like not seeing us. As far as I can tell, there are no cameras on us.'

'We can't be sure, but I haven't seen anything to indicate we're being watched. Although, one of them did get inside. They're showing that they're one step ahead. Playing with us.'

'If they got in before, they'll do it again. When they come for us,' Ruth stated, 'we attack. We need to remain calm.'

'I can't remain calm. I'm already feeling claustrophobic. If I have to spend another night in this fucking freak show of a place, I'll go mad. I need to get out of here.'

'We've almost finished watching the footage. There can't be much more left. If they found a way out, so will we.

'You really think they escaped?' Jess asked. 'I'm beginning to doubt it.'

'They had to have found a way out. How else did they load the short clip on social media? Let's watch the rest and follow their lead.' Although Ruth sounded optimistic as they locked themselves in the bedroom, she feared how the footage would finish. The next few minutes would either give them encouragement or seal their fate.

27

JESS AND RUTH WATCH THE FOOTAGE FROM FIVE YEARS AGO

S taggering, Danny held his neck.

The camera fell to the floor, the screen darkened, and Maria's screams rang through the lodge. Everyone was shouting, panicked, frantic voices.

'Oh Christ! What have you done?' Emma shouted.

'Danny. No, please, Danny. Wake up. Please, Danny, wake up,' Maria wailed.

'This isn't happening. It has to be a dream. It can't be... It can't be happening,' Emma cried. 'Oh my God!'

The three of them shouted at each other in shocked, frightened voices, and for a few moments, it was hard to make out what they were saying.

Maria continued pleading, 'Please, Danny. Don't die on me. I'm so sorry.'

'There's so much blood,' Emma said. 'Grab something. Anything.'

'What?' Matt asked, almost gormless. 'What should I grab?'

'Fucking hell. A towel, something to stem the blood. Oh, sweet Jesus! He's dying. Hurry. Stay with us, Danny.'

Maria's pleas were deafening. At the top of her voice, she yelled, 'Please wake up Danny. You can't die!'

Footsteps were heard racing along the floor, and Matt returned seconds later.

'Here,' Emma said, 'help me tie this around his neck. Support his head. We have to try and stop him bleeding.'

'You're making it worse!' Maria hollered. 'Stop the blood. It's spraying everywhere.'

'Matt, take her over to the kitchen out of the way. I need to try and concentrate.'

'I'm not going anywhere. This is your fault, Matt. If you hadn't brought us here in the first place, knowing what you did, this would never have happened. If he dies, I'm going straight to the police. I'll tell them what you've done.'

'Please,' Emma pleaded. 'Now isn't the time.'

The clip finished with Maria practically howling. It sounded like she was slamming her hands on the floor.

Then the noise stopped.

It seemed much later in the evening. Matt was wearing the same clothes: a blood-spattered shirt and jeans. The camera appeared to be set up on the breakfast bar. He was strolling back and forth in the living room, alone, appearing stressed, his eyebrows deep on his forehead, his fingers tapping his pocket, pushing the other hand through his hair. As he continued pacing the floor, you could hear whimpering sounds from the back bedroom.

On the floor by the front door, Danny's lifeless body lay in a pool of blood.

Suddenly, Matt turned, the tips of his fingers resting on his teeth. He knelt beside the body. With the back of his hand, he touched Danny's face. 'I'm... I'm so... I don't know what to say. I'm so sorry, mate.' He burst into tears. 'I'm so, so sorry.' With his hands over his mouth, the muffled cries continued.

Once composed, he walked to the back bedroom.

Maria was shouting. It sounded as though her lungs would explode, and at any second, the windows would smash, the glass bursting into hundreds of pieces.

As Matt walked back along the hallway and into the living room, he turned, yelling, 'I didn't mean for any of this to happen. You can't blame me. Please.'

Again, she roared at him, her voice strained. 'It is your fault!'

He continued pacing. Every few seconds, he looked at the dead body and appeared more agitated.

The bedroom door slammed, and Emma walked through the back hallway into the living room. As she approached Matt, he seemed unsure whether to hug her or back away.

'Hold me,' she instructed.

Crying, his face buried in her shoulders, his body shook, and he placed his arms around her.

'What are we going to do?' asked Emma, her tone subdued. 'She doesn't want to call the police. She's hyper-ventilating. The thought of going to jail is crippling her. She's cracking up in there.'

'She's blaming me. She's the one who stabbed him.'

'Stop,' Emma ordered. 'This isn't helping.'

'We have to call the police. We have no choice.'

Emma pulled away from her boyfriend, clearly agitated, as if she had another idea. Looking around the living room, eyes darting between corners, she held his face. 'We're stuck out here in this Godforsaken place, we're under attack, and there's a dead body lying by the front door. How are we going to explain this to the police when they turn up? We're all in this together. She's my best friend, Matt. I don't want her locked up any more than she does. I'd do anything for her. Anything.' Emma checked behind her, facing the hallway leading to the back bedroom, and turned back. 'We're going to have to hide the body.'

'What?' Matt asked, pulling away from her. The shock was evident on his face, and he started scratching at the skin of his arms.

'You heard me. We drag Danny outside, hide the body, and wipe away the blood in here. Otherwise, we all go down. We're an accessory to his murder. She wouldn't have stabbed him, only you opened the front door. It's as much your fault as it is hers.'

'Are you out of your mind?' Matt asked.

'As I explained, she's my best friend. I'd die for her. It's the only way we can resolve this.'

As the final clip rolled, Matt, Emma, and Maria were standing by the kitchen window.

The camera was turned, facing them. It was unclear if Maria and Emma knew it was recording. If they did, they never said anything.

'Go on, Maria, tell him. Tell him what you told me,' Emma pushed.

'I... I can't go... go down for this. My biggest fear is being locked up in confined spaces.'

'You and everyone else,' Matt hissed. 'It doesn't give you an excuse to get away with murder.'

'I'll die in prison. I'll kill myself before the police arrive. I swear to God. I'll kill myself.' Maria lay on the floor, hands on the sides of her head, and sobbed.

'Stop!' Emma cried. 'Just stop it, please stop. Don't talk like that.' As she crouched by her friend, Maria begged them to help her.

'Fuck this shit,' Matt said. 'She's going to get us all arrested. 'I'll help, okay? But we never fucking mention this again. Turning and looking at the body, he instructed, 'Grab his legs. There's the old well outside. It's deep. We'll place his body in there.' His voice was stern and authoritative. 'If I'm agreeing to this, we all help.'

Shuffling noises were heard.

Frantic, stressed voices reverberated through the lodge.

Finally, the front door opened, followed by the sound of Danny's legs being dragged across the floor and outside.

There was a gap of about ten minutes.

Jess was speechless as she clicked the mouse to forward the recording, unable to comprehend what she was watching.

Stunned, Ruth shifted her body to rid the numbness.

When they came back inside, Matt appeared to move the camera onto the kitchen worktop, giving a complete view of the living room and catching Maria racing to the back bedroom.

'This is ridiculous. We're never going to get away with it. What have we done, Matt? What if they find the body?' Emma waited as if wrestling with her conscience. A moment later, she rushed to Maria.

'I have to delete this shit,' Matt sighed. As his hand went over the camera lens and the picture blacked out for a moment, loud beeping noises came from the back bedroom. Placing the camera back on the breakfast bar, still recording, he shouted, 'What was that?' Alarm shrouded his face, his mouth open, and his eyes narrowed, short, quickened breaths as he spun and rushed across the living room. 'What were the beeping sounds I heard?'

Racing out of the back bedroom, Maria said, 'Oh my God! I have reception.' Her face was heavily smudged with mascara, with black lines under her eyes and face. Her cheeks were bright red, almost like her face was about to spontaneously combust. 'I'm... I'm calling the police.' Bringing her mobile phone to her face, she began dialling.

With force, Matt whacked the phone from her hand, and it crashed to the floor. 'Are you crazy? Have you completely lost your mind?'

'What are you doing?' she shouted. 'It's our chance to get out of here. To get help.' Crouched, she picked up the phone and stood, again trying to make a call.

Again, frantically whipping the phone from her hand, he threw it at the wall. Grabbing Maria, he shook her hard. 'Do you know what we've just done?' His desperate pleas seemed to fall on deaf ears as he stood, looking astonished as Maria knelt on the floor.

'I was in the toilet,' Emma said as she came out of the bedroom. 'What's going on?'

'Maria has reception. The Wi-Fi is back on. She's calling the police.'

Turning to her friend, with her hands clamping Maria's face, she spoke softly and as calmly as possible. 'Listen to me. That can't happen. If the police come, we're all in the shit. You get that, don't you? We need to clean up the blood at the front door, and in the morning, we get the hell away from here.'

She broke away from Emma's hold, stumbling backward. 'I need my phone.'

With a harsh voice, Emma shouted, 'You're not listening!

We have just hidden Danny's body. We dumped him in the well. It was your decision. Remember?'

'Huh? Danny? No, he's on the floor by the front door.'

'She's delusional. She's going to give us away. How are we going to handle this?' Stepping back, Matt covered his face with his hands, the agitation evident.

Charging across the living room, Maria grabbed the phone, holding it to her face. 'The screen's cracked, but I think I can still make a call.'

Rushing behind her, Matt placed his arms tight around her waist and rotated her body, so she faced him. 'Listen to yourself. Listen to what you're saying.'

Calmly, she said, 'Can you get Danny out of the well? We can leave now. We can call for help.'

'Danny is dead. You stabbed him in the neck. His lifeless body is lying at the bottom of the well. We've covered up the murder. You said you'd kill yourself if we called the police, remember?'

'No,' she insisted. 'You killed him. I remember now. It was you. I'll tell the police that when they arrive. You'll go to prison, not me.'

Shaking her, spit surging from his lips, he yelled, 'You have to listen! We are all responsible.'

'You killed him. You and Emma. Go and get him from the well.'

'She's totally bloody lost it.' With both hands, Emma grabbed her friend.

Swinging her arms, she slapped Emma in the face and walked to the front door. 'I'm going for help. You both killed him. That's what I'll tell the police. I'll tell them that.'

With a forearm on her throat, Matt held her against the front door. 'You're not understanding this situation. You're not thinking straight.'

'No. leave me,' she hissed, her voice raspy and strained. 'I know what happened. My mind has never been clearer.'

Grabbing each of Maria's arms, they forcefully dragged her through the living room and into the bedroom to the right of the hallway.

Although they went out of view, the camera picked up their voices. A door slammed, and screaming echoed through the lodge.

'Keep her in there a second,' Matt ordered. 'I'll grab something to wedge against the door handle. Have you removed the bedroom window key so she can't open it?'

'Yes. And I have her phone as well. I can't hold this door for much longer. Hurry,' Emma instructed from the hallway.

Matt walked to the boiler cupboard, his footsteps pounding along the floor. The door opened. 'Okay, I have a broom. There's a mop and bucket here and a bag of tools. We have to clean up the blood by the front door.'

'Hurry,' Emma ordered, 'I'm struggling to keep her contained.'

Crunching sounds reverberated as Maria thumped the door.

'Okay, this should hold her until we decide what to do. The handle is jammed. I don't know how long we have.'

'Oh Christ, Matt, how are we going to cover this up? We're in trouble. The first chance she has, she'll confess. We're screwed.'

'Guard the room with your life. Let me know if you hear the glass smashing. She could try to escape. We may have to lock her in the boiler room.'

The crunching sound continued, and screams reverberated through the lodge.

Again, the sound of footsteps as Matt rushed back into the living room. 'I have a plan. Wait in the hallway and make sure she doesn't get out.'

'What plan?'

'We have Wi-Fi. I have to do something. You're not going to like it. But we need to frighten her. As a threat, I mean.'

'A threat? What are you talking about?'

'Okay. Bear with me. I'm going to grab the laptop and edit the recording. I'll post it on YouTube. It's so Maria knows I'm serious. It will be our story, visiting this place. Don't worry; I'll cut out everything that happened regarding Danny's death. But it's the only way to buy Maria's silence. She'll be too scared to do anything, and the uploaded video clip on YouTube will be a reminder she can never tell anyone. A stark warning.'

'I'm not getting it?'

'I have to keep her quiet. There's always the threat of her going to the police. If that happens, we'll spend the rest of our lives locked up—the three of us. I have video editing software. The clip will only be a minute or two. I'll morph the faces and dub the voices. No one will know who we are. The real copy, showing Maria murdering Danny, I'll hide under the floorboards until we get out of here. I saw a handful of tools under the boiler. It's the only way we'll buy her silence.'

'You're going to hide the evidence under the floorboards? How are you going to retrieve it?'

'Someone's   trying   to   get   into   the   lodge—the tyres bursting, the torchlight outside, and the bangs on the front door. Once the clip's loaded, we'll get out of here.'

'You really think we'll escape? They could still be out there.'

'We... We have to try. That's why I'm going to hide the hard drive in a safe place. When Maria knows what I've done, there's no way she'll say anything. When this has blown over, I'll come back for it. That's all I can think of right now. If they find the hard drive, we're ruined. They'll know what we've all done. Hiding it under the floorboard is our only option right now. Please try and understand what I'm doing. If Maria threatens to confess, I'll blackmail her. I'll have the real copy showing her murdering Danny. It's our way to keep her silent.'

'That's just cruel,' Emma said.

'It's the only way for us to get away with it.'

There was a gap of about two seconds, and then it showed Matt kneeling on the floor with a hammer and a long screwdriver resting next to him. The floorboard was up by the front door.

Again, the camera appeared to be resting on the breakfast bar.

Emma stood in silence next to him.

'Okay, the floorboard has stayed intact. I worried it might break. My Dad was a builder. I learnt loads from him as a kid. Right, I've edited the recording and posted it to YouTube. Hopefully, it will get shares from other accounts. I've tried to make it as mysterious and bizarre as possible, so it gets a few hits. Maria needs to understand if she tells anyone what we've done, there'll be repercussions. It should be enough to keep her quiet.' In the kitchen drawer, he found a black pen and an envelope. 'I'll secure the hard drive in the envelope and hide it under the floor so it's easy to find when I return. Our main priority now is escaping from here.'

'I feel sick. This is a disaster,' Emma said.

'Look, there's no alternative. It's what has to happen.'

'I'm going to check on her. She's too quiet.' Emma disappeared from the frame as Matt swept the floor, removing wood splinters, tools, and old nails, placing them in an industrial bag.

'Matt, she's gone?'

'What?' he called from the front door.

'Maria. She's escaped from the bedroom.'

'That's impossible.' Grabbing the camera, Matt pointed it along the living room to the hallway.

Emma was standing by the bedroom door. 'Turn the camera off.'

'No. I need to keep recording.' He scanned the bedroom. The window was closed and locked—the handle in a horizontal position. There was no sign of broken glass. The bathroom was empty, again, the window locked. 'No. This can't be happening. How did she escape? It's not possible. She has to be in here.' On his hands and knees, he steered the camera under the bed. 'Where the hell is—'

A hatch cut into the floor burst upwards and hammered against the back wall. A figure, disguised with bandages wrapped heavily around their face and head, placed their arms on the floor on either side of the hatch and lifted themselves into the bedroom.

Emma screamed as the figure approached her.

At the last second, Matt ran out of the bedroom, ramming the broom against the door handle.

'Matt? You bastard. Open the door!' Emma screamed. 'Matt, please hel—'

As Matt charged into the living room and towards the front door, he kneeled by the gap in the floorboard, and the recording ended.

Jess closed the laptop and looked at Ruth. 'The hatch in the opposite bedroom must be hidden behind the bed. That's our way out.'

28

SATURDAY EVENING

A palpable sense of anticipation filled the air as Jess opened the bedroom door opposite hers and gripped a leg of the bed. Ruth grabbed the opposite leg, and they pulled it away from the wall. It was weighty and cumbersome, and the legs squealed as they scraped on the wooden floor.

'I can't believe what Matt did,' Ruth said. 'Locking his girlfriend in the bedroom. This bedroom. So he could escape. How cruel can someone be?'

With her leg pressed against the wall, Jess pulled the bed sideways so she could squeeze around it. 'I guess it's why he never came back to retrieve the hard drive. Knowing he had Emma murdered, we have to assume that's what happened, probably Maria too. It was dangerous returning, and he probably went into hiding.'

'And dumping Danny's body in the well. It's... horrible to imagine.' A shiver rushed through Ruth's back as she looked across the hallway and out Jess's bedroom window. The well was just a few yards from the lodge.

'I know,' Jess answered. 'His body is down there, and no

one knows. The people who have walked past it, not knowing what happened. It's terrifying.'

'Do you think Matt is still out there?'

'Who knows? But if he is, he's living with some serious guilt.' Sidestepping along the floor, with her back brushing the wall, Jess edged to the head of the bed. Glancing down, she saw the hatch. 'Oh my God! It's still here. Yes. It's our escape route.'

'I don't know about this,' Ruth announced. 'They know it's here. They could be waiting.'

'Hold up,' Jess responded. Rushing into her bedroom, she stood to the right of the window and peered across the fields. Her eyes slowly scanned the area as if in slow motion. 'I see the figure.' Quickly, she moved out of view.

'Did they see you?'

'I don't think so.' Looking again, careful not to be spotted, Jess leant forward. 'No. They're standing to the side of a field by the hedges and facing towards the front door.' Grabbing the hard drive, Dictaphone, torch and mobile phone, she closed the bedroom door. 'Now's our chance. We've got to make a run for it.'

Back in the opposite bedroom, on bended knees, Jess gripped the small circular handle, placed a forefinger through it, and lifted. The hinges groaned as if in protest.

With a shared nod, the women stood looking underneath the lodge.

Jess sat, placing a hand on either side of the hatch, slowly lowering her body through the gap and onto the ground. Old branches snapped under her trainers, leaves crumbled, and her feet penetrated soft moss, making a squelching sound. The stench was rancid, clawing at her lungs and making her wheezy: old decaying grass, rotten fungus, and mushrooms.

Helping Ruth through the hatch, they crawled on their hands and knees, feeling the sting of nettles on their skin as they emerged from under the lodge.

As Jess stood, reaching behind to help Ruth to her feet, she said, 'Let's keep low. We can't risk being seen.' Looking at the same spot in the fields, she saw the figure had gone. Keeping as low as possible, Jess trudged away from the lodge and onto the narrow road. 'There's a van parked at the cottage.'

Joining her, Ruth looked down into the valley. 'Well, that's scuppered our plan. We can't go down there now.'

'I say we head towards the main entrance. We can keep hidden in the woods.'

The women embraced as if drawing strength from each other, turned, and ran towards the trees behind the lodge.

The air was heavy with the damp smell of earth and vegetation, and every rustle of leaves and snap of twigs under their feet caused alarm. Lactose built in their calves, their breaths short and choppy, and they dodged low-hanging branches that seemed intent on snaring them into their grasp.

'Can you see anyone?' Ruth asked, looking between the trees to her right. She halted abruptly, feeling a sharp ache in her ankle from her boots. Her gaze followed Jess, who stopped ahead, scanning their surroundings.

'Nothing. But they'll know we've left the lodge soon enough. We have to keep going. How's the ankle?'

'Bloody painful. Trust me to dress like I'm on the catwalk.'

As they neared the hay barn, Jess swung her arm out to stop her friend. Strange glowing lights flickered in the distance. Hiding behind the trees, they watched as a group of around fifty people began filtering inside.

Abruptly, the van they'd seen parked outside the cottage pulled up, and they observed as the driver, their face concealed with a bandage, stepped out.

Making their way to the back of the vehicle, they opened the doors and lifted the limp body of a woman.

The clouds parted, the cold breeze pushing against their skin, and Jess looked up, seeing the edge of a full moon emerging. 'It's the same van from the footage. The creep from the petrol station. He's conducting a ritual. We have to do something.'

Tom Wilder walked through the hay barn with Alice slumped over his right shoulder—the flickering glow of candles held aloft by each person lighting his path.

The followers sat on wooden crates, others on hay bales and old barrels. At Tom's command, they removed their masks; purity was an integral part of the ritual.

Placing Alice on a hay bale in the far corner of the barn, Tom removed the bandage around his head and switched on the lights. 'Brothers and Sisters, it's great to see so many familiar faces. Thank you all for making this gathering such a success. So, is everyone ready?'

A raucous cheer erupted around the barn. The excitement was evident as people shuffled on their seats, grins on their faces, and eyes glued to the makeshift altar.

By his feet, Tom grabbed a long piece of rope and tied it around Alice's body, securing her tightly to the hay bale. 'Shortly,' he continued, 'we'll extract the chosen one's blood. You've all been here many times. I don't need to explain the benefits of what we get from each new catch. Let us recognise the sacred purpose that unites us all. We seek immortality; we seize our destiny, our opportunity to claim the eternal life that is rightfully ours. I will pass around the goblet, and you will each take a small sip. Please ensure there's enough for everyone. Greed will not be tolerated here. A sip. No more. We shall partake in the ultimate act of devotion, the key to unlocking the secrets of eternity. Let us embrace this moment, for it shall be our salvation, redemption, and legacy for all time.'

Behind him, Alice stirred. Lifting her head, she suddenly realised what was happening.

'Help. Let me go. I'm not supposed to be here. What is wrong with you freaks?'

Gasps echoed through the barn as the followers watched on in anticipation.

'For the first time,' Tom said, his voice raised to overthrow the screams, 'we'll summon a new spirit. I've learnt much about his ways, and I feel so excited to introduce you to him. His name is Astaroth, the prince of knowledge, the keeper of secrets. He who holds the key to eternal life and boundless wisdom. It is Astaroth whom we will worship tonight, for he is the embodiment of all that we seek – power, knowledge, and immortality. So, let's begin. It's time to ask him to join us.'

At the back of the hay barn, Jess and Ruth stood with their ears pressed against the wood.

'He's talking about summoning a demon,' Jess whispered. 'This... This ritual he conducts, every full moon, relates to the stories surrounding Sheers Woods—the paranormal activity. I knew it. We have to get her out of there.'

Pressing her fingers against her forehead, she worked at the stress knot, trying to rid the ache.

'How are we going to do that? Have you seen the number of people in there?'

'They're going to kill her, Ruth. These people are twisted. That's why Beth, the florist, warned me not to come here. She knew what happened. It's why no one would talk to Matt at the restaurant. The locals are scared. This is the reason. We have a chance to do something about it. To finally stop the terror that has overshadowed Sheers Woods for so long.'

'What do you suggest we do?' Ruth asked as she watched her friend creep to the entrance of the hay barn.

Removing her phone, Jess eased back the bowed doors, her muscles tight and teeth clenched at the thought of being heard. Lifting her phone, she began to record.

'You're not serious,' Ruth whispered as she joined her. 'Tell me you're not serious.'

'It's the only way to stop them. This is the evidence we need. We can finally put an end to their depraved secret.' Through the phone screen, they watched as the woman carried from the van tried desperately to free herself from the rope. Tom Wilder stood to her left, facing away from the gathering and towards the back of the barn. There were around fifty in total; all sat staring at Tom—men and women, weird masks by their feet and their hands out, palms facing upwards as if waiting to accept something.

As Tom spun around, Jess and Ruth leant back and out of shot, hiding behind the wall carved with strange symbols.

'Did he see us?' Ruth asked in a hushed voice.

'I... I don't think so.'

Tom began humming, and everyone joined in. The low-pitched sound was eerie and uncomfortable to hear.

'Followers, the moment we've been waiting for is here.'

Again, Alice screamed, 'Someone help me, please. I'm not supposed to be here. Let me go.'

With his arms out, Tom ordered, 'Repeat after me—Astaroth, the prince of knowledge, the keeper of secrets. Join us.'

Everyone repeated the words.

Tom recited the sentence over and over as everyone copied his exact words.

'When his back's turned,' Jess announced, 'I'm going up there. I have to untie her.'

'No,' Ruth ordered, suddenly worried she was heard. 'I won't let you do it. Are you mad?'

'Hold the phone. Record everything. If I'm caught, run for it. Get to the entrance and as far from here as possible.'

Ruth took the phone and grabbed her friend's arm. 'Please, listen to me. You can't do this.'

'I have to help her.' Holding Ruth's left hand and gently squeezing, she turned and ducked low, passing the symbols on the wall, her pulse quickening with each step and careful not to draw attention to herself.

A group of three women sat on a barrel, their faces gleaming, eyes focused and still as if in a trance. As Tom turned, facing the back and chanting a song in an unfamiliar language, Jess joined them.

They didn't appear to notice her.

She sat still, fists tightly closed, running her thumbs along the knuckles of her forefingers, and glanced behind her, seeing Ruth peeking around the wall and filming everything.

Slowly, Jess dropped to her knees and crawled towards

the front. Her heart seemed to roar through her ears, and she worried someone would hear.

Near the front, four women and two men sat on the edge of another barrel, again in a trance-like state. Their eyes were closed, and they hummed to themselves. This time, as she turned around, she saw Ruth shaking her head.

As Tom turned back around, Jess dropped and sat on the floor. It felt like she was playing What's the Time, Mr. Wolf? A hand touched her shoulder, and she froze, too worried to look.

'Are you new?' A gruff man's voice asked.

Jess nodded without turning around.

'First time?'

Again, a nod.

'Welcome, Sister.'

Another nod. *Piss off now and mind your own business,* Jess thought. *I ain't your sister.*

Up at the front, as Alice tried to wriggle free, Tom placed his hands over her body.

'Silence, everyone,' Tom ordered. 'Remain seated, open your eyes, and let us rejoice in what's about to happen.' On his own, he repeated the words, chanting as if stuck on a loop, over and over, each time louder. 'Astaroth, the prince of knowledge, the keeper of secrets. Join us.'

The barn fell deathly silent.

Again, Tom asked, 'Astaroth, the prince of knowledge, the keeper of secrets. Won't you please join us?'

A palpable stillness descended on the barn.

Beside Jess, candles started flickering, and the smell of sulphur and rotten flesh was apparent. She covered her mouth, fearing she'd vomit.

The weathered timber panelling, forming the shell of the hay barn behind where Tom stood, whined as if stretching. A low growl suddenly resounded through the hay barn, followed by gasps from the congregation.

Jess backed away, watching the fear in everyone's eyes and hearing people whisper to one another.

'It sounds angry. I don't like this,' a man said, sitting beside her, addressing his companions.

'Something has definitely joined us,' another man said, 'but it sounds so enraged.'

The growl increased, more intense, resembling a wild beast, its primal resonance echoing through the barn.

Fighting the harsh shiver down her back, Jess flinched.

Then, a shadow appeared as if emerging from the very darkness itself and began drifting across the back wall.

The apprehension was one of alarm, dread of the unknown.

At the back, Tom seemed unaffected by the sinister presence. The chilling shadow began to take form, resembling the silhouette of a large creature with elongated horns as it oozed along the ceiling. Abruptly, it seemed to morph into a small cyclone, possibly three or four feet long, and hovered above Alice's face.

'Get away from me,' she yelled as she slung her head from side to side. 'Leave me alone.'

The barn was gripped with unease as the shadow seemed to disappear inside Alice's mouth. Her body convulsed as if having a fit.

Reaching to the ground, Tom grabbed a knife in one hand and a syringe in the other, holding them over Alice's right arm. 'And now, the part we've been waiting for. I will tear her skin and have the first taste. Let's extract some blood.'

Instantly, Alice emitted a low growl. Her words appeared

to echo in a deep, guttural voice as she muttered a different language, and smoke began seeping from her nostrils.

As people shuffled in their seats, Tom could sense their unease. As he walked around Alice, she kicked him, sending him a few feet across the barn, and he landed hard against the wall. Her head swung to the left, her eyes rolled back in their sockets, and froth spilled from her mouth. 'You will all die.'

As people stood and made their way out of the barn, Tom shouted, 'Remain here. Everyone. I said to remain here. That's an order.' His words fell on deaf ears.

Jess stood and rushed through the crowd, quickly untying the ropes and releasing Alice. Leaping up with an unexpected burst of strength, she whacked Jess with her left arm, sending her backward across a barrel. Charging at Tom, who was still on the ground shielding himself with his arms, she lifted him, hurling him against the back wall. His body went straight through the decaying wood, and he lay injured on the ground. Picking up the knife, Alice spun towards the congregation as they exited the barn in disbelief. As she rushed at them, their screams rang through the valley. Outside, she dropped to the ground, writhing in pain, and crawled away from the barn into the woods.

Ruth stood behind the wall, dumbfounded, having filmed everything.

Jess ran to her, and they hugged tight.

'Shit. Are you okay?' Ruth asked, handing her mobile phone back, unable to stop her hand shaking.

'I... I don't know. It was awful. That poor woman.' As Jess inhaled, the smell of rotten flesh was still evident. 'We need to follow everyone down to the entrance. Let's get the hell out of here. Quick, come on.' As Jess ran through the doors, she looked for Alice. Although skeptical, she still thought she could help.

The full moon beamed from above, the clouds slowly parting, and Jess removed her torch and shuffled to the edge of the field, seeing Alice crawling through the grass. Her arms were straight, her hands pressed into the earth and supporting her body, and her legs dragged behind her like a limp animal taking its last steps.

Racing to her, Jess shouted, 'Wait. I want to help you. I'm so sorry for what happened. Please let me help.'

Turning on her back, Alice collapsed and reached her left hand in the air.

Jess grabbed it, watching as her face began to implode and collapse. Her eyes rolled back, her skin became dark purple, and a gentle groan pushed from her lips. Then she died.

Behind Jess, the familiar growl reverberated through the trees, saturating her surroundings. 'Ruth, we need to run. Now.' Spinning around, she rushed to the hay barn, hearing a vehicle start.

As it pulled away along the road, Ruth knelt, banging on the back windows.

29

SATURDAY EVENING

From outside the barn, Jess watched the van charging along the narrow road towards the congregation. For a moment, it appeared Tom Wilder was going to drive through the middle of them. At the last moment, he steered into the fields, the horn bellowing as he navigated around them.

Jess considered calling out and asking for help, but she knew whose side they'd take.

All she wanted to do was drop to her knees, pull her hair, and scream at the top of her voice. It was her fault that Ruth had been kidnapped. Her doing. If she hadn't been such a martyr and they'd kept going, they would have reached the main road and found help. Ruth had turned up for one reason—concern for her friend's safety. Now, Jess had let her down.

Summoning the strength from deep within her stomach, she began jogging through the desolate fields.

So much was processing in her mind. The scenes from the hard drive she found played out. Matt, seeing the body being loaded into a van at the petrol station. The group following it into Sheers Woods. Danny being murdered, and his body dumped in the well. The memories flooded her consciousness. And Emma, desperate for help, pleading with Matt as he callously locked her in the bedroom for his own selfish motives—to save himself. Had he got away? Was he still out there, possibly in the shadows, hiding and worried that one day someone would find his recording and tell the story?

She thought about the poor lad who'd called to the lodge to warn her and seeing bandage-faced person dragging a sack through the fields. Tom Wilder. He'd blocked their path earlier in the day and donned the same disguise at the barn, but his arrogance was such that he believed he could drop the facade and reveal his true self at the ritual without consequence.

Then there was the gravedigger, making out it was safe and how he'd call the police and get them help. Another chilling thought processed. Was he getting the grave ready to hide the body in the sack?

Hatred pulsed through her veins. The determination to save Ruth and expose the evil that lurked here drove her forward.

Forcing her body to keep going, guided by the intense light of the full moon and her torch, Jess could see the lodge on her right. The security lights were off, the area drenched in tranquility, and to a layperson, it looked so inviting.

Something caught her eye.

A figure stood in a field near the lodge.

The same figure that had been watching her and Ruth earlier.

∾

I'm doing good, Andrew Egan thought to himself. *They're still locked inside. Tom will be proud.* Marching in circles, he began jumping on the spot to dim the noise in his head. He was born with a rare brain defect that developed into psychosis and paranoia. The condition, known medically as a neurodevelopmental disorder, affected his brain's ability to process sensory information and regulate emotions. As a result, Andrew experienced frequent episodes of distorted thinking, hallucinations, and delusions. Darkness was the main trigger. As a child, he'd often lie awake for hours, convinced the walls were speaking to him or people were hiding under his bed.

Whenever he tried to talk to his father, he'd get a beating, often bruised for days. His mother, Marge Egan, was more understanding and always made it easier for him to deal with his condition. She'd often hold his hand for hours, trying to convince him that it was all in his head and nothing bad would happen.

Joe refused to listen to Marge, and when she spoke about medication and getting their son psychiatric help, he threatened to kill them both.

As Andrew stood facing the lodge, sweat poured down his face. He became breathless and sluggish. Removing the bird mask, the relief instant, he basked in the fresh air as it whipped against his skin.

I'm sorry, Tom. I'm really sorry. Don't be annoyed.

Abruptly, he checked the radio and saw the charging light had diminished.

'Uh oh. Uh no. Trouble. Too much trouble.' Pressing the side button, he spoke, hoping Tom would hear him. 'Still here. Still at the lodge. I'm watching them like you said. Over. Are you there? Over. Hello, Tom. Over.' Releasing the button, he hurled the radio to the ground, stamping on it.

'Stupid, stupid thing. Rubbish. Totally shit. I hate you. You're over now, how about that?' The crunching noise under his boots was satisfying, but Andrew knew there'd be repercussions.

He wanted to run, just like his son, Timmy. Escape from his father and never see him again. It would be so easy to walk to the entrance, along the road, and disappear. But he'd never survive. His father told him this many times. Andrew, he'd say, it's a mean world out there. You're stupid, and people will only befriend you to take the piss. To mock you. You're different from the others. You wouldn't last a second in the real world.

His mind drifted to the night his mother left. Andrew was lying in his bed, and he saw lights coming from the grave. As he got up and walked to the window, he saw his father rolling her into the hole he'd dug. She was still wearing the white nightdress stained with blood, and her favourite slippers.

Andrew still missed her.

During one of their trips to town, Joe parked up and went into a hardware store to buy soil. While sitting in the passenger seat, a woman tapped on the window and asked Andrew for any spare change. Attracted to her and not used to female attention, he grabbed a few coins from the front of the car and asked her why she wanted money. She'd explained to Andrew that she ran away from home due to her abusive parents and moved from town to town, sleeping rough.

Over the next few weeks, every Wednesday, Andrew accompanied his father into town, chatting with Madeline and giving her whatever change he could take from the cottage. When she told him she was moving on due to the police hassling her, Andrew gave her his address and said he'd look after her. A few nights later, while Joe was sleeping, she called to the cottage. Andrew began jumping excitedly, keeping her hidden from his father for days. He fed her, let her hide in the basement when Joe was around, and brought her into his bed at night.

One morning, his father came home early for lunch and caught them sitting on the sofa, caressing each other. Joe hit the roof, and when he found out she was pregnant, he went ballistic. Once he'd finally calmed down, he told his son she could stay. But there were ground rules. No one could know she was living with them. That meant she couldn't leave the cottage under any circumstances.

While giving birth, he called on an old friend to deliver the twins, but due to complications, Madeline died a few days later.

Tears rolled down Andrew's face as again, he watched his father burying a body in the graveyard. Part of him suspected his father of killing her, too.

Now, as he made his way to the lodge, hopping and yelping loudly, worried he hadn't seen any movement, he felt a heavy blow to the back of his head, and he crumpled to the ground, unconscious.

Jess had to be quick. It may only be minutes before Andrew came around.

With a swift, careful motion, she pulled his right arm out of the sleeve and gently rolled Andrew onto his side, pulling the feathered outfit from under his body and away. As she picked the bird mask off the ground, Andrew grabbed her ankle, and stumbling backward, she reached for the heavy log, smashing his fingers and then catching him full pelt on the bridge of the nose. Again, Andrew lay unconscious on the ground.

Once the outfit was on, Jess delved into the left pocket, feeling the hairpiece she'd seen hanging over the clothes-line. Hurling it at Andrew's face, she turned and set off through the fields to the cottage.

The feathered costume was itchy and uncomfortable, the mask was awkward to run with, and Jess contemplated putting it on. She ultimately decided against it, figuring it might hinder her movements if she needed to defend herself.

Suddenly, under the full moon's glow, the silhouette of the cottage nestled amidst the dense woods.

As she walked along the cracked, uneven concrete path, a security light above the front door kicked into motion, and she gasped, rooted to the spot. Her heart thumped loudly in her chest, and a cold sweat trickled down her body. Crouching behind a bush, she waited to see if anyone came to the front door. With no apparent movement, she parted the rough bushes, the security light still glaring, and peered through the living room window, seeing only blackness.

With bated breath, Jess gripped the door handle and tried to force it downwards. She jiggled it back and forth, urging it to open, but nothing worked.

Shit. What did I expect? she thought. *There has to be another way.*

As she sneaked along the path to the back of the cottage, she saw headlights in the distance.

They were approaching fast.

∼

Braking hard, Tom sent Ruth hurling against the seats in the back of the van. Like a warrior preparing for battle and adorning their armour, he wrapped the bandage tightly around his head before exiting the vehicle and opening the rear doors.

'Get out.' He watched as she crouched, her eyes wide and fearful. 'I said, get out. You and your friend have fucked everything up. I don't have time for this.' Leaning into the van, he grabbed her hair and pulled her onto the ground.

Ruth's screams were piercing, and Tom retaliated by kicking her hard in the ribs.

'No one can hear you.' Bending forward, he spoke in her right ear. 'You'll both pay for your actions. That's a promise. Do you know how much fucking organisation goes into the meetings? No. You both had to interfere. Well, now it's my turn to do the right thing.' Tom heard someone behind him. Spinning around, he saw the figure, wearing the bird mask and feathered outfit. 'You stupid prick. I told you to watch them. What happened? Andrew, I asked you a question?'

Ruth winced on the floor, diverting Tom's attention.

'Get up. I haven't got time. Help me, Andrew. Grab her legs.'

Her head was pounding, and a vein in the side of Jess's temple throbbed so hard she thought it would burst. Although cold outside, the heat was intense under the mask, and its weight felt more like that of a motorcycle helmet. The feathered outfit irritated her skin, and any second, she'd start itching. Dread invaded her body, worried she couldn't hold Ruth and the mask slipping off would be a significant problem. Taking a gulp of air, smelling Andrew's stale sweat, she reached down and grabbed Ruth's legs.

'Wait,' Tom ordered. 'Where's the radio? Did you lose it?'

Jess nodded and felt a hard shove, which caused her to step back.

'I asked one thing,' Tom stated. 'Just one. Not to let them escape from the lodge. Why couldn't you follow the simple instruction?'

Another push, harder this time, caused Jess to fall against the cottage wall. Any second, the oversized boots would slip off her feet, jeopardising the disguise. Although she was around the same height as Andrew, and the feathered costume covered her arms and legs, she couldn't give Tom a reason to suspect her. In desperation, she pushed away from the wall and began galloping on the spot, feeling the boots sliding off her feet.

'Enough!' Tom shouted. 'Wait here, you idiot. If I want a job done, I'll do it myself. You'll only drop her. I'm putting her in the basement. Then I have to look for the other one.' He bent down, lifting Ruth, placing her over his shoulder, and opened the front door to the cottage.

Her cries for help reverberated through the hallway.

A few minutes later, Tom turned off the lights and came outside. 'Watch the cottage. If she escapes, I'll kill you. That's a promise. I'm taking the van. I must find the other one. She's out there somewhere. There's no way she'll leave without her friend. If she comes here, I need you to be ready. Can I trust you?'

A nod.

'Don't let me down.' Tom got into the van and drove away from the cottage.

As the lights disappeared along the road, Jess removed the mask and breathed in the crisp night air, feeling the sense of urgency, and knowing time was running out.

30

SATURDAY EVENING

Dumping the feathered outfit, mask, and boots in a large bin outside the cottage, Jess pushed the front door and stood barefoot in the bleak hallway. There was no sign of the gravedigger she and Ruth had met earlier, but she had to assume he was close.

The smell hit her instantly, infesting her nostrils. A rusty, blood-like waft hung in the air like rotten meat. The stench was heavy and sour, with an underlying foulness, like gone off milk or a garbage truck left in forty degrees heat.

Instantly, she covered her mouth with her hand and started dry retching like an eating trial on one of those reality TV shows.

'Ruth, are you there? If you can hear me, tap on something,' Jess murmured, but there was no response.

Shining the torch to the stairs on her right, she saw an old mahogany frame, rife with woodworm and knots, supporting the steps leading to the first floor. Dust mites danced in the torchlight, and the smell of death drowned the air where she stood.

Opening the first door on the left, she stepped into the living room. Newspapers were piled high, a couple of fishing rods leaning against the wall, a small TV in the corner perched on a rickety old table, and black-and-white photos of a man and small child adorning the wall. As far as she could tell, there was no telephone, and there wasn't time to sift through the clutter. 'Ruth, can you hear me?'

Backing away, Jess shined the torch along the dingy hallway which cut through the shell of the cottage like a gaping wound, its walls infested with mould and bacteria. The paint, having long surrendered to the dampness, was flaked and crusted, revealing a mix of decay and deterioration.

At the kitchen door, she grabbed an old brass handle, loose, barely attached with rusted screws.

Locked.

Through the grimy, discoloured glass, she shone the torch over the kitchen. Bowls sat on the rickety table with cutlery balancing on their edges, mugs, stained plates, cardboard cereal boxes, and newspapers scattered on flimsy chairs. Dirty dishes piled high over the sink at the back of the kitchen, and the walls and ceiling were stained yellow from cigarette smoke. An ashtray overspilled with butts sucked to within an inch of their lives rested on the grubby worktop. More newspapers covered the back window, stuck to the glass as if blocking the world from this infested, hideous place. The tiled floor was covered in balls of screwed-up, blood-soaked kitchen roll.

It's disgusting. I've never seen anything more horrendous in my life, Jess thought.

'Timmy, are you okay?' The distant voice came from underneath the floor.

Dropping the torch in shock, Jess was momentarily

plunged into darkness and crouched, finding it lying against the wall. She knocked the glass end with her hand, pleased that the light flickered back on.

Again, the young voice. 'Timmy. Where are you?'

Directing the torch down another hallway branching away from the kitchen, she steered the light on a door at the far end.

The floorboards bowed, moaning under her feet. The smell was still strong, and it felt like she was in one of those fun houses at the local fairground. Any moment, the walls would close in and crush her body. She was suddenly disorientated, like the hallway was a rope bridge, swaying side to side, scary mirrors twisting her features, and the stairs mere conveyor belts, spewing out unsuspecting visitors at the exit and readying itself for the next victims.

Leaning against the wall, she gulped the foul air, closed her eyes, and steadied herself.

Reaching the door at the end of the hallway, she found a key in the lock, rusted and thick, and she felt like Alice In Wonderland at the tea party.

A firm clunk resounded as she turned the key anti-clockwise and pushed the door open.

The light was off, and like the rest of the cottage, the room was damp and infested with dust mites. Old wooden chairs sat in the corner, aligned along the back wall, the paint chipped, cushions worn, and legs bowed. A heavy-looking wardrobe stood by the opposite wall.

'Timmy. Is that you?'

Jess flinched, forgetting for a moment about the voice. Shining the torch in the corner of the bleak room, she saw a hatch cut into the wooden floor with a combination lock securing a flimsy metal flap.

Gently tiptoeing across the room, the air from her lungs

whistling through her nostrils, she crouched and gently pulled the lock. From underneath her, a muffled whine emanated, reminiscent of someone gagged.

Through a gap in the hatch, Jess whispered, 'I'm here, Ruth. You're safe. I have to break the lock.'

'Timmy. Where's Timmy?' the voice asked again.

Grabbing a chair from the corner of the room and turning it sideways, Jess began smashing the lock. 'Come on. Break.' Another swing, missing the lock by a few inches. Holding the chair, her elbows bent, body twisted, and her lips gripping the torch, she whacked the lock again, hearing a crunching sound and seeing the lock fly across the room. 'Yes.'

Lifting the hatch, she saw her friend slumped in the corner, bound and gagged on the basement floor.

Adjusting her eyes to the light, Ruth blinked. Her cheeks were heavily creased from the scarf pulled tight around her mouth, and her face smudged with mascara from her tears, but she was alive.

Quickly, Jess rushed down the steps, turning on the light and untying her. 'Are you alright? Stupid question, I guess.'

With a heavy sigh, Ruth nodded and winced with the pain in her ribs as she tried to stand.

Jess helped her to her feet. 'I guess we're even now.'

'Not by a long shot,' Ruth answered. 'You owe me lunch for the next year.'

After embracing, Jess saw a shadow in her peripheral vision, crouched under a rickety wire bearing a dim lightbulb.

'Where's Timmy?' the girl asked, the fear evident in her voice.

'Timmy's... er... Is anyone else down here?' Jess asked, changing the subject.

'Have you seen Timmy?'

Assisting Ruth up the steps and out of the basement, Jess instructed, 'Keep low and out of sight. I don't know where the old man is.' She told Ruth about Andrew and how she'd jumped him outside the lodge, wearing his disguise to get into the cottage. 'I'm going to bring the girl with us.'

'Is that a good idea? She's delusional. We don't know if we can trust her?'

'I have to take the chance. I can't leave her here. I need you to watch from the window. Tom is out looking for me. If you see headlights, shout.'

'Okay. Hurry.'

Back in the basement, Jess squatted to appear less vulnerable. The girl had undoubtedly been kept down there for some time and was traumatised. 'What's your name?'

Her head eased to one side as if listening intently. 'Fran. It's... It's short for Francesca. Where's Timmy?' she asked, her voice timid and resonating off the basement walls.

'My name is Jess. Jess Turner. I want to help you. They can't keep you down here like this. Do you understand me? Please, come with us.' With her arm out, she beckoned the girl over. 'It's okay. I won't hurt you.' As she stepped closer, Jess could see her stained nightdress. She was barefoot, her feet blackened and blistered. Similar to the young lad who had called to the lodge, her skin appeared dull, with a yellow complexion, and her eyes were sunken into her skull. As she got closer, Jess could smell her rank breath as though she hadn't brushed her teeth in months. Her hair was blonde, straw-like, dry, and smelt of burning wood.

'Where's Timmy?' she asked again.

Taking the girl's hand, feeling her rough, chapped skin, Jess turned off the light, and climbed the stairs, leading her out of the basement. With the hatch left open, she turned and lowered her body, placing her hands on the girl's shoulders. 'Okay. You must keep as quiet as possible. You can't make a—-'

'Jess,' Ruth interrupted. 'I see a torchlight in the fields. It's coming this way.'

'Shit. Andrew.' Jess kept the torch low on the floor and stepped to the window. 'What are we going to do?'

'Is it Timmy?'

Ruth covered the girl's mouth, desperate to keep her quiet.

As the figure approached the window, Jess stepped to one side of the frame, and Ruth grabbed Fran and pulled her to the other side.

'What's he doing?' Jess asked.

'He's trying to see inside. I think he knows we're here?'

'Don't make a sound,' Jess whispered, her voice trembling. Preventing a sneeze, she listened to her chest go in and out, her heart almost thumping against her ribcage.

Backing away from the window, the figure, unmistakably male, paused briefly before the footsteps gradually faded along the path towards the front door.

'Quick, Ruth. We need to find somewhere to hide.'

'Where? What about the wardrobe?'

'Too conspicuous. There must be somewhere along the hallway. Let's take the girl. Quick.'

'Oh shit. Alright. Come with us. We need to keep hidden.' Ruth grabbed Fran's arm and rushed out of the bedroom.

Jess followed, watching her friend try a door on the right.

'It's locked,' Ruth said.

'Try another one,' the stress evident in Jess's voice. 'He's coming.'

The front door slammed. They could hear rapid strides along the hallway by the front door.

Ruth tried a door on her left, flipping the handle down and pushing it open. 'Okay, stay silent. You understand? Don't make a peep.'

The girl stared blankly as though she were disconnected from reality.

Once the three of them were inside, they kept the light off and eased the door closed.

The decaying smell seemed worse in this room.

Beside Jess, the young girl whined. Pawing the bleakness, she found her lips, covering them with her hand, feeling warm breaths push from her nostrils against her skin. 'Please,' Jess said. 'You must be silent.'

Her muffled, heartbreaking pleas for Timmy continued.

'Can you hear anything?' Jess muttered.

'Nothing. Do you think he's—?'

Suddenly, another door slammed further along the hallway. The footsteps quickened as though the person was charging around the house.

Holding the torch, Jess slowly made her way to the back of the room and tried the window. 'It's locked.' As she turned, shining the torch, a shadow crept along the gap under the door. 'He's outside.'

They could sense someone standing in the hallway, possibly about to rip the handle down.

Ruth's grip around the young girl's mouth tightened.

Jess tensed, worried they were about to be caught.

And then, in a split second, the odds of them escaping tipped in their favour.

The footsteps gradually faded, disappearing into the room at the end of the hallway.

'What is he doing?' Ruth asked.

Gripping the handle and gently opening the door, Jess stepped into the hallway.

'He'll hear you,' Ruth hissed. 'Stop. Come back.'

A finger over her lips displayed her intention to face the threat. 'Stay here. Don't make a sound.'

As the man stood over the hatch, he bent forward, peering into the dim basement.

Aided by the faint moonlight through the window, Jess charged at him, seeing only his shape from behind through the shadows. Extending her right leg, she kicked him to the bottom of the stairs. Slamming the hatch shut, she called to Ruth. 'Quick. Help me with the wardrobe.'

'Where is he?' she asked, dashing into the room.

The young girl stood behind her in the hallway.

'Under here. Grab the wardrobe; we'll topple it.' Stepping away from the hatch, Jess grabbed one corner, Ruth the other, and they shimmied it across the floor. Moving around it, they pushed, their bodies pressed against the wall. The wardrobe toppled over, landing on the hatch with an almighty thud, causing shockwaves across the room.

Grabbing the girl's hand, Jess led her through the hallway and outside.

Ruth followed close behind.

Leaning her back against the cottage wall and gathering her thoughts, Jess held the girl's hand and searched the area, looking for headlights in the distance.

Beside them, Ruth crouched, hands covering her face, and gasped with the sheer horror of their predicament.

'Am... Am I coming with you?' Fran asked.

Stunned to hear her ask a question other than where Timmy was, Jess smiled, pushing a hand through the girl's hair. 'Oh, sweetie, you have to come with us. It's... It's not safe for you here. You understand that, don't you?'

The girl nodded with sadness in her eyes, bringing her hand to her mouth and biting on her knuckles. 'Are we going in the new car?'

'The new car? What new car?' Jess questioned.

'Through my... my bedroom window, I saw Grandad opening the garage. He put it in there. I came down, and he caught me. That's why... why he put me in the basement. He always puts me there as a... a punishment.'

'Can you show us where the garage is?' Jess asked. 'Take your time, and don't stress.'

'Around there.' Fran pointed to the back of the cottage. 'He... He put the car in there.'

With newfound hope, Jess and Ruth exchanged glances, their eyes alight with the possibility of escape, before they hurried along the path.

The brick garage, part of an extension built onto the back of the cottage, was constructed of weathered bricks. Patches of moss clung to the rough surface, and the mortar had faded to a dull grey. There were no windows, and a metal shutter secured the building with a robust combination lock.

'We can't break this,' Jess said after tugging the lock. Turning to Fran, she asked, 'Do you know the numbers?'

With a shake of her head, the young girl answered, 'No.' Pointing to the fields, she continued, 'But he does.'

For a moment, Jess thought someone was behind them. Feeling the hair standing on her arms, a hot flush developing on her chest, she turned, looking to where the young girl was pointing. 'Who, Fran? Who can you see?'

'Grandad. Look, see the glare?'

Through a gap in the trees, they saw what appeared to be an industrial light set up in a field.

What's he doing?' Jess asked.

'My Grandad often digs at night.'

'Okay,' Jess said. 'We have to get the combination for the padlock.'

'You're just going to march up there and ask him? Good luck with that,' Ruth remarked sarcastically.

'Do you have a better idea? Look, we're on the home stretch. That evil fuc... That... That man is our only hope. We have to try.'

Sneaking to the edge of the field, they watched him, seemingly oblivious to their presence. He wore the same clothes as earlier, and an industrial lamp provided enough light for him to see. With a shovel, he excavated soil from an ancient grave, dropping it in a mound nearby—the inscription on the gravestone dated back over half a century.

'I thought he buried bodies,' Ruth whispered, 'not excavated them.'

As Joe finished digging, he walked to a nearby tree and dragged a white sheet that looked like it concealed a body.

'Is that Timmy?' the young girl asked, gripping Jess's hand.

'Turn away. Please, you must turn away.' Picking up a large stick, Jess hurled it at the bushes near the cottage.

'Who's there?' Tom, is it you? Andrew?' Lifting the industrial lamp, he turned full circle, winding the lead around his boots. Once he'd worked free, he bent forward, placing the lamp in the same spot, and walked over to the bushes. 'I said, who's there?' Grabbing the radio clipped to the side of his trousers, Joe pressed the side button. 'Andrew. Can you hear me, over? Come in, Andrew. Christ! I hate these things.' With his thumb pressed hard on the button, he spoke more harshly this time. 'You bloody imbecile, talk. Can you hear me? Andrew?' Hurling the radio to the ground, Joe trudged towards the cottage.

'Shit,' Ruth muttered, 'he's going to find him in the basement.'

Jess rushed to the edge of the grave and peered into the hole, shining the torch. 'The bastard is hiding the body where it will never be found. He's... He's dug up an old grave, and he's going to dump the body on top of the coffin.' Reaching into the pocket of her leggings, she removed her phone.

'What are you doing?' Ruth asked.

Without turning, Jess said, 'I'm going to take photos so this sick bastard never gets away with it.' Lowering onto her knees, she parted the sheets, revealing her boyfriend, Ben.

31

SATURDAY EVENING

'**B**en. Oh no. Please, God, no! Wake up. Wake up, Ben.' With two fingers touching the side of his neck, Jess shouted, 'There's... I think there's a pulse.' Crouched by her boyfriend's side, she turned. 'We have to get him to a hospital.'

'How?' Letting go of the girl's hand, Ruth hurried over. 'Are you sure he's still alive?'

'I... I think so.' Gently slapping the side of his face, his skin cold and clammy, Jess tried to rouse him. 'Come on, Ben. Wake up. Ben, don't die on me.'

Ruth placed her fingers in the same position at the side of Ben's neck. 'There's definitely a faint heartbeat. We have to get him help.'

'What have they done to him?' In the corner of her eye, Jess saw a light by the cottage. 'He's... He's coming. Quick. I have an idea.' Grabbing the girl's hand, she rushed across the field and hid behind the tree where Ben had been slumped. 'There's another one. Oh shit. This is madness.' As she shone her torch over the bloodstained sheets, she knew it was Timmy. Facing the young girl away, she ordered, 'I need you to stay focused. Sit down on the grass and close your eyes. Can you do that for me?' Uncertain if the girl had seen the body, she watched her sit. 'Eyes closed, remember. No cheating.'

'I like to count,' Fran stated.

'Counting is good.'

'One. Two.'

'No, Fran. In your mind.'

'Okay.'

'We have to keep quiet,' Jess advised. 'Don't make a peep.'

Ruth was squatting with an arm around Fran's shoulder and covering her eyes with her right hand.

The torch was getting closer. Suddenly, they heard the old man talking as he approached the field.

'What have you done? I know you're here. Come out. I said, come out.'

As Fran gasped, Ruth placed a hand over her mouth and ordered, 'Keep quiet. Eyes closed, remember?'

'Come out, you bitches. I know you've been in the cottage.' As he shuffled to the edge of the grave, he picked up the radio.

Keeping low, Jess rushed at him, grabbing the shovel from the mound.

As Joe turned, she whacked him in the face, and he stumbled back, dropping into the grave and on top of the coffin.

The crunch of wood was severe, and Joe lay on his back, looking up at Jess. With a strained voice, he spouted, 'You stupid bitch. I... I can't move. My back. I've hurt my fucking back.' Lifting his neck, he winced.

'What's the combination code for the lock?'

'I can't move.'

'I said, what's the combination?' Aware Ben was in a critical condition, Jess said, 'Fine. Let's try another way.' Ramming the shovel into the mound, she began spilling soil over him. Tarpaulin packed the grave around the coffin, making it easier to cover his body.

'What are you doing? I can't move. I'm in bloody agony. Get me help.'

Beckoning Ruth over and instructing her to scoop the soil with her hand, Jess continued with the shovel, spilling it into the grave.

Before long, Joe's feet and body were covered. The soil hit his face, irritating his eyes, and went up his nostrils and into his mouth.

'What have you done to my boyfriend?'

'Tom... Tom inject... I can't breathe.'

Holding the shovel, her hair damp with sweat and sticking to her face, Jess stood. Her fingers were numb and stiff, and a callous developed on the palm of her hand. 'What did Tom do?'

'He injected him with chloroform. I... I was instructed to bury him alive to get back at you. I don't want... want to do this anymore. He's out of control.'

Looking over at Fran, still sitting on the grass with her eyes closed, remembering how she'd been locked in the basement, her heartbreaking cries for her brother, Timmy, and peering over the graveyard, imagining all the bodies they may have hidden, Jess said, 'I think you are as well.' As she continued to spill soil on his face, he mouthed the combination.

'It's 666.'

'I should have guessed,' Jess muttered. Tossing the shovel on the ground, a surge of adrenaline tore through her body.

Feeling lightheaded, she steadied herself and raced across the field towards the garage.

Ruth followed, holding the young girl's hand.

With the torch clenched between her teeth, Jess aligned the numbers and pulled the lock. 'It's not working. I don't think he's given us the right code.' It felt like the blood emptied from her body, the excitement suddenly replaced with dread.

Squatting by the lock, Ruth said, 'Here. Let me look. It's okay. You have it upside down. It's all nines.' Gently moving the dials, she positioned the sixes, and the lock opened.

Peering behind to ensure no one was coming, Jess eyed Ruth, placed her fingers under the shutter, and lifted. The screech was harsh on their ears as the chains rattled on the pulley.

Halfway up, the shutter jammed, and Jess tried to gently rock it left and right. Using her weight, she leant against it, forcing it down and hearing a loud clunk. With her hands under the shutter, she lifted again, pushing her arms upwards like a weightlifter in competition, waiting for the telltale beep signalling success as they held the barbell aloft.

The smell of paint and oil hit them instantly. The air was heavy with the intense aroma, and it felt like their lungs were filling with the toxic fumes.

Fearing that someone may be hiding, waiting to jump them, Jess shone the torch. She could see wooden shelves adorned with an assortment of old spray cans, containers brimming with nuts, bolts, screws, and boxes of tools. Old, stained rags hung on a line stretching through the garage, and a punchbag dangled from the ceiling with a gaping hole and the stuffing spilling out.

Shining the torch across the garage, she saw Ruth's car.

Just as the young girl had said.

'Okay. Sit in the back and put your seatbelt on,' Jess instructed.

'Are we leaving for good?' Fran asked.

'It's for the best. You understand, don't you?' Watching the young girl's eyes drop to the floor, she continued. 'They're not good people. They'll end up killing you, just like they killed Ti—' Managing to stop herself, Jess closed the door and got into the passenger seat.

Ruth got in beside her, relieved that the keys were still in the ignition. Starting the engine, she bit her lip, her body clenched, hands tight on the steering wheel, and pulled the car slowly out of the garage, through the hedge, and into the field, stopping beside Ben. He was lying on his stomach, his right cheek resting on the cold ground.

As Jess opened the passenger seat, she raced over to him, aided by the lights from the vehicle.

His eyes were open, his skin deathly white, and he was trying to moisten his dry lips with his tongue.

'Ben. Thank God! We need to get you to the hospital. You're going to be okay. Can you hear me? Blink once if you can hear me.'

Gently, his eyes closed and opened.

'You need to help us. Ruth's here. We're going to place you in the car. You need to stay strong, baby. Then we can get you help.'

Opening the driver's door, Ruth knelt beside Ben. 'Grab under his arm. I'll grab the other one. Okay. On three. One. Two. Go.'

As they desperately tried to lift his body, their feet slipped on the wet grass.

'Ben, you have to help us. I know it's difficult, but try as hard as you can.' Lifting his right arm, then his left, Jess placed his hands on the door frame. 'Pull yourself up. Come on, you can do it. Ben, come on.' She watched his hands clench, gripping the frame and pulling his body forward. 'Yes. That's it. Keep pulling.'

Grabbing his jacket, she and Ruth helped until the front half of his body was on the seat. Lifting his legs, sliding and falling on their knees, they pushed until he was slumped on the back seat.

Getting into the passenger seat, Jess twisted her body and held Ben's hand. 'He's so cold. Am I... Am I going to lose him?' Stemming the tears as they rolled down her face, she swallowed the lump in her throat, wanting to cry until there was nothing left. She had to remain positive. They still weren't in the clear, and Ruth needed her to guide them out of Sheers Woods.

'We're not going to let him die. These bastards can't win.' Ruth started the car and reversed onto the narrow road. 'Which way?'

'Oh, Christ. I don't know. Tom's still out there looking for me. I say we avoid the lodge. It's probably the first place he'll look.' Leaning the phone against the window, Jess hit the record button, needing as much evidence as possible. 'This road should lead to the main entrance.'

In the car's headlights, the shadow of the trees carved menacing shapes as if watching. Their branches appeared to twist in the wind, claws leaning in and ready to grab them, crush them to death, and spit them out. The eerie mist had returned, suffocating the woods like a pillow held over someone's face. The darkness pressed in around them like a dense canopy shielding the outside world, and the weird silence provoked an unsettling atmosphere.

'How's he doing?' Ruth asked, her foot pressed down on the accelerator, struggling to cope with the sharp bends.

'His eyes are closed. His breathing seems to be slowing down. I... I can't lose him. He's my life. It's all my fault.'

'Don't. Don't say that.'

'It's true. He came out here because of me. I've been so stupid and stubborn.'

'You're a journalist. Aren't we all?' They approached another hash bend, and Ruth saw it too late, swerving at the last second, hitting the brakes, and slamming into a hedge. 'Sorry.' Adjusting the rear-view mirror, she saw lights appear behind her. 'Oh shit. We have company.'

'What do you mean?' Turning, Jess saw a glow through the fields, around a hundred yards from them. Two tiny specs, gaining, becoming brighter. 'They're coming this way. Should we drive into the field and turn the lights off?'

'No. They're bound to see us. This is never going to end.' Pulling away from the hedge, Ruth hit the accelerator, watching as the lights got closer.

A groan came from the back seat, and Ben began twitching.

'He's deteriorating. I think he's having convulsions. Ben, stay with us. We're getting help. Please, baby, stay with us.' Facing Ruth, she said, 'You need to lose this maniac. Drive faster.'

'I'm trying.' Ruth's eyes blurred, and she blinked hard, seeing the road as one long conveyor belt, round and round like a broken treadmill, speeding out of control and unable to stop. The stress clouded her mind. The fear of dying and never leaving the woods gnawing at her brain. In the rear-view mirror, the lights resembled glowing fireballs about to burst through the glass and consume her body, burning her to a crisp.

The smack from behind brought her back to reality.

Undoing her belt, Jess knelt on the seat, facing the back. She could see Tom Wilder grinning, his eyes wide and focused on them. 'Speed up. We have to lose this prick.'

'How? He's going to ram us off the road.'

'Hold on.' Grabbing the seat, Jess watched as Tom sped up and rammed them from behind a second time. 'This guy is a fucking nut job.'

'I'm glad I'm coming with you. I think my family are nut jobs too,' Fran commented.

Only for the tense situation, Jess and Ruth would have laughed. Somehow, it didn't seem appropriate.

'Can we drive through the woods?' Jess shouted.

'It's too dangerous.' Glancing at the speedometer, the display showed thirty-three miles per hour. The steering wheel shook with the rough terrain, and the tyres struggled to grip the road. The sharp bend ahead came too fast, and Ruth was forced to drive through a hedge and into a field. The wheels span, flicking mud, and the car's front end crunched against the ground.

Behind them, the lights followed closely.

'I'm approaching a line of trees. I don't think I can get through. There's no other way.'

'You have to try. Keep calm. You can do it.' Jess looked to the left, seeing the trees stretch to the edge of the field. 'Focus. Keep going.'

As Ruth squeezed the car through a gap, she saw the van following. 'He's still with us. I can't shake him off.' Again, the van smacked into them, jerking them forward. Grappling with the steering wheel to avoid the oncoming trees, Ruth saw something in the headlights—a woman standing alone in the field and staring at them. 'Oh, shit.' With a hard turn to the left, the car skidded to a halt. 'Where did she go?' In the wing mirror, Ruth saw her again, staring at the van behind them.

Tom Wilder was driving too fast and didn't have time to brake, driving the van straight into a tree and going headfirst through the windscreen.

32

SATURDAY EVENING

The sign hung on the wooden frame, swinging in the breeze. "Welcome to Sheers Woods. Enter at your own risk."

How very apt, Jess thought.

'Is... Is he dead?' asked Ruth.

'I think so.'

'Did you... Did you see her?'

'I was holding Ben's hand. Who did you see?'

'The woman from the ritual. It was her. She was standing in the field.'

'That's impossible. I watched her die.'

'It was her, Jess. 'It's right here, isn't it?'

'Yeah. Take a right. We should get a signal shortly,' Jess said, tapping her phone screen, still seeing "No Service." As a vehicle approached on the other side of the road, she felt overwhelmed. Sheers Woods was like a parallel universe, a nightmare you'd never wake from, and seeing a normal world seemed alien to her. It felt like she'd been trapped there forever, as though life had passed her by, forgotten about her. It was hard to explain. As if she'd been frozen in time. Now, her focus was on getting Ben help and dealing with the horrors of Sheers Woods later. Suddenly, her phone began pinging. 'Oh my goodness! We have reception. Struggling to stop her hand from trembling, she opened Google Maps and searched for a hospital nearby. 'There's one in Amersham. It's only a couple of miles.'

'Thank God! How's he doing?'

'Shivering. He's still very pale.' Jess dialled 999, placing the phone on loudspeaker and instructing Ruth where to go.

A woman spoke almost instantly. 'Emergency services. Do you require police, fire, ambulance, or coastguard?'

'Er, police.'

Then, another voice, husky and calming. 'Police emergency line. What's the nature of your emergency?'

How the hell do I explain this, Jess thought. 'Hello. I've... I've been staying at a lodge in Sheers Woods, Amersham. I was assigned to investigate a viral clip. To cut a long story short, I was under constant attack. There was hair on the clothesline due to someone being scalped, a person dressed as a bird, a body dragged through the woods, a.... a ritual, an old man hiding bodies in the graveyard, a... a possessed woman who collapsed as I held her hand and a body in the well. Oh, and the leader of the cult crashed into a tree and went through the windscreen. I think he might be dead.'

'Take a breath and run that by me again,' the stunned operator asked.

'Look, my boyfriend has been poisoned. We've just turned up at Amersham Hospital. I have to go, but you have my phone number.' Jess hung up, got out of the car, and raced to the accident and emergency entrance. 'Please, can you help? My boyfriend has been poisoned.' She watched the medical staff rush to the car and take Ben into one of the trauma bays.

Jess, Ruth, and Fran were led to an emergency waiting room.

After a few minutes, a middle-aged woman with a friendly smile walked in and spoke to them. 'Hi. I'm Nurse Higgins. Can you tell me what happened?'

Recalling what the old man had said while lying in the grave, Jess explained, 'My boyfriend has been injected with Chloroform.'

'Do you know how long ago he was injected?'

'Today. But I don't know what time exactly.'

'Does he have any medical conditions?'

'Um, no, not that I can think of,' Jess answered. 'He had asthma as a child.'

'Okay. The head nurse will be here soon. We'll keep you updated on his condition. Please try to relax. He's in the safest possible hands.'

33

ONE MONTH LATER

'The service was beautiful. So many people turned up. I was so proud. You would have been, too.' Wiping the smudged mascara from under her eyes, Jess slowly lifted her head, looking to the sky. Soft, white clouds bulged like pillows, drifting lazily across the expanse. Among them, one cloud caught her eye, resembling an angel with outstretched wings cradling a harp in its delicate hands. 'I'm... I'm so sorry. It's my fault. I know people tell me I can't blame myself. But I do.' Coughing, she wiped her blurry, tear-stained eyes with a tissue and placed it in the sleeve of her black cardigan. She'd bought a black skirt for the funeral, which was too long and dragged on the ground. The flat slip-on shoes were cutting the heels of her feet. Staring at the grave, she saw the array of flowers with messages of condolence. The newly turned soil emitted a damp and earthy scent.

Everything reminded Jess of that hideous weekend in Sheers Woods. The bouquets on the grave evoked memories of Beth, the woman who'd asked her to leave the florist with the harsh warning to turn back. The grave. How the old man had promised to help them get out, and later, they'd seen him excavating earth in an attempt to hide Timmy and bury her boyfriend alive. Even the cards attached to the flowers reminded her of the night Timmy called to the lodge, giving her a note with a warning to leave before it was too late.

'I'm not used to this,' Jess continued. 'I don't know what to say. If I'm honest, I feel a little stupid.' Sobbing, she tried to pull herself together, wiping her eyes with her sleeve. 'I'm so sorry. If I hadn't gone there, this would never have happened. You'd be here, holding me, telling me how proud you are, and making everything right. You'd tell me how brave I am. But you're the bravest person I've ever known. You came out there to help me. You'll always be a hero. I ... I took a couple of weeks off. The doctor said I was suffering from PTSD. It couldn't have been for nothing. I had to right all the wrongs. Bring justice to their wickedness. I worked on the documentary. Doug was great. He said to take as much time off as I needed. I pieced everything together with the notes from the Dictaphone and the recordings. When I handed over my written report, photos, and docufilm, Doug said I'd possibly be up for the Pulitzer Prize—one of the most prestigious awards in journalism. But I'm not holding my breath. We'll see. Anyway, I'm going now. I'll be back tomorrow. I love you so very much. My hero.'

Jess felt a hand on her shoulder and turned around, seeing her boyfriend, Ben.

'That was beautiful. Jess, you have to stop blaming yourself. You weren't to know it was your father at the cottage. Christ! The stress you were under.'

'I pushed him down the stairs of the basement. He broke his neck. We tipped the wardrobe over so he couldn't get out. How is it not my fault?'

'The police have released you on bail. The solicitor assured you the judge would be lenient, considering the situation. The strain and severe pressure. Everything you went through. It would break anyone. You said yourself that the room was dark, and the figure was bent over. You weren't to know it was your father. Come on. We need to rebuild your strength. Let's go for a coffee and a bite to eat.'

As they left the cemetery hand in hand, Jess got on her tiptoes and kissed her boyfriend's cheek.

'Thanks, Ben. I love you so much.'

'I've got to go to work for a few hours. They're struggling to put one of the sets together. I'll be back by ten at the latest. I'll pick up a takeaway on the way home if you like.'

'It's Saturday evening. Tell them you're busy?' Jess insisted, feeling a sudden slump at the thought of Ben leaving her.

Leaning over, his face clean-shaven, he kissed her on the lips.

Jess could taste lemon and citrus on her mouth. 'Please don't go. You've just moved in here with me. If it continues like this, you might have to find alternative accommodation.' She playfully threw a cushion at him, hitting his chest.

Hoping they'd cuddle on the sofa, watch a film, and share a bottle of wine, Jess fought the disappointment. It felt like the air had been released from her body, and she'd slump off the sofa and onto the floor. 'One condition then. You bring back a curry—a bottle of wine and flowers. There's no compromising here.'

'You got it.' In the hallway, he grabbed a scarf from the

railing, wrapping it tight around his neck, and fixed the collar of his brown jacket. 'Right. I'll see you a bit later.'

'Shall I drop you to the station?'

'I'm good. I could use some fresh air.'

The front door closed, and Jess sarcastically blew kisses from the living room window, seeing Ben pull his scarf with a sheepish smile playing at the corner of his lips as though embarrassed.

He blew kisses back, laughed, and rushed along the road towards the train station.

'Hey. I was thinking of calling over tomorrow. I'll do Sunday lunch. Are you up for it?' Jess held the mobile phone in front of her, seeing the dark bags under her mother's eyes and confusion in the empty stare.

'I'd... I'd like that. I'm sorry I couldn't go. I'm not... up to it yet. You understand, don't you?'

'Of course. You were there yesterday at the funeral. It was extremely tough. No one says you need to go all the time.'

'How did the grave look today?'

'It's a lovely spot,' was all she could say. How could she answer such a question and make everything sound better? 'How are you feeling?' Jess realised she'd followed up with an equally challenging question.

'Good and bad days,' she answered, her voice strained and hoarse. 'Where's Ben?'

'He's had to go to work. They're having trouble with the set. He'll be back later.'

'That guy's going to have a heart attack. He works too hard.'

'He sure does.'

'He looked healthy at the funeral. I'm glad he's recovering. The glow is back in his face.'

'He certainly gave us a scare,' Jess answered awkwardly, struggling to find the right words. After her father died, she wondered if her mother wished it was Ben who had died instead, although if she had, Jess never saw the signs. 'Are you sleeping?'

'I'm sleeping. The doctor gave me tablets. He recommended that I see a bereavement counselor. But I don't believe in those. Time is the greatest healer. I keep hearing that... that Andrew person in my head.'

Sitting back on the sofa, Jess tucked her feet under her body. Her left shoulder began aching, so she switched the phone to her right hand. 'Try to ignore it?'

'I saw him on the news after they caught him.'

'Yeah. Racing along the main road and away from the woods. I hope they throw away the key. His trial is coming up soon—and Joe's. From what my solicitor says, they'll never get out. Tom got his karma, killed instantly as he went through the windscreen.'

'Jess. Please. There's been enough strategy.' Her mother looked to the floor, composed herself, and raised her eyes back to the screen. 'I was saying about Andrew. It's the first thing I hear in the morning and the last before I go to bed.'

'What do you hear?'

'Oh, that gruff sneer of his. It's so... piercing. I remember the reports in the paper. I saw a clip on the news. It makes my blood boil. How he described seeing Bob pull up beside the lodge. He sent your poor father to his death. Telling him you were down at the cottage. The police found the car. He'd walked through the fields. But the words Andrew used in the interview. Boasting. "I sent him there. I knew he'd never come back. I did good. Tom would be proud." It grates me to know there's such evil in the world.'

'I'm so sorry,' Jess said, her eyes suddenly filled with tears and spilling down her cheeks.

'Listen to me, and listen well. Whatever you think, it's not your fault. You were doing your job. You're so driven and enthusiastic. You didn't ask your father to go out there. I begged him to wait. I said you'd call, but he was adamant.'

'I pushed him into the basement.'

'It's a tragic accident. Nothing else. We'll get through this. Stop blaming yourself, you hear me?'

'I hear you,' Jess answered, grabbing a box of tissues from the side unit, and blowing her nose. Her mobile phone started beeping as a call came through. 'I have to get this. I'll see you tomorrow. Does 2 pm work?'

'That works great. See you tomorrow, love. Stop beating yourself up, Jess. It's going to be hard. We'll get through this together, one day at a time. I love you so much.'

'Love you too, Mum.' Ending the call, Jess wiped her teary eyes and squinted through the blurriness. The screen showed "No Caller ID" across the top. 'Hello, Jess speaking.' She listened, expecting to hear someone explain how they'd gotten her number through a contact, a friend of a friend, or social media and if she had a couple of minutes spare to talk about the weekend spent at Sheers Woods. 'Jess speaking. How can I help?' With no response, she ended the call. It rang again a second later with the same display on the screen. 'Hello? Is someone there?'

Suddenly, a faint, muffled cry for help pushed through the phone speaker as though coming from a distant tunnel underground.

Struggling to hear, Jess asked, 'Who is this?' Again, the

distorted, echoey noise came through as though emanating from within the depths of a cave. As she listened intently, trying to figure out what they were saying, it seemed the voice began playing backwards, first slowly and then it speeded up.

Gripped with fear, it felt as though something clutched her throat, crushing the life from her. Her heart seemed to slow down, battling to push the blood around her body. As though paralysed, her fingers stiffened, and the phone dropped to the floor. Closing her eyes, she counted to ten, composing herself, frightened she was having a stroke. Wriggling her fingers, she lifted her shoulders and stretched her back. Pressing her hands into the soft cushion, she stood, reached for the phone, and ended the call.

She jumped as it rang again.

This time, Ruth's name appeared on the screen.

'Oh, thank goodness,' Jess said as she answered the call, her breaths rapid and laboured.

'Hey. You sound as though you've been running.'

'No. Just the paranoia I'm condemned to suffer with for the rest of my life. Flashbacks, guilt, tense, always on edge. Hey, welcome to my world.'

'Where's Ben?'

'Out. Working. He's always working.'

'Look. I'm passing through on the train. I can be in Cricklewood in around twenty minutes. Do you fancy a drink?'

'Christ! Yes. Absolutely.'

'Great. See you in The Crown.'

∾

In the bathroom, Jess brushed her teeth, wiped her mouth with a towel, and applied lipstick. After running a brush through her hair, she turned off the light.

A gurgling sound reverberated behind her.

Switching the light back on, she walked to the toilet, seeing the water bubble like volcanic ash. *What is going on?* she thought, pressing the button, and hoping the cold water would flush it away. Waiting, the cistern filled, and the water settled. Abruptly, it began churning again, and steam filled the bathroom. 'For Christ's sake!' Then, the voice she'd heard on her mobile phone seemed to come from within the drains. Again, it played backwards, echoey and hollow, like someone trapped underground.

Racing into the hallway, she slammed the bathroom door, grabbed her keys from the breakfast bar in the kitchen, and left the flat.

Outside, she leant a hand against her car, panting, worried for her sanity. Since spending the weekend at the lodge, she'd had hallucinations, suffered from paranoia, and often woke in the middle of the night in cold sweats, seeing Ben lying next to her and managing to stem the panic. It was getting worse. Her doctor had prescribed medication, but it would take some time for them to take effect.

Gulping the cold air, she stepped back from the car, seeing the tyres begin to deflate. 'You're not real. This isn't happening. I'm not at the lodge. I'm safe now.' Blinking hard, the rush of blood made her woozy, and she turned, walking along the road to the pub.

A bouncer smiled, nodding his head. 'Evening.' He opened the door, and Jess walked in.

Although it was just gone 7 pm, the pub was already busy. Jess could hear live traditional Irish music coming from the back. The sound of banjos, tin whistles, an accordion, and a fiddle made her feel relaxed. There was something about live music that comforted her.

The bar, a centrepiece of the establishment, crafted from polished mahogany, ran the length of the pub's interior, immediately drawing attention with its authentic elegance, exuding warmth and character.

Bar staff carried trays of food and drinks to people sitting in the restaurant area, while others sat at small circular tables and engaged in lively conversation.

Ruth stood at the bar, waving. She blew a hard breath as if to suggest she didn't think it would be so busy.

'Hey. My goodness. You look great,' Jess stated as she hugged her friend.

'And you.'

Although Jess thought she was just being polite, she took the compliment.

'What would you like to drink?'

'I shouldn't, really. I'm on tablets. One glass of wine should be alright.'

'Merlot? Large?'

'Go on then.'

They sat in the corner by the front door.

Ruth wore an elegant, long brown jacket and placed it on the back of a chair. Her black skirt and white blouse complimented each other and looked chic.

Jess felt underdressed in a pair of grey leggings, a red jumper, and one of Ben's coats. 'So, how's work going? I'm sorry it's been a while. I couldn't face talking to people.'

'Hun, I get it,' Ruth said, her voice soft and sympathetic. 'You don't ever need to apologise. After that weekend, fuck, I can't even believe it was real. I gave Doug two weeks' notice. I pulled a sickie, blaming stress so I didn't have to face going in. I'm not cut out for journalism. Sheers Woods made me realise how dangerous the job is and what it entails. It ain't for me. I'm going to enrol in a college course. Fashion. It's a safer bet. My cousin has got me an interview with a design house. At least I'll gain practical experience and earn money while I'm learning. It's a safer option.'

Sipping her wine, Jess grinned, and her cheeks flushed. 'I'm with you on that.'

'So, I hear there's a battle going on?'

'Battle?' Jess placed the wine in front of her and picked the edge of the table as a distraction from the anxiety.

'Yeah. Netflix. Amazon. Shudder. You're made.'

'Oh, I've been contacted by numerous agents. They want to make a documentary. I don't know how much money I'll get. I haven't given anyone an answer yet. I'm still thinking about it.'

'Bloody hell, Jess. What's there to think about? This is so exciting.' Ruth saw the tears in her friend's eyes. 'I'm so sorry for what happened. The funeral was beautiful. Your father will be looking down and so very proud.'

'Sorry I couldn't talk. It was a difficult day.'

Ruth extended her hand, gently placing it over Jess's. 'I understand. Stop apologising. You're not still blaming your-self, are you?'

'Oh, I don't know.' Her voice was strained with emotion, the lump severe in her throat, and Jess tried swallowing it away. 'Somedays it's harder to cope than others. I keep seeing him, bent over the hatch. Me rushing over, kicking him down the stairs, and him breaking his neck. I some-times wake, hearing a ferocious snap. I killed my father, Ruth. How am I going to live with that?'

'One day at a time. Easy steps. It will get easier to live with.'

'Mum and Ben have been great. You too. I don't know what I'd do without you all.' Downing the wine, Jess pushed the chair back and got another round of drinks, bringing them back to the table.

'Go easy,' Ruth said. 'The tablets, remember.'

'Maybe I'll get pissed. That will help dim the noise. Mum said she's haunted by Andrew's words. How he sent Dad down to the cottage. Almost boasting and how Tom would be proud.'

'Bless her. I read they want to excavate the graveyard in search of bodies. Imagine what that will do to the families left behind.'

'It's harrowing. I can't comprehend what loved ones are going through. Joe Egan dug graves and hid corpses for years after they trafficked limbs. So evil.' She shivered, her body suddenly shaking. 'They found Danny's remains in the well. I guess we know where the others are now, thanks to Joe. I'm sure they'll be found when they start digging.'

'They were all in it together. Tom, Andrew, and Joe. I can't believe they kidnapped people, removed their limbs, killed them, and buried their bodies. It's like a horror movie. I heard a couple of local police were in on it as well. Taking part in the rituals. I guess it's how they got away with it for so long.'

'At least there's been loads of arrests,' Jess said, suddenly beaming. 'The police were able to identify the followers from the recording we made of them all fleeing the hay barn. That's one good thing.'

'Yeah, that and the masks they left behind. Thank goodness for DNA. I need to run. I'll walk you home. Oh, how's Fran doing?'

'She's good. She's still in temporary foster care, but the social services are pushing for emergency adoption procedures. I call to see her every few days. She looks so much stronger and healthier now.'

'Oh, one thing I'm confused about,' Ruth stated. 'They never found the woman who Tom carried into the barn.'

'That confuses me too,' said Jess. 'I held her hand as she died.'

34

SATURDAY EVENING

'I'm almost done here,' Ben said with eagerness in his voice. 'I'm going to be finished earlier than I thought.'

'Amazing. Don't forget the takeaway on the way home.'

'Noted.'

'Oh, and flowers and wine. That's a must.' Jess suddenly felt uneasy about mixing too much alcohol with her tablets and thought, *One more glass can't hurt.*

'I'll be home in an hour.'

'Okay. See you then.' Placing the phone in the pocket of her leggings, she opened both the main door and the one to her flat.

The lights were on in the hallway, and she walked slowly to the kitchen, still bothered by the phone call from earlier. She grabbed a glass from the cabinet, filled it with water, and gulped it down in one go, frowning as she swallowed, the cold liquid stinging her lungs. After a second glass of water, sipping it this time, she placed the glass in the sink and walked along the hallway and into the living room. Turning on the light, she sat on the sofa, grabbed the remote control, and switched on the TV. Her mood had lifted, and the cloud that had earlier hung over her had disappeared, knowing Ben would be home soon. She disliked him working so many hours, but it was something she'd have to get used to.

A buzzing sound echoed from the hallway, and Jess flinched, feeling her heart skip a few beats. 'He can't be home already?' Muting the TV, she pushed off the sofa, walked to the hallway, and lifted the entry phone receiver. 'Ben?'

No answer.

'Ben, is it you?' she asked again. Carefully placing the receiver back, she walked to the living room window. A streetlight flickered from the pavement; the road was empty, and no one was at the front door. 'Strange.' As she sat, the buzzer sounded again. This time longer. Leaping off the sofa, she charged to the window—still no one at the front door. *It's kids playing around,* she assumed, trying to remain calm. Fear began to churn in her stomach, and panic threatened. Turning away from the front window, the buzzer immediately echoed through the hallway. She turned back, staring at the main door, and it stopped. Again, she faced away from the window, staring at the back wall of the living room. The buzzer punched through her ears. Abruptly shifting around to the window, it stopped.

Clutching the sides of her head, Jess said, 'Please stop. I can't take this anymore.' Stepping back towards the hallway, the buzzer persisted, grating her senses, and she grabbed the receiver. 'Who is this? Leave me alone. I'm going to call the police.' Footsteps charging behind her made her drop the receiver and spin around. The hallway was empty—only the sound of the receiver knocking against the wall.

Bang.

Bang.

Bang.

Frustrated, Jess yanked it downwards, snapping the cord from the cradle.

Suddenly, the door to her flat started knocking. Someone was standing in the main entrance—five loud taps in succession.

Edging along the hallway, she placed her eye to the spy hole.

The main entrance seemed deserted.

Opening the door, Jess peeked through the crack, unable to see anyone, and pulled it back further. She gazed at the main door, seeing it closed. Stepping out, she looked at the door on her left leading to the upstairs flat, which was also closed. Debating whether to knock, she decided against it. The neighbours weren't friendly, and she'd only feel stupid and judged if she called them down.

As she stepped back inside and slammed the door, someone knocked so hard the vibration caused her to jerk forward. 'This is crazy,' she shouted, rotating towards the front door, and looking through the spy hole. A loud gasp elevated from her throat, and every nerve tingled in her body. A woman sat in the corner of the main entrance with her face in her hands. She shook violently as if distressed and began slamming her body against the wall.

As Jess reached for the door handle, she hesitated, deciding not to open it, and slid the chain across to secure it. Trying to interpret what was genuine and imaginary, she closed her eyes, pinched the skin of her right forearm, and slapped the sides of her face with both hands. 'Come on. It's not real. It's not real.'

As if in slow motion, her eyes opened, and she peered towards the corner of the main entrance.

The woman was gone.

With a hefty sigh, feeling the blood return to her body, her shoulders dropping, she gave herself words of encouragement. *I can do this. I've been through so much, but I have people who care. People who love me. It will take time, but I'll get...*

The woman appeared from nowhere, crawling at high speed along the floor. She stood and then barged against the front door, her face pressed to the spy hole.

Jess stumbled backwards. Finding her footing, her hands placed on the wall for support, she leant against the front door, seeing the woman tilt back and slam her head against the wood. Again, she repeated the action.

Blood poured from her forehead, and she wiped it, placing her fingers in her mouth.

As Jess raced into the living room and slammed the door, the sound of splintering wood continued.

Her phone rang. Jess pulled it from her pocket and saw the FaceTime request from Ruth.

'You look like shit. What's happened?' asked Ruth.

'She's... She's here.'

'Who? Who's there?'

'The... The woman from the ritual. The one Tom carried to the barn.'

'She's dead. You said it yourself. You held her hand as she took her last breath, remember?'

'But what if she's not dead? 'What if she's still out there? The police never found a body.'

'Where did you see her?' Ruth asked, keeping her voice calm, knowing her friend was vulnerable.

'Outside. In the main entrance. She was sat in the corner.'

'Okay. Reverse the camera. Let me see. I'm here on the line. Nothing is going to happen.'

'I... I can't go out there.'

'Yes, you can. You've been through so much with what happened at Sheers Woods and the terror you endured. And... your father. Jess, it's bound to have an effect. But you'll get better. I know you will. Keep taking your tablets. You have people who love you. Come on, go to the front door. I want to prove to you it's not real and that you have nothing to worry about.'

Jess tapped the screen, reversing it, and focused on the living room door.

'Go on,' Ruth said, her voice reassuring to ease the stress. 'I'm here. Nothing's going to happen.'

As she opened the living room door, Jess felt the phone shaking in her hand. On the hallway wall, the cradle hung askew from the force of her ripping the receiver away. Facing the front door, she looked for any telling cracks in the wood, but there was nothing to indicate any damage. Silently, she crept along the hallway floor to the spy hole and peered through it. The main entrance was empty. 'She's gone.'

'See. I told you.' Ruth could hear the heavy sigh through the phone, the relief palpable. 'What time is Ben coming back?'

'Uh, should be soon. Thank you, you know, for being there.'

'No need to thank me.'

Walking into the living room, she closed the door and switched the screen back. 'What is wrong with me?' she asked, pulling a chair back and sitting at a small table near the window.

'It's going to take time. You need to rest, and don't put

pressure on yourself. Why don't you and Ben go away for a weekend?'

'Maybe. His job is so demanding. I'll chat to him when he gets home.'

'Okay. Enjoy your evening. It was lovely to catch up. I'm here if you need me. Just ring.'

'Thanks, Ruth.' Ending the call, Jess opened the laptop and searched for the name Astaroth, the demon Tom had summoned during the ritual. Due to her commitment to piecing everything together, she hadn't done much research on it. After duplicating her notes and the recordings, she handed copies over to the police as evidence and, while taking time to recover, went to work on her report.

Now, she felt it was time to understand what had appeared at the ritual.

A picture showed Astaroth depicted as a nude man with feathered wings, wearing a crown, holding a serpent in one hand, and riding a beast with dragon-like wings and a serpent tail.

Underneath was a description.

Astaroth is commonly depicted as a male figure with angelic or demonic features. He may be portrayed with feathered wings, often carrying a sceptre or other regal symbols. Some depictions show Astaroth with animalistic traits, such as a serpent's tail or horns. His appearance can vary depending on different cultural and artistic interpretations.

Astaroth is believed to possess great knowledge and persuasive abilities, often tempting individuals with promises of wealth, power, or worldly pleasures. In occult traditions, Astaroth is sometimes invoked for purposes of divination, astral projection, or other esoteric practices.

However, such dealings with Astaroth are considered dangerous and may lead to spiritual or psychological harm.

In some cases, during rituals, if Astaroth is summoned, it will choose a victim, possessing and killing them within minutes. It's believed that anyone who comes into physical contact with this person will also die.

Jess slammed the laptop shut, fighting the palpitations in her chest. Then, she grabbed her phone and FaceTimed Ruth.

'Hey. Is Ben back?'

'No. I have to read you something. Bear with me.' Opening the laptop back up, Jess recalled, word for word, everything she'd read. When she finished, she looked at the screen, noting how Ruth's eyes were squinted and her jaw was clenched.

'It's ridiculous. You don't believe that, surely?'

'So where is she?' Jess asked with alarm in her voice. The screen flickered. She shifted in the seat, arm outstretched, trying to get a better signal. 'Are you there, Ruth? Ruth?'

'Yes. I'm struggling to see you. The picture's not great. You're blurred. Oh, hi, Ben.'

'Ben's not back yet,' Jess confirmed.

'Then who's behind you?'

Glancing over her shoulder, she looked to where her friend was pointing and back to the phone. 'No one's behind me'

'Yes, there is. Can't you see them?'

Again, Jess looked. 'There's no one there.'

As the picture cleared, Ruth shouted, 'It's her. Jess, get out of there. Jess, get out. Jess?' The picture went blank, and Ruth tried continuously to call back.

Moments later, the front door opened, and Ben called from the hallway, 'I'm home. Are you hungry? Jess?'

Removing his jacket and scarf and placing them on the rail, he walked into the living room and saw his girlfriend lying on the floor. She was wheezing heavily, smoke came from her mouth, and her face began to implode. 'Oh my God! What's happened? Jess, what's happened?' As he crouched beside her, she shook her head as if to tell him to leave.

Ben grabbed her hand and watched her take her last breath.

The End.

ACKNOWLEDGMENTS

Thank you so much for choosing The Footage and I hope you enjoyed it.
You can sign up to my mailing list and keep up to date with other projects I have planned.
Just go to:
https://www.stuartjamesthrillers.com

Firstly, I'd like to say a huge thank you to my family for your extreme patience and listening to my ideas constantly. I love you so much.
I feel you know my thrillers as well as I do.

I want to thank a few people who helped immensely with the research of The Footage.
To my wonderful friend Ali Hickman-Jameson who is a retired Police Sergeant and is always so very helpful. You really are an amazing lady.
To finding an incredible editor in the wonderful Nikki Bocelli. Thanks for everything.
Also to the lovely Dee Groocock for your proofread. You are such a lovely lady.

A huge thank you to everyone on my Facebook arc group for your ongoing support. I can't thank you enough. I can call each member of the group a friend and I'm so glad you're a part of the team. Thank you for being there.

We have almost 140 members and I'm so, so grateful to you all.

Special thanks to the Facebook groups who continually promote my works and support me so much.
The Fiction Cafe.
The Reading Corner Book Lounge.
UK Crime Book Club.
Donna's Interviews, Reviews and Giveaways.
Also to the incredible book bloggers who have supported my journey so much and to all you wonderful readers and authors.
And lastly, special mentions to Susie at Prescription Books, Zoe O'Farrell, Kate Eveleigh, Emma Louise Bunting, Emma Louise Smith, Michaela Balfour, Kiltie Jackson, Wendy Clarke, and Debbie Schutt for the support and your friendship.
I'll be forever grateful.
You really are amazing and I can't thank you enough.

Make sure to keep up to date with projects I'm working on and sign up to my mailing list at:
https://www.stuartjamesthrillers.com

Also, you can follow me on social media.
I love to hear from readers and will always respond.
Twitter: StuartJames73
Instagram: Stuart James Author
Facebook: Stuart James Author.
TikTok: Stuart James Author

That's it for now.

Once again, thank you so much for choosing, The App.
Hopefully, I'll have a new adventure with Billy Huxton and
Declan Ryan from Creeper, coming soon.
Love to you all and keep safe.
Stuart James.

Printed in Great Britain
by Amazon

57433029R00155